Candace Camp
Gina Wilkins
Allison Leigh

From This Day Forward

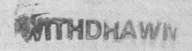

HARLEQUIN®

TORONTO • NEW YORK • LONDON
AMSTERDAM • PARIS • SYDNEY • HAMBURG
STOCKHOLM • ATHENS • TOKYO • MILAN • MADRID
PRAGUE • WARSAW • BUDAPEST • AUCKLAND

Recycling programs
for this product may
not exist in your area.

ISBN-13: 978-0-373-83732-8

FROM THIS DAY FORWARD

Copyright © 2009 by Harlequin Books S.A.

The publisher acknowledges the copyright holders
of the individual works as follows:

NO REGRETS
Copyright © 2009 by Candace Camp

ALWAYS A GROOMSMAN
Copyright © 2009 by Gina Wilkins

THE DADDY TRACK
Copyright © 2009 by Allison Lee Davidson

CONTENTS

NO REGRETS

Candace Camp

* * *

For Barbara and Kenneth Chalmers, who in
one more year will have their own 60th anniversary.
You're a wonderful example to us all!

Dear Reader,

I was intrigued with the story of Jack and Claire and how they met and fell in love back in 1949. In thinking about the story, it seemed right to set it in my own hometown of Amarillo, Texas. It was great fun to dig into the research for this period—looking up half-forgotten streets, talking to relatives, finding pictures and information on the Nat Ballroom, where my mother and father had gone dancing while they were dating.

I had many conversations with my sister Barbara, who was a teenager at the time, and her husband, Kenneth. They helped me greatly by recalling all sorts of things, from how many articles of jewelry a "lady" could wear to what the coolers of the day looked like, from what attire was suitable for a picnic date in the Palo Duro Canyon to what was involved in the G.I. Bill of Rights. Jack's car is even based on Kenneth's automobile.

Hopefully you will enjoy, as I did, this brief visit to a simpler time and a wonderful generation of people—and the city in which I grew up.

Sincerely,

Candace Camp

PROLOGUE

Christmas
Amarillo, Texas

CLAIRE MURPHY turned at the sound of the front door closing, followed by soft footsteps in the hall. "Rebecca? Nate? We're in here, dears."

"Gran?" A moment later Claire's granddaughter stuck her head into the room, looking surprised. "You're still up?"

Claire smiled and exchanged a look with her husband, who sat beside her on the couch. "Yes, we're still rather night owls, I'm afraid."

Nate, her grandson and Rebecca's cousin, appeared behind Rebecca. With the same long build as most of the Murphy clan, he easily gazed over Rebecca's head at Claire and winked. "Grabbing a chance to enjoy the peace and quiet, huh?"

Claire's blue eyes twinkled, matching the mischievous glint in her grandson's. "Maybe. At eighty-two, even the most beloved of great-grandchildren can make one a trifle tired."

She didn't look tired in the least, despite her age. Tall and slender, her snowy hair cut into a chin-length bob, she was dressed in dark wool slacks and a soft cashmere sweater in a deep, vibrant shade of red. Pearls glistened at her earlobes and throat, and she looked every inch an elegant grande dame, the sort whose still-lovely face and gracious manner hid a backbone of iron. But when she smiled, her eyes lighting up with amusement and a love of life that nothing had ever been able to quench, she was just their warm and approachable grandmother, the one who laughed at their jokes and listened to their woes and even, now and then, went to bat for them with their parents.

"Come on in and join us." Jackson Murphy stood up from his place on the couch beside Claire. "We're just enjoying the fire and drinking some hot buttered rum. Let me get you a cup."

Jackson was as tall as his grandson, his hair still thick, but now white instead of the raven-wing black of earlier years. A lifetime spent largely outdoors had lined his skin, but it was easy to see the handsome young man he had once been in the strong bones of his face.

"I'll get the cups," Nate assured him. "You just sit down and enjoy the fire. The cider still on the stove?"

"Yes. Cups are in the cabinet beside the sink," Claire said.

Jackson resumed his seat beside his wife, reaching over to pick up Claire's hand and lace his fingers through hers. Claire glanced at him and smiled.

Rebecca, watching them, felt a little clutch in the

area of her heart. They're still in love, she thought, with a flash of surprise and pleasure. It wasn't something she'd ever considered before, just accepting the fact that Gran and Granddad were there, forever linked in her mind, an indivisible unit. But they had once been young and single, like she was; they had met and fallen in love and gotten married, like all the couples she dealt with on a daily basis in her wedding-planning business.

"How was the movie, dear?" Claire asked now, interrupting Rebecca's thoughts.

"Oh…okay, I guess." Rebecca shrugged.

"She's being kind," Nate put in from the doorway. He came forward and handed his cousin a steaming cup. "It was awful. On the way home, Rebecca told me that if I ever talked her into watching something like that again, she would never speak to me."

"A shoot-'em-up seems like an odd choice for Christmas," Jackson commented, nodding.

"Odd doesn't begin to describe it, Granddad," Rebecca told him emphatically. "Next Christmas we're going to a movie I pick."

Nate groaned. "A chick flick? Please…"

"It would have been better than *Steele Thunder III,*" Rebecca pointed out. "If only your sisters had gone, too, we would have had you outnumbered."

"Going to a movie always seemed an odd Christmas tradition to me," Claire commented.

"Way to get the rambunctious kids out of the house." Jackson grinned. "Same reason Laurie and Susan took their little ones this afternoon."

"Yeah. See?" Nate pointed out, grinning at his cousin. "It could have been worse. You could have been stuck at a movie about a talking dog."

"Hmm…" Rebecca adopted a thinking pose. "Let me think—talking dog versus wooden actors…"

Nate laughed. "All right. All right. I give up. Next year you get to choose."

"Well, I certainly hope that both of you plan to visit us sooner than that," Claire put in. "You should both come this summer. We'll have a July Fourth celebration—how does that sound? And this time maybe you two will bring guests."

"Uh-oh," Rebecca said, rolling her eyes at Nate comically. "Here it comes—the 'When are you going to settle down' speech?"

"Don't be impertinent, missy," Claire told her, with a teasing grin that belied her stern words.

"Just wait," their grandfather chimed in. "Next she'll pull out her 'we haven't many more years to live and we want to see you settled before we go' speech."

"Hush, you." Claire gave her husband's arm a playful slap. "You'll make my grandchildren think I'm manipulative."

"Honey, they've known you all their lives. They know you run everything."

"Gran, you find me a girl as perfect as you are, and I'll marry her," Nate declared.

"Nate's right," Rebecca agreed. "It's pretty hard to measure up in this family. I mean, look at Mom and Dad. Nate's parents. You and Granddad. You guys all have such great marriages. It's hard to find something like that."

"Oh, I don't know." Claire smiled, her face softening. "As I remember, your grandfather wasn't that hard to find. He walked right up to my door."

"Really?" Rebecca looked from Claire to Jackson and back. "When? What happened?"

"Oh, heavens, you don't want to hear about that old stuff," their grandfather said, waving a dismissing hand.

"Yeah, we do," Rebecca assured them. "I don't think I've ever heard how you two met."

"That's right," Nate agreed. "Go on…tell us, Gran."

"Well…" Claire began, her voice falling into the rhythmical cadence of a practiced storyteller. "It's true. Jack simply appeared on our doorstep one day. It was in May of 1949. I was back in Amarillo for the summer, staying with my parents. I'd just graduated from the University of Texas, and the law school had accepted me for admission that fall. I was twenty-two and sure I had life by the tail."

She smiled reminiscently, her eyes looking into a past her audience could not see. "I remember, I was standing in the hall upstairs, looking out the window at the street, and I saw this flashy Dodge coupe pull up in front of the house."

"It was not flashy," Jackson protested. "It was a beauty—a 1948 DeSoto, black with chrome trim."

Claire gave him a decidedly inelegant dig in the ribs with her elbow. "I swear, you liked that car better than me."

"Now, sweetheart, not better…" he teased.

"Anyway…" Claire went on, ignoring his comment. "As I watched, the driver's door opened. And this long, lanky fellow got out and started walking up the sidewalk to our house…."

CHAPTER ONE

"MAMA, there's someone coming up to the house." Claire leaned a little closer to the window, peering out.

"Don't shout, dear," Emily Winters admonished her daughter as she came out of her room down the hall, adjusting the pearl strand around her neck. She was an attractive middle-aged woman, gray beginning to intermingle with the dark blond in her hair, which she wore swept up and curled into a careful French roll on the back of her head.

The resemblance between Mrs. Winters and her daughter was clear, though Claire's hair was a soft brown and hung in a long, sleek bob that stopped just short of her shoulders. Their faces held the same elegant beauty, and Claire's eyes were the identical shade of blue.

Emily's mouth tightened in disapproval as she saw Claire in front of the window, holding the curtain aside to peer out. "Don't stand in front of the window gaping, Claire. It's common."

Not appearing "common," Claire knew from long experience with her mother, was Mrs. Winters's chief concern. "I was just bored," Claire explained.

"So I looked out. And I saw someone stop in front of our house."

"Who? It seems an odd time." Emily glanced at her slim gold watch.

"I don't know. I've never seen him before." Then, with the spark of mischief that frequently got her into trouble with her mother, Claire added, "But he looks awfully cute."

"Really, Claire." As expected, her mother frowned.

The doorbell rang downstairs, and Claire turned, starting toward the staircase.

"Let Bonnie get it, dear," Mrs. Winters admonished. "No doubt it's just the Fuller brush man."

"Bonnie's busy cooking," Claire replied, already running lightly down the steps. She paused to flash a grin back at her mother. "And he's too cute to be the Fuller brush man."

She continued down the stairs, and, with a sigh, Mrs. Winters followed her at a more dignified pace.

The man was even taller than he had looked coming up the walk, Claire realized as she opened the door and saw him waiting on their doorstep. He was also, she thought with a little jolt, even better looking.

He was half-turned away, gazing at their yard, and he swung back at the sound of the door opening. His eyes were a bright clear green, startling under the straight black slashes of his eyebrows. In the moment before he smiled, Claire had an impression of a thin, angular face, cheekbones pressing sharply against tanned skin, and a firm jaw and chin. Then his lips curled up into a smile, and Claire felt as if her heart did a flip.

He stared back at her, his automatic smile freezing on his face, then suddenly he seemed to come to himself, and he said, somewhat tentatively. "I—Mrs.—I mean, I'm looking for the Winters's house."

There was, Claire thought, a hint of East Texas in his speech, and his voice drifted up a little in questioning at the end of this sentence.

"I'm Claire Winters."

"Claire?" He said her name as if he knew her, and his eyebrows lifted as though surprised. "I'm sorry." He grinned a little ruefully. "You must think I'm crazy. I just—I was picturing you as a scrawny kid. But of course you've grown up by now."

"Do I know you?" Claire frowned, trying to put a little of her mother's frost into her tone. But she found it hard to do; there was simply something too engaging about this man's smile. Somehow she felt as if she ought to know him even though she was certain she had never seen him before.

"No, ma'am. But I feel like I know you. I'm Jackson Murphy. I knew your brother Dennis. We were in the Army together…"

At the mention of her brother, Claire felt the old familiar tug at her heart and the beginnings of tears in her eyes. But she smiled, recognizing the name. "Jack Murphy!"

He smiled back, his eyes looking straight into hers, warm and, like hers, touched a little with sadness. "Yes, ma'am. That's me. Jack Murphy."

"Come in." Claire stepped back to let him enter, turning to the side to look at her mother.

Mrs. Winters had stopped on the last step of the staircase, one hand on the railing and the other at her pearls, seemingly frozen into place, her eyes large and almost frightened.

"Mama, look, it's Dennis's friend. Jack Murphy. You remember Dennis writing us about him."

"Yes, of course." Mrs. Winters gave a brief, mechanical smile and moved down into the entryway. "How do you do, Mr. Murphy?"

"Ma'am." He nodded politely at Emily. "I—please accept my condolences. Dennis was a…a good man. A good friend."

This time the gesture that touched Emily's lips could scarcely be called a smile. "Thank you. Well… it…it's been a long time, now."

"Yes, ma'am."

Mrs. Winters turned toward Claire. "Why don't you show Mr. Murphy into the parlor, dear? I'll tell Bonnie to bring us some iced tea. You will have a glass of iced tea with us, won't you, Mr. Murphy?"

"Thank you, that sounds very nice, ma'am."

Mrs. Winters turned and headed back toward the kitchen. Claire pivoted in the opposite direction, crossing to the formal living room at the front of the house. She knew that her mother was less concerned with getting refreshments than with taking a moment to collect herself. The mention of Dennis still had the power to throw her, even after five years.

"I'm sorry," Jack said as he followed her into the living room. "I hope I didn't upset your mother."

"No, please, don't worry yourself about it. As

Mother said, it's been a long time. It's just that…well, I guess it sort of takes you by surprise nowadays, hearing his name. After so long."

He nodded, looking uncomfortable.

Claire smiled, gesturing toward one of the chairs arranged in a conversational grouping at right angles to the couch. "Really, don't worry. It's fine. Please, sit down."

"Sorry for acting like such a dolt at the door," he went on, his grin recovering its easy charm. "Obviously I knew you must be grown after all this time. It's just that Den always called you his kid sister…"

"I was fifteen when he enlisted. And he was always annoyingly big brother-ish." Claire's wistful smile took the sting out of her words.

She glanced toward the mantel, lined with framed photographs, then went across to pick up one of them and bring it back to Murphy. "This is the two of us. That's when Den was sixteen."

Claire, too, looked down at the silver-framed picture in Jack's hands. Dennis stared back at them, slender and grave, the suit he wore oddly making him look even younger than his age. Beside him was Claire, also in her Sunday best, white gloves on her demurely folded hands. She had been, she thought, all eyes and knobby knees, still a child though she was trying her best to look grown-up.

"Yep. Didn't often look so serious, though," Murphy said, studying the pictures.

"True." Claire smiled. Her brother had always been lighthearted, a golden boy who glided through life with a joke and a smile. If he had suffered the usual pangs of adolescence, Claire had not known about it.

"You look like him, a little." Murphy handed back the picture, and once again his grin flashed. "Lot prettier, though."

Claire tried to ignore the little leap of her heart as she took the photograph and placed it back on the mantel. It was silly to let a meaningless compliment fluster her. It wasn't as if she were a young girl, not knowing what to do about a little innocent flirtation. She had graduated from college, after all, and she hadn't exactly been dateless the whole time she had been there. Jack Murphy was not the first man to tell her she was attractive. Not even the first handsome man to do so.

However, if she was honest, she had to admit that he was one of the few who had made her pulse speed up just by smiling at her.

Feeling a little gauche and aware of his eyes on her, Claire walked back to her seat on the sofa. She looked at her hands, then cleared her throat and looked up at him. She could feel the pulse beating in the hollow of her neck, and she hoped he could not see it.

"Here we are." Her mother entered the room, carrying a tray, and the awkward moment was broken.

With relief, Claire turned to her and stood up to take the tray, but Jack beat her to it, jumping up and reaching out to take the silver tray from Mrs. Winters's grasp and set it down carefully on the coffee table in front of the couch.

"Bonnie had just made a fresh pitcher, so we are in

luck," Emily Winters said, smiling in her usual coolly polite way.

Her mother had recovered, Claire could see, from the momentary jolt of being reminded of her son, and she was once again in her gracious lady mode. It had always been a role her mother played; she enjoyed her position as a social leader in their small city. In recent years, however, she had become more and more entrenched in the role until it seemed to Claire that Mrs. Winters was now more country club matron than the mother Claire had grown up with.

"So you knew our Dennis," Mrs. Winters went on smoothly, offering their visitor one of the glasses of tea.

"Yes, ma'am. We were in the '36th' together. Whole war."

Mrs. Winters' smile remained firmly in place. "How nice," she said as if he had just said they had been next-door neighbors or played tennis every Saturday morning.

"So you were in Italy together," Claire said.

"Yes, ma'am. And France."

"The Battle of the Bulge?"

"Now, Claire." Mrs. Winters's face acquired a brittle look. "We mustn't drag our guest through all his old war experiences."

"Oh, I don't mind, ma'am," Murphy hastened to assure her. "If you wanted to hear about Dennis and—"

"That's perfectly all right," Mrs. Winters said in a politely remote tone.

Jack Murphy looked a little nonplussed, as though he was not sure what the older woman's statement meant, but he had no time to speak before Claire's mother moved on to say, "Why don't you tell us about yourself? Are you a Texas boy, as well?"

"Yes, ma'am. East Texas, little town called Big Sandy."

"What a quaint name. You spent your whole life there?"

"Yes, ma'am. Until the war came along."

"And was your father a farmer?"

"No, ma'am. He worked in the oil fields most of the time. Lots of oil around there. Van Zandt County. Tyler."

"I see. How interesting."

The corner of Jack's mouth quirked up. "Well, I have to admit it never seemed too interesting to me. At least, not the working in the field part. Oil, now, that's a different story. I've been at UT since I got discharged, studying petroleum engineering."

"My. You seem to be an ambitious young man."

"Well, the GI Bill seemed like too good a deal to waste."

"I've been at the university the last four years, too," Claire put in.

"Really?" Murphy looked at her.

"Yes, I graduated this year."

"Well, I'm sorry we never met." Again that trace of amusement touched his mouth. "Though I'm guessing we didn't exactly run in the same circles."

"It's such an enormous school," Mrs. Winters put in. "I always hated for Claire to go to such a large, anonymous sort of place. It seems quite easy to get lost. SMU or Texas Women's College would have—"

"Mama…" Claire said in the long-suffering tone of one who had heard this argument many times before.

"Yes, I know, dear. At any rate, that's all water under the bridge, and you're home now." She smiled at her daughter.

"So did you graduate this year, Mr. Murphy?" Claire asked.

"Yes, I did. And, please, call me Jack."

"Jack." Claire smiled at him. It seemed far more enjoyable saying his name than the occasion warranted, and she was aware of the faintest tinge of heat along her cheekbones. "And you must call me Claire."

"I'd like that."

"And what do you plan to do now that you've graduated, Mr. Murphy?" Mrs. Winters stuck in, pulling the young man's attention back to her.

"Well, I've already got a job with Hammond Oil. I've been working for them while I've been at school. But first I thought I'd take off a few weeks. See the country. I wanted to drive out to California and spend a few days in Los Angeles, maybe even go up to San Francisco. So I thought, well, I'd come up to Amarillo to get on Route 66 and pay my respects to Dennis's family. He was…" He paused. "Well, he was a good man, and I know he'd have wanted me to see you. Tell you anything you might want to know."

"Very considerate of you, I'm sure," Mrs. Winters replied, once again avoiding any mention of her son. "Ah, there…I believe I hear Mr. Winters's car in the driveway. He must be home from work. I'm sure he

would love to meet you, Mr. Murphy. Why don't you
stay and have supper with us?"

"I'd love to meet him, but I wouldn't want to put
you out, ma'am," Jack demurred.

"It's no trouble," Claire put in quickly. "Really.
Bonnie always fixes more than enough for us, and it
won't take a minute to add an extra place."

Claire suspected that her mother's invitation had
been made more out of a desire to wriggle out of any
more conversation about Denny and his death in the
war than out of any real desire to have Jack stay for
supper. But Claire had no intention of letting the opportunity slip out of her hands. She did not pause to
examine why she felt this way. After all, she was not
the sort of girl who went on alert in the presence of any
eligible male. But there was something about this man
that intrigued her, and she was glad of a chance to talk
to him more.

There was the sound of footsteps in the hallway, and
a moment later Claire's father strode into the room. A
tall man, somewhat stoop-shouldered, he wore a dark
three-piece suit and carried a briefcase. Claire rarely
pictured him any other way. Alan Winters was an
attorney with a thriving civil practice, and he routinely
immersed himself in his work, often bringing home
material to work on in his study after spending two or
three hours with his family.

Claire had always felt closer to her father than to her
mother. She had little interest in her mother's pursuits
of bridge games and luncheons at the country club.
From the time she was a child, Claire remembered seeing

her father come and go every day, and it had always seemed to her that he took part in an exciting world that existed outside the one in which his family lived. It was the world of banks, with their high dark wood counters and cool, smooth marble beneath one's feet, of tall stone buildings and sidewalks that glittered in the sun, of the high-ceilinged post office with its enormous colored murals stretching up the walls and huge red granite Texas stars embedded in the floors. It was to this magical place that she ventured now and then with her mother to shop at one of the big department stores downtown or go to a movie with her family. But her father got to go there every day, and his life, she had thought, must be special indeed.

She had vowed that one day she, too, would enter that world. She had gotten her first opportunity when she was in high school. The war had taken not only the young men her brother's age, but had also pulled many young working women to the high-paying factory jobs that one could find in the larger cities. Her father's secretary and his receptionist had been among those who left. Swamped with work and unable to find suitable replacements, Alan Winters had turned to his bright and capable daughter. All through high school, Claire had worked in his office after school and on Saturdays, and it was then that she had become certain what she wanted to do with her life. She wanted to practice law, just like her father.

Her best friend Josie had wrinkled her nose in distaste at the thought of Claire's spending her spare time amidst the dusty old books in her father's office, but Claire had loved it, and from that moment on, she had aimed her life in a path straight to law school. No amount of argument from her mother or amusement from the men she had dated or puzzlement from her sorority sisters had been able to deter her from her goal.

"Well, hello," her father said pleasantly as he strode into the room. "I see we have a guest."

Mr. Winters went first to his wife's chair, bending down to plant a quick kiss on her cheek, then turned toward Murphy, his gaze quietly curious.

"Darling, this is Mr. Murphy," Emily Winters began.

"He served with Denny in the war," Claire explained as she stood up to greet her father.

"Oh. Ah, I see." He stepped forward, his face warmer, holding out his hand for the younger man to shake. "A friend of Dennis—well, welcome to our house."

"Thank you, sir. Jack Murphy."

"Den wrote us about him," Claire went on.

"Of course. Yes, I remember the name. Dennis… um…" He cleared his throat. "Dennis relied on you."

"Thank you, sir. I hope so. I certainly relied on him." Again Jack offered his regrets over the fact of Dennis's death, a statement that Mr. Winters received somewhat more gracefully than his wife had done, though his face was tinged with the sorrow that had settled there frequently in the last few years.

Mr. Winters clapped his hand on the younger man's shoulder and said, "Why don't we go back to my study for a drink before dinner and give these lovely ladies a chance to get ready?"

Since Claire, despite her mother's frequent urgings,

rarely gave in and dressed up for the evening meal at home, she would have preferred to have been included in the gathering in her father's study. However, she could not really begrudge her father the opportunity to chat with her brother's friend alone, and, besides, tonight Claire welcomed the chance to improve her appearance before they sat down to eat.

She was not, of course, going to follow her mother's habit and apply a fresh layer of makeup or put on one of her nicer dresses and heels or clasp a strand of pearls around her neck. The yellow and white-striped sundress she had worn all day was perfectly fine for a dinner at home and, anyway, she quite liked the way it looked on her. But there was no reason not to apply a little lipstick and brush through her hair, and she didn't think it would be out of place to put on a pair of earrings, as well.

While she was not in the market for a husband as so many of her friends were, that didn't mean she couldn't enjoy a little flirtatious attention from a good-looking man, did it? And Claire was quite certain that the way Jack Murphy looked at her indicated an interest in her as more than just his late friend's sister.

From the way he stood up when she entered the dining room thirty minutes later, his green eyes sharpening and a smile curving his well-shaped lips, Claire knew that her bit of primping had been worth it.

Unfortunately, however, dinner with her parents allowed no opportunity to explore that interest—or even to engage in a bit of mild flirtation. Her mother directed the conversation, keeping it on as impersonal a level as was possible. It was almost as if, Claire thought, her mother was trying to hold off Jack Murphy, to keep a firm division between him and her family.

Her father was no better. Claire had no doubt that he had discussed Dennis and his death with Jack during their male tête-à-tête over bourbon before dinner, but now he steered clear of the subject as firmly as Claire's mother. He was only trying, in his gentlemanly way, to keep all distressing subjects from his wife and daughter, Claire knew, but it irritated her. Maybe her mother wanted to avoid any reminder of Dennis or his death, but Claire would rather know the grim details than remain ignorant. All the barriers her mother erected cut her off from Dennis's memory just as surely as they walled off her pain.

"Do you plan to stay in Amarillo for a day or two, Jack?" Mr. Winters asked jovially. "Or are you itching to get started for California?"

"Oh, Amarillo looks like it might be worth spending some time here," Murphy said, his gaze going to Claire before he turned toward her father at the end of the table. "I've never been here before."

"It's an interesting city," Mr. Winters said. "Mrs. Winters is a native, but I moved here from Arkansas. Fell in love with it immediately. It has its own kind of beauty. You should see the canyon, shouldn't he, Claire? Palo Duro Canyon," he elucidated.

"Yes, it's quite a sight," Claire agreed. "Like the Grand Canyon, only smaller. You can drive down into it and go exploring. Just don't get caught by one of the low water crossings."

"Indians used to winter there—the canyon provided

shelter for their horses, you see." Mr. Winters went on for a few more minutes about the history of the canyon.

"There are other things to do here," Claire put in when her father wound down. "There are even nightclubs."

"Really?" Jack grinned at her, his eyes lighting in interest.

"Oh, yes." Mrs. Winters decided to enter the conversation again. "The Nat is quite well-known, I believe. I have heard it said that it has one of the finest dance floors in the southwest. Benny Goodman and other famous bands have played there."

"It started out as a swimming pool." Mr. Winters could not resist a discussion of history of any kind. "The Natatorium is its full name, you see. The dance floor's laid right on top of the pool. Most unusual, I think."

"Well, it sounds like quite a place." Again Jack Murphy's green eyes went to Claire. "What about you, Claire? You go dancing there?"

"Yes, I do." Claire grinned, a challenging light suddenly twinkling in her eyes. "In fact, I'm going there tomorrow evening."

"Is that a fact?" His gaze held hers. "Well, maybe I'll see you there."

"Maybe you will," Claire agreed, her cheeks warming. "Maybe you will."

CHAPTER TWO

"REALLY, CLAIRE." Mrs. Winters turned a stern look on her daughter. Supper had ended and Jackson Murphy had left. He was barely out the door before Mrs. Winters swung around to face Claire, disapproval stamped on her face. "You acted in a most unbecoming way this evening."

"Now, Emily," Mr. Winters put in mildly. "No reason to get on the girl."

"No reason? She was positively forward with that young man."

"Forward!" Claire protested.

"There was no reason to tell him you were going to the Nat tomorrow evening. He acted as though he intends to show up there. And why not—you practically invited him."

"What's wrong with that?"

The corner of her mother's mouth turned down. "For one thing, you're going there with Harlan. What if this young man shows up and asks you for a dance?"

"Then I'll dance with him," Claire retorted.

"Oh, really, Claire. Don't be absurd."

"I'm not. What's wrong with having a dance with him? I liked Jack Murphy."

"He seemed like a nice enough young fellow," Alan Winters agreed. "Dennis's friend. I shouldn't think there would be any problem in Claire's accepting a dance with him."

Claire looked at her mother, raising her eyebrows in a challenging way. Emily Winters pressed her lips together tightly, her face unyielding.

"There," Alan said pleasantly, as if everything had just been settled. "No reason to be upset. Now, if you ladies will excuse me, I'm going to finish up a little work in my study."

He walked off down the hall, shrugging out of his suit jacket as he went. It was his one concession to informality, shucking off his jacket and undoing his tie when he settled down to work at home.

Emily waited until the door of his office closed before she took up the verbal cudgels with her daughter. "Claire…you know as well as I do that you should not encourage that boy. Your father is a kind and generous man. He treats everyone with equal courtesy—the hallmark, I might add, of a true gentleman. But a woman has to demonstrate more restraint. Especially an attractive young woman. Men so often take things the wrong way."

Claire stared at her mother. "A dance? What do you think is going to happen in one dance? I'm not talking about marrying the guy. Jack Murphy is going to be here a day or two—maybe—and then he's gone to California. I doubt I'll ever see him again. What could be so horrible about dancing with him?"

"There is no reason to adopt that tone with me, Claire. I know you like to think that you are a modern young woman, that you can live your life exactly as you please. But there are standards. And men still judge you on how you act."

"What men? Mother, what are you talking about?"

"Well, Harlan Ames, for one," Mrs. Winters shot back. "You have a date with Harlan tomorrow night. He is your escort. How do you think he will react if Mr. Murphy just shows up there, asking you to dance with him?"

"I'm not *engaged* to Harlan." Claire was stiff, her arms straight by her sides, her fists knotting. "And it isn't a date. Harlan is picking me up, but there are a bunch of us going. Susan and Bob and the Fortner boys. Barb Hollowell and her cousin Marj are coming with Dave Sutton. We're all going to be there together. It's just fun, not pairing off. I'll probably dance with all those guys. It's what you do—even when you're a couple, when you go out with a group, everybody dances one dance with each other."

"Yes, but Jack Murphy isn't—"

"Isn't what?" Claire asked when her mother paused, and her eyes lit dangerously. "Jack Murphy isn't what?"

"Well, he's not one of your set."

"What difference does that make? Does that mean I can't dance with him?"

"Of course not. It just means…well, you don't know what he's going to think or how he's going to act. And the company you keep reflects upon you, Claire."

"Jack Murphy was my brother's friend." Claire spoke in a low, flat tone, her voice fairly vibrating from the effort it took to control it. "If Denny approved of him, I have no doubts about him."

"It's an entirely different thing, and you know as well as I do that Dennis was a—an exceptionally friendly person, the sort who accepted anyone."

"He wasn't *friends* with just anyone."

"How do you even know that this young man was really his friend?"

"Dennis wrote me about him. He told me that Jack was a great guy, that I would like him. And he was right. I do like him."

"No doubt you do. But that doesn't mean that Harlan—"

"I don't care what Harlan Ames thinks!" Claire snapped. "And I don't understand why *you* care. He isn't even my boyfriend!"

"He could be," Emily pointed out. "If you gave him half a chance, Harlan would jump at the chance to date you. You know he would."

"I don't want to date him."

"Why ever not? I just don't understand you, Claire." Emily frowned, her face set in frustration. "How can you simply ignore one of the most eligible bachelors in the city? He has a good position at the bank—"

"Because his father is the president of it."

"That's scarcely a black mark against him. Most young women would think that was a plus. Harlan and his sister will inherit a great deal."

"I'm not interested in Harlan's money."

"Of course you wouldn't marry him solely for his money," Emily agreed reasonably. "But surely it's something in his favor. He comes from an excellent family, and he can take care of you in very good style for the rest of your life. He's a handsome young man, as well, and a good conversationalist."

"Mother, I know all Harlan's qualities. I've known him since I could walk. He can be funny and fun, and he's a good dancer. But I have no interest in marrying him."

Emily Winters crossed her arms in front of her and regarded her daughter balefully. "If you gave yourself a chance, you might find you felt differently."

"I won't. Mother, I could never fall in love with Harlan. And, anyway, marriage is the last thing on my mind at the moment. That's years and years away. I have law school to get through first, and then..."

"Law school!" It was clear from the look on Mrs. Winters's face that this topic was even more upsetting than her daughter's lack of interest in an eligible bachelor. "Honestly, Claire, don't tell me you are still going on about that."

"I don't know why you would think I wouldn't be. I told you when I got home that I'd been accepted into UT law."

"Yes, and I'm sure that's a great honor, my dear, but that doesn't mean that you have to accept."

"It's not a question of having to. I *want* to. Being a lawyer has been my dream for years. You know that."

"I blame your father for this," Mrs. Winters said bitterly. "If he hadn't let you go to work in that office of his, this never would have happened."

"Perhaps not. But I'm very glad it did."

"Have you even thought about us, Claire?" her mother asked. "Have you considered how it will reflect on your parents?"

"I would hope you would be proud of me!" Claire exclaimed. "You make it sound as if being an attorney is disreputable. Father is a lawyer. You always seemed proud of that fact."

Mrs. Winters grimaced. "Don't be flippant. You know as well as I do that it's not the same thing. You are a girl. You have no need to work. It's one thing to have a college degree. Girls of your sort are expected to go to college and acquire a higher education. But law school is another matter entirely. Law is a career. Why, it will look as though we couldn't afford to support you. As if you had to work."

"Mother…"

"Besides, it's so unfeminine. All that arguing and standing up in court. People will think your father and I have failed."

"It has nothing to do with you and Daddy. Going to law school is entirely my decision. What I do with my life is my decision."

"It's our decision, too, since we will be the ones paying your way through law school," her mother retorted.

"What are you saying? That you're going to cut off my funds? It won't stop me. I'll just work my way through school."

"Oh, really, Claire, you haven't the least notion of what it's like to work at a real job, much less to do so while you're trying to pass your courses."

"Then I'll learn. Other people have done it. I can get some extra money by selling the pearls Grandmother gave me."

"Claire Anne Winters!" Emily stared at her daughter, aghast. "Sell your pearls? What has come over you? Sometimes I hardly recognize you anymore."

"Really? Well, I hardly recognize you anymore, either." With that parting shot, Claire turned and stalked out of the room.

When she reached the hallway, she turned and glanced down it toward her father's study. She hesitated for a moment, then turned and walked to his door and knocked. At her father's invitation to enter, she stepped inside. Her father, glasses perched on his nose, his shirtsleeves rolled up and his hair mussed, glanced up at her a trifle vaguely.

"Hello, Claire. Was that you and your mother I heard? Are you arguing?"

"Yes. It seems to be the only thing we do anymore." Claire closed the door behind her with a snap. "She doesn't want me to go to law school."

"Oh." Alan Winters released a long sigh and leaned back in his chair, taking off his reading glasses and laying them on the desk before him.

"Yes. Oh." Claire came forward and sat down in the chair facing his desk. "Is that what you think, too, Daddy? Are you unhappy I'm going to law school? Do you think I'm a disgrace to the family?"

"A disgrace!" Her father's mouth curved up humorously. "For getting accepted to law school at UT? I'm very proud of you, my dear. That's quite an accomplishment."

Claire smiled, relaxing in her seat. She had always been closer to her father in temperament and outlook than she was to her mother. It had been Claire who had listened with interest to Mr. Winters's stories about his cases at the dinner table while Dennis and Emily had been patently bored.

"Thank you," she said to him now.

"I'm sure your mother didn't mean that you had been a disgrace. She loves you very much. It's just—well, your mother wants you to be happy."

"But this is what I want. This is what will make me happy."

Her father hesitated, then said carefully, "I know you think so right now. But your mother is a very practical woman. And she's experienced more of life than you have. You mustn't discount her opinions."

Claire stiffened a little in her chair. "What are you saying? Do—do *you* think I shouldn't go to law school?"

"I think you're very deserving of being admitted," he told her obliquely. "And, of course it's an honor."

"But you don't think I should go…" Claire guessed, her stomach sinking.

"Well, it—it's not something you need to do."

"I do need it. I don't understand. You always wanted Dennis to follow in your footsteps, you and Mama both. You and he used to argue about his becoming an attorney. You didn't want him to waste his brain, his abilities."

"Yes, but, sweetheart, Denny was a boy."

Claire stared at him, stricken. "But you are the one who always told me I could do anything I wanted, that I was as bright and capable as anyone else."

"Yes, of course, dear, you are. I meant every word

of it. Clearly you are just as smart as the others who were admitted."

"Smarter than a good number of them," Claire replied tightly. "You know as well as I do that I had to have better grades than many of the men they admitted. I had to be top of my class."

"I'm sure you did. Claire, sweetheart, no one questions your intelligence."

"Then what do you question? You told me I could achieve whatever I wanted, be whatever I wanted."

"Well, I meant within reason, of course," her father replied, a hint of impatience creeping into his voice.

"Within reason!" Claire could hardly believe this was her father saying these things. She could feel the traitorous threat of tears at the edges of her eyes. "What is so unreasonable about wanting to become an attorney? There are other women who are attorneys. I wouldn't be the first."

"Yes, of course, there are female attorneys, and you know that I do not believe that a woman should be denied an education simply because she's a woman."

"That's what I had always *thought* you believed."

"But there's no reason for you—I mean, you don't have to work. I am well able to support you. I'm more than happy to buy you clothes, whatever you want. Have I ever stinted on such things?"

"No. But that's not the point."

"You are an attractive young woman with plenty of prospects. You should be out having fun, not sitting in some dusty law library, poring over casebooks." He smiled at her fondly.

"Oh, you mean I should be—what, shopping? Painting my toenails? Gossiping on the phone with my friends?"

"It's a waste of the system. You'll go to school for a year or two, maybe you'll finish and get your degree. You might even practice for a time. But at some point, Claire, you're going to want to get married and settle down. You'll quit your practice. You'll want to stay at home with your children. It's only natural. And you will have taken a place in law school from someone else who could have used it."

"A man, you mean." Claire felt as if her jaw had locked up; she could barely get out the words. "A man who didn't do as well in college as I did, who wasn't as smart as I was."

"Well, probably so, but he, you see, will use his legal education."

"And so will I! How do you know that I'm going to marry? Or have kids? And even if I did, why would I suddenly want to stay home and take care of the house? I've never wanted to do that before. When I'm done with law school, there will still be plenty of time for me to meet someone and get married. I can practice law and have children."

"You think that now. But it will be different when you meet the right man, sweetheart." He smiled at her, and the trace of paternal condescension in his face galled Claire.

"So falling in love automatically makes a person stupid?" Claire asked, knowing that she sounded bitter and sarcastic, but unable to stop herself.

"I didn't say that."

"That's what you meant. Or, I guess, what you meant was that it makes a woman stupid. I presume you don't believe a man wants to quit thinking or being useful because he falls in love or decides to have a family. But when a woman falls in love, she's suddenly interested in, oh, say, aprons and cupcakes, not contracts or torts. Is that it?"

"You're twisting my words. Of course you wouldn't become incompetent in any way. It's simply that your interests, your talents will turn in a different direction. It's only natural. You'll want to raise your children, to make your home just like you want it. And what husband is going to want you to work? It wouldn't reflect very well on him or his ability to provide for his family. He'd want you to quit work when you married—or at least by the time you have children. You must see that, Claire."

Claire sighed. Probably what galled her the most was that he was right. Men wanted to be the sole provider, the head of the household. She knew, deep down, that by pursuing a law career, she might very well be giving up any chance at love and marriage. If even her own father, one of the fairest and most intelligent men she knew, felt this way, it seemed very unlikely that she would find any man who did not mind her ambitions.

"Maybe marriage isn't for me, Daddy," Claire said, standing up.

"Don't say that!" Mr. Winters's face wrinkled in concern. "Sweetheart, of course you'll marry. You're such a lovely, intelligent girl. The right man will come along."

"I'm not sure I want to marry," Claire admitted. "Not if it means giving up...everything else." She looked at her father.

Mr. Winters's frown deepened. "Honey, you don't understand—you'll realize later what I'm talking about. "

"Maybe so." She looked away, then back at him. "I like the law. I enjoyed working in your office. I was good at it. Wasn't I?"

"Yes." He sighed. "Much to my regret."

Tears filled her eyes, and she turned away quickly to hide them. Why had her father never told her that he felt this way? Her anger had drained away, leaving behind a confused sorrow. She had always been sure of her father's approval even when her mother had opposed her. It felt so odd to know that this time she had no intention of abiding by his wishes.

Claire walked to the door and opened it, then paused, looking back at him. "It's pretty ironic, isn't it, that you used to want so much for Denny to go to law school, that you got upset with him because he didn't have enough ambition—and now you're upset with me because I have too much."

She turned and walked away, not pausing for his response.

CHAPTER THREE

CLAIRE GAZED OUT across the dance floor, aware of a strong feeling of restlessness. The faceted mirror ball that hung from the ceiling caught the light and fractured it over the dancers moving about the floor in a fox-trot.

She had looked forward to this evening, glad to get out of the house and away from the new awkwardness between her and her parents. Most of the day had been spent avoiding her mother. Claire had given over an inordinately long time to bathing and doing her nails and hair, then had tried on and discarded several different outfits before she had finally settled on her full black circular skirt and soft gray jersey knit top.

However, she was honest enough to admit that keeping herself busy and away from Mrs. Winters was only part of the reason for spending so much time on her looks this evening. Like her mother, Claire suspected that Jack Murphy had been flirting a little with her yesterday at supper——and that he had shown a certain interest in her statement that she was going to be at the Nat tonight, dancing.

But she had been here for over an hour and still had not seen any sign of him. She had danced with all the young men in their party, including Harlan, and Bill Harris, whom she had known in high school, had come over to chat a little and had asked her onto the floor for a fast jitterbug. But none of it had proved to be very much fun. Harlan had been drinking a great deal—indeed, she suspected that he had had a few drinks before he even came to her house this evening to pick her up—and he was acting a bit too proprietorial for her comfort.

Perhaps, she thought, it had been a mistake to go out with Harlan several times since she had returned home from college. She had not considered tonight a date any more than she had considered the time or two they had gone swimming at the club with some of their other friends as dates. After all, the only time she had actually been alone with him was last Friday when they had seen a movie at the Paramount. But she had noticed tonight that Harlan had slung his arm along the back of her chair casually as they chatted with their friends, and when Bill had sat down to talk with her after their dance, Harlan had shot the other man several dark glances.

Claire decided that she would have to curtail their evenings out. The last thing she wanted was for Harlan to start thinking the way her mother was—that their relationship was something more than friendship. She sighed, thinking that the summer might prove to be most boring if she was going to have to avoid Harlan, and she cast another sweeping glance across the room.

There, standing on the edge of the shining maple-planked dance floor, was a tall, slender man with thick black hair. He turned his head in her direction. It was Jackson Murphy.

Claire's heart began to pound. Recognition touched Jack's face as he saw her, and he smiled. Claire smiled back, and he started across the floor toward her, skirting the dancers. She cast a look down at her lap to hide the glow of triumph that she suspected stamped her features, but she could not deny the giddy feeling that permeated her body. He had come here to see her; she was certain of that. She had not been mistaken in the interest she had seen in his eyes.

She raised her head. He was only a few feet from the table now, and again they smiled as their eyes met.

"Well, Miss Winters," he said, stopping beside her. "Fancy meeting you here."

"It is a popular spot," Claire replied. "But, please, it's Claire, remember?"

"Claire."

"Won't you join us?" she asked, and he pulled up a chair and sat down with alacrity. "Let me introduce you to my friends. Jack, this is Harlan Ames. And next to him is Susan McElroy." She moved around the table, naming all her friends who weren't presently out on the dance floor, ending by looking at the man beside her and saying, "And this is Jackson Murphy. He was a friend of my brother's."

"Really?" Harlan's eyebrows lifted, and his gaze was anything but friendly. "You're from Amarillo?"

"No. East Texas, actually. Dennis and I were in the war together."

"Oh. I see."

Jack turned his gaze back to Claire. "This is quite a place," he told her. "Just like you said. Good band."

"I'm glad you like it."

"I was hoping that you'd do me the honor of giving me a dance," he went on.

"Claire's here with me," Harlan interposed quickly before Claire could reply.

Claire shot a pointed glance at Harlan, then turned to Jack. "Thank you, I'd enjoy a dance."

Harlan moved in his chair, but Claire ignored him and stood up. Jack jumped to his feet, offering her his arm. They walked out onto the dance floor, where the couples had begun to circle slowly as the band started a waltz.

"So is that guy your boyfriend?" Jack asked conversationally.

"No. He's not even my date," Claire replied shortly.

"I got the feeling he didn't like me," Jack went on with a grin, turning to face her as they reached the dance floor.

"I think Harlan's beginning to assume more than he should."

Claire took the hand he held out and moved into position, her other hand going up to his shoulder. His arm curled around her, his palm settling on the small of her back. Claire had danced with many men; she had never been a wallflower. But it felt different somehow to have Jack Murphy put his arm around her, to have her hand nestled in his, to look up into his face. It made her a little breathless, uncertain.

What was happening here? She wasn't quite sure, and for a girl who always knew where she was going, that was an unsettling experience. But, she realized, it wasn't really unpleasant. In fact, what she felt, she knew, was excitement.

He was a smooth dancer, not the sort who pushed you around the floor, but neither was he the noodle-armed kind where you had to guess where he was headed. It was easy to fall into the rhythm with him. Yet, at the same time, she was very aware of his close-ness, his arm around her, his hand clasping hers. She could smell the faint scent of his aftershave, feel the warmth of his body. She found herself wondering what it would be like to have his arms encircle her tightly, to be pressed against him in an embrace and feel his lips on hers.

Her cheeks warmed at her thoughts; she hoped the color didn't show up in the dim light of the dance floor. His hand tightened a little on her back, pulling her closer. Claire did not resist; her entire body sud-denly felt much more alive, tingling with awareness. She was sorry when the music came to a close and he released her.

Claire looked up, giving him a quick smile. She felt faintly embarrassed, knowing what her reaction to him had been, and she wondered if he had any idea how she had felt. And what had he felt? He had definitely moved closer to her; surely that meant that she was not the only one to feel something.

"Why don't you come join us?" Claire suggested as they strolled back to the table where her party sat.

"I don't imagine your friend Harlan would like that."

"I told you, Harlan has no claim on me. I'm here with a group of friends. If I ask you to join us, I don't see that he has any say in the matter."

A corner of Jack's mouth twitched up. "I suspect old Harlan won't see it quite that way."

"Well, if you prefer not to sit with us, that's fine…"

He chuckled. "Oh, no, I didn't say that. I would very much like to sit with you—just warning you that Harlan may raise a stink."

Claire knew he was right. As they got closer, it was easy to see that the situation at the table had already become a trifle strained. Harlan was pushed back from the table, his arms crossed over his chest, staring moodily toward the dance floor. His friend Bob was leaning toward him, talking earnestly, and most of the others at the table were studiously ignoring Harlan. As Claire and Jack reached the table, Susan, on the other side of Bob, rolled her eyes at Claire and made a little nod toward Harlan.

Marj was dancing with one of the Fortner boys, and the other Fortner was gone, as well, so Claire sat down in one of the empty chairs they had left rather than taking her former seat beside Harlan. Jack sat beside her. Across the table Harlan looked up and glared.

"What? Now you're not even going to sit next to me?"

Claire gazed back at him coolly. "You didn't look like you wanted company."

"There's some company I don't want," Harlan replied with a pointed look at Jack.

Bob, beside Harlan, cast an apologetic glance toward Claire and Jack as he clapped a hand on Harlan's shoulder. "Hey, Harlan, why don't you and I go outside and have a smoke?"

Harlan didn't look at him, just shrugged off his hand. "Why are you hanging around here, Murphy? Don't you have somewhere to go?"

"Not at the moment," Jack replied easily.

"I invited him to join us, Harlan," Claire told him, her voice hardening.

"I'd like to know what the hell you think you're doing!" Harlan jumped to his feet, planting his palms on the table's edge and leaning across toward Claire.

Beside Claire, Jack rose smoothly to his feet, his body tensing and his eyes alert and watchful, his hands hanging loose and ready. "I think you ought to sit back down, Mr. Ames," he said, his voice low but steely. "You don't want to make a scene here."

"Oh? Is that what you think?" Harlan cast a disdainful glance at him. "Well, I'm not talking to you. I'm talking to her." He jabbed a finger in Claire's direction.

"Harlan, you're drunk." Claire also stood up. "I'm not talking to you when you're like this."

Ignoring her words, Harlan went on, still leaning heavily against the table. "What the hell do you think you're playing at? You trying to make me jealous?"

"Excuse me?" Claire's eyes flashed, and color rose in her cheeks. "No, I am not trying to make you jealous. Your jealousy is the last thing I want."

"Then what's all this flirting with him?" Harlan's voice rose, and people at the tables around them began to turn and look.

"Harlan, come on. People are watching." Bob reached out and took his friend's arm.

Harlan jerked his arm away. "I don't give a damn! Let 'em look!" He cast a scornful glance at the table nearest them, then turned back to Claire.

"I danced with Mr. Murphy," Claire said tightly. "I have every right to do so. The fact that you picked me up at my house tonight doesn't mean that you have any claim on me. I'm not your girlfriend."

"Then what the hell have you been doing for the past two weeks?" he exclaimed.

"I have been socializing with my friends," Claire shot back. "Or, at least, that's what I thought I was doing. I wasn't aware that being around you and my friends somehow made me your property."

"You know what? You're just a tease! That's what you are."

"Okay. That's it." Jack moved quickly around the table, stopping right beside Harlan, so that Harlan was forced to twist around and step back to look up at him.

"What the hell do you think you're doing?" Harlan swayed without the support of the table, his head craned back to look at the taller man.

"At the moment I'm trying to keep you from making a fool of yourself. Or, at least, any more of a fool than you already have." Murphy planted his palm on the other man's chest and exerted pressure.

Harlan, already unsteady on his feet, folded into the chair behind him. He began to sputter and try to rise, but Jack leaned forward and put a firm hand on him, holding him down.

"I suggest you stay there. Drink some coffee and let your friends take you home."

"Why, you—who the hell do you think you are—I ought to punch you!" Harlan again started to rise, and Jack casually swept a foot under Ames's ankles, knocking up his feet and sending him back down heavily into his chair.

Jack fixed him with a cold, hard stare. "You don't want to fight me, son."

Claire, looking at them, realized that Jack was probably only four or five years older than Harlan, but there was a look of hard-won experience in Murphy's face that made the other man appear a boy beside him.

Jack turned toward Claire. "Would you like for me to take you home, Claire?"

"Yes, I would. Thank you." Claire reached over the table and picked up her evening bag.

"Wait! Claire!" Harlan stared at her, dumbfounded. "You can't leave!"

Claire simply raised her eyebrows, then turned away, tucking her hand into Jack's offered arm.

They walked off. Claire heard Harlan's voice behind her, but she didn't look back. Hopefully Bob and the others would talk some sense into Harlan, and he wouldn't try to follow them.

Jack whisked her through the front doors, and they paused outside the fortresslike facade of the large ballroom. The evening breeze was cool on Claire's reddened cheeks and stirred her hair, lifting it away from her face. She offered her companion a small, embarrassed smile.

"Thank you. I'm sorry for the way Harlan acted back there."

"Not your fault." His shoulders rose in a nonchalant shrug. "I hope it didn't ruin your evening."

"No. I was bored, anyway," Claire admitted with a grin.

"Would you like to go somewhere? Grab something to eat or get a cup of coffee?" He glanced around. "I think there's a café on the other side." He gestured toward the cross street, where an extension consisting of a café had been built onto the ballroom to give it an entrance on Route 66.

"No." Claire shook her head emphatically. "I don't want to go back in. There's a coffee shop open this late downtown, if you want to try that."

"Sure."

It felt a little odd, Claire thought, getting into Jack's car. He was very close to being a complete stranger to her, but she had no fear of him, only a low, thrumming sense of anticipation.

"Nice car," she commented, casting about for something to say.

"Thanks. I worked for Hammond while I was going to college—so I didn't have to depend entirely on the G.I. Bill. And when I got through school, I decided to give myself a graduation present." He shot her a sidelong glance. "I told myself it was practical. I'll be traveling a lot on my job."

"So you should have a comfortable car. Sounds reasonable."

"Doesn't it?" A grin flashed across his face. "A pickup might have been more practical, but…"

"Not as attractive."

"Exactly."

He followed the directions she gave him, and they drove through the mostly empty streets toward the center of town, chatting casually about Austin and the places there that both of them had frequented while they were in school—the cool waters of Deep Eddy Pool and Barton Springs, the all-night Nighthawk restaurant, the Owl Club north of town for dancing.

When they reached the coffee shop, Jack parked and they went inside, settling into one of the high-backed booths. There, in the small brightly lit coffee shop, they fell into a momentary silence, suddenly a trifle awkward.

Claire picked up one of the menus just to have something to do with her hands, but when the waitress arrived, she ordered only a cup of coffee. She set the menu back down on the Formica table and glanced across at Jack. He was watching her, his green eyes steady under the straight black slashes of his brows. Claire's gaze went to his mouth—his upper lip sharply cut, his lower lip full—and she found herself wondering what it would feel like to have that mouth on hers, a thought that immediately embarrassed her. She dropped her gaze back down to the table.

"So now that you've finished college," Jack said finally, breaking the silence, "what do you plan to do?"

"I'm going to law school." Her words were almost defiant, and Claire raised her eyes, meeting his squarely, waiting for the inevitable comment. She had heard them all, she thought, from exclamations of sheer astonishment to jokes about looking for a lawyer husband. She wished, she realized, that she wasn't going to have to hear him denigrate her choice.

His eyebrows went up a little, and he smiled, but there was an odd, bittersweet quality to the curve of his lips and a touch of sadness in his eyes. "That's what Den thought."

"What?" She stared at him, completely thrown by his response.

"Dennis. He told me you were smart as a whip. He knew you were going to do something big. He said once that you kept writing him about working in your dad's office and he laughed, said he reckoned it was going to be you going to law school, not him."

Claire's throat closed and tears stung her eyes. She pressed her lips together tightly.

"I'm sorry," Jack said quickly, reaching out to lay his hand over hers on the tabletop. "I didn't mean to make you unhappy."

Claire shook her head. "No. It's fine. Thank you. It didn't make me unhappy—well, maybe a little, but mostly…" She blinked away her tears. "Mostly it makes me so proud and—" Claire swallowed and sighed. "I still miss him sometimes."

"Yeah. Me, too." He paused, then went on, "He'd be proud of you, I'm sure."

"I hope so." Claire smiled at him. "I'm glad you told me. Most people seem to think I'm kind of crazy."

He raised an eyebrow. "Crazy? Why? For wanting to be a lawyer?"

Claire nodded. "My mother wants me to settle down and marry somebody like Harlan Ames."

"Good Lord. Why? Does she have something against you?"

Claire giggled. "No. At least, I don't think so. She's never seen Harlan the way he was tonight. She just likes the fact that his father is a banker. Mama is a bit of a snob—you may have noticed." She sighed. "Appearances mean a lot to her—what people will say. How things look. She thinks it makes my father look bad somehow if I go to law school. It seems like— well, I think she's been worse about it ever since Den died. She started to cling more and more to all these *things*. The country club. Her charities. Jewelry. Stuff that seems even less important to me than it used to, after Dennis died."

"Things affect people differently, I guess."

"I know. And I think I understand the way she is— at least a little. If she concentrates on all these things, maybe it makes it easier to not think about Dennis, like she's trying to fill her life up with stuff so there's not any room for all the sadness."

"That makes sense."

"But why does she have to run my life the same way she runs hers?" Claire exclaimed in frustration. "Why do I have to live here and do all the things she does? It's as if she wants me to have the same life she's had."

"Well…maybe she just is afraid of losing another child."

Claire stared at him. "I never thought of that. You

might be right." A smile burst across her face, dazzling him. "Thank you."

He smiled back.

Claire realized that his hand still covered hers on the table, strong and warm. A quiver of sensation ran up from it and deep into her body. His touch…his smile… Why was it that he, out of all the men she had known, set off sparks in her? How did it happen that Harlan Ames did not interest her in the slightest, yet whenever she looked at Jack Murphy, all she could think about was kissing him?

CHAPTER FOUR

THEY STAYED until the coffee shop closed an hour later, ignoring the looks sent them by the waitress and the number of times she strolled by to ask if they wanted anything else. Claire found herself talking about any and everything with Jack. She recounted memories of things she had done with Dennis when they were little, of trips they had taken back to the Arkansas home where her father had grown up. She talked about her high school years and the classes she had enjoyed at the university.

And she had listened, rapt, to Jack's stories about the war, about landing in Italy and then again in southern France, about slogging through rain and mud and snow. She had laughed over reminiscences of his boyhood in the sultry heat of East Texas, of feeding the chickens and milking the cow and the other chores that had fallen to him while his father was working in the oil fields near Longview.

Finally, after a flat announcement from the waitress that it was closing time, they left the café, driving slowly back to her house. It was near midnight, but Claire hadn't the slightest interest in going home. If she could have thought of somewhere else to go, she would have gladly suggested it.

But all too soon Jack was pulling up in front of her house. With an inward sigh, Claire turned to him, saying, "I had a lovely time tonight."

He smiled. "Even with Harlan causing a scene?"

"Even with that."

"Don't go in yet." He turned off the engine and turned to face her.

"I have to pretty soon or Mama will start turning on all the lights."

"Really?"

Claire let out a little laugh. "Yes, really. Whenever I come home, it's like I'm sixteen all over again." She shrugged.

She didn't add that most of the time she didn't care about her mother's behavior. This was the first time since high school that she had been brought home by someone with whom she would have liked to steal a few more quiet moments alone.

Claire was turned toward him, her arm braced on the back of the seat. He reached out and interlaced his fingers with hers, looking into her eyes. Claire's heart tripped in her chest, and she was suddenly, intensely aware of her own physicality—the blood pumping through her veins, the air rushing in and out of her lungs, the dryness of her throat, her skin prickling in anticipation.

"I'd like to see you tomorrow," he told her, his thumb moving lightly, slowly up and down the side of her finger. "Would you drive down to Palo Duro Canyon with me? Show me all the sights?"

Claire smiled, excitement rising in her at the re-alization that Jack wasn't leaving for California yet, that she would have another chance to see him, talk to him…be with him.

"That sounds lovely," she replied, hoping that she didn't sound quite as eager as she felt.

"Great. What time? Around noon maybe? I thought we could have a picnic down there."

"Perfect. I'll bring the sandwiches."

"Oh, you don't need to—"

"Nonsense. You're staying at a motel. I have a kitchen. I'll fix the sandwiches."

"Okay," he gave in with a grin. "You make a good case."

"Very funny."

He leaned toward her, his movements slow and deliberate, and Claire knew that he was about to kiss her, that he was, in fact, giving her time to pull back if she wished to.

She also knew that she had no intention of pulling back. Her pulse was thrumming, her chest tightening. She leaned forward. Jack drew in his breath sharply, and his mouth closed on hers. His hand was still entwined with hers, and his fingers tightened involun-tarily, though he made no other movement to hold her.

They kissed, the moment seeming to last forever while at the same time rushing forward. Claire trembled under the force of a sudden, intense hunger, and she felt a corresponding tremor in him. Heat flared where their flesh touched and traveled straight down through her, pooling in her abdomen.

Reluctantly he pulled back. Claire stared at him in the dim light, her eyes wide, her mouth soft and slightly open. For a moment, he seemed to teeter on the edge of something, the air electric with tension between them. Then Jack drew in a deep breath and moved away, unlinking their fingers and turning to face forward again.

He ran his hands back through his hair, taking another moment, then said in a low voice, "I'll walk you to your door."

"You needn't."

Jack tossed her a grin. "And have your mother say I'm not a gentleman?"

He opened the door and came round to open hers. They walked to the front door, not speaking, but his hand came down to take hers again. It seemed very natural, Claire thought, as if that was where her hand belonged. She turned at the door and smiled at him. She knew that she would have liked him to kiss her again, but she suspected that he would not do so here on the well-lit front porch, not with the threat of Emily Winters watching.

So she smiled and said, "Tomorrow then? Noon?"

"Noon." He smiled and gave her hand a squeeze, and Claire turned, opened the front door and slipped inside.

She was relieved to find no parent lurking in the foyer, and she hurried into the living room to push the drapes aside a fraction and look out the window at Jack Murphy as he trotted down the sidewalk and got into his car. The car rolled away, and she let the draperies drop.

A smile spread across her face, and she trailed out of the room into the foyer, reaching out to lock the door. Turning, she ran lightly up the stairs. She felt, she thought, as if she were floating, and she had to press her fingers to her mouth to hold back a giggle.

She understood now what it meant to be walking on air.

"You're going where?" Claire's mother stared at her across the breakfast table.

Emily had already eaten breakfast with her husband before he left for the office this morning, but, as was her habit, she was enjoying a second cup of coffee at the table with her daughter as Claire ate.

"Palo Duro Canyon," Claire repeated though they both knew that her mother had heard her correctly the first time. "Jack Murphy asked me to go with him."

"He's still here?" Emily frowned. "How did this come about? Did he interrupt your date with Harlan last night?"

"Mama, I told you, it was not a date. And he didn't interrupt. He very politely asked me for one dance. Harlan, on the other hand, was quite obnoxious and started a scene. Jack very nicely offered me a ride home."

"Jack Murphy brought you home?" Emily's frown deepened. "You mean you left Harlan at the ballroom?"

"Yes, I did. He'd had too much to drink, and he was being very unpleasant. Bob tried to get him to hush, but he wouldn't pay any attention. Hopefully Bob drove him home because he wasn't in any condition to do so himself."

"Oh, dear. This hardly sounds like Harlan. He's usually such a nice young gentleman."

"He's been known to drink too much, Mama. It's hardly something that anyone spreads around, especially to parents. But I noticed that he had gotten worse when I was home at Christmas."

Her mother looked pained, but dropped the subject of Harlan. "Still…I don't like the idea of your accepting a ride home from a man we don't know."

"He's a nice man, Mama. I promise you. And he was a friend of Den's."

"That doesn't necessarily make him an acceptable man for you. Men can be friends with the most unsavory characters and people hardly think anything about it. But with a woman, it's an entirely different matter."

"I am sure that my reputation will survive being driven home by Dennis's friend even though I haven't known him since childhood."

"There's no need to be sarcastic, dear. I am simply looking out for your best interests."

Claire sighed. "I know you are, Mama, and I'm sorry if I was short with you. But I do wish that you would trust my judgment."

"But I do," her mother replied, looking surprised. "Still, a girl your age is inclined to be a little…well, naive, and you have always had such a good heart. You overlook the, ah, differences in people. I'm sure Mr. Murphy's upbringing was vastly different from yours, and while that may not seem like a very big thing to you now, trust me, in time it can loom quite large."

"Then I guess it's a good thing that he won't be

around much longer, isn't it?" Claire reached out and patted her mother's arm. "Really, Mama, don't worry. I'm just going down to the canyon for a picnic. It's not a big thing. Really."

Claire reminded herself of the same thing as she went up the stairs later and began to get ready. A trip down into the canyon for a picnic lunch didn't require such careful make-up or selection of what to wear— any more than it required her make deviled eggs, as well as thick ham sandwiches or to wheedle Bonnie into frying up some of her delicious apricot tarts.

She was going to unnecessary trouble, Claire knew. It was pointless, really, since Jack Murphy would be heading to California soon, probably the next day. But she could not bring herself to cut short her primping or drop her elaborate preparation of the lunch basket. Sure, it wasn't going anywhere—it couldn't, given that they'd probably never see each other again after today—but that didn't mean she couldn't enjoy the day. She liked Jack's company; he was interesting to talk to, and he made her laugh. And, she was honest enough to admit to herself, she wouldn't mind a repeat of last night's kiss.

Claire had had her share of kisses. But Jack's kiss last night had been something special. She couldn't remember another kiss that had made her feel as if she was about to dissolve into a puddle. When he'd pulled back from her, she felt as if she were glowing from within. She wasn't sure why his kiss had been so electric, why she had been flooded with heat. But she had not been able to get it out of her mind all morning.

Indeed, it had taken her a long time last night to fall asleep; her nerves had been positively humming.

Claire was waiting at the upstairs window when Jack arrived, though this time she forced herself to wait and let Bonnie answer the door. After all, she wasn't a novice at dating; she knew it was a mistake to seem too eager. But when she came down the stairs and saw him waiting for her, leaning against the door, his sleeves casually rolled up to reveal his tanned, muscular arms, Claire could not keep a grin from bursting across her face.

Jack straightened, his eyes lighting up in a gratifying way as he returned her smile. "You look awfully good for hiking around."

"Who's says I'm going to be hiking around?" Claire teased, giving him a wide-eyed look. "I thought I was just there to point out the sights. My intention was to sit under a shade tree and watch you clamber up the rocks."

He raised an eyebrow at her. "Think so, huh?"

Claire laughed. "Anyway, a sundress is cooler. It gets pretty hot down there." She knew that she had chosen this particular halter-topped sundress more for the way her shoulders looked in it than for its cooling properties, but there was no reason to tell him that.

She went into the kitchen for the picnic basket, and Jack picked up the small bright red and white metal cooler for their drinks and perishables. They carried them out to his car and stowed them in the back seat, then set off on their drive.

It was, Claire discovered, just as easy to be with Jack on the ride down to the canyon as it had been the night before. They laughed and joked as they drove, seemingly never at a loss for a topic. In a way, it seemed as if she had known Jack all her life, Claire thought, and yet at the same time, there was a frisson of excitement that ran through her simply because she was with him.

Palo Duro was at some remove from Amarillo, and once they reached it, it was a slow, winding driving down into the floor of the canyon. They stopped at a rock park building partway down to look at the vista, then continued to the bottom, eight hundred feet below the rim. They drove along the road curving through the canyon floor, pausing now and then to look up at the high walls, banded in colors of yellow, rose, white and maroon. Low water crossings led over the shallow creek that snaked through the canyon. White poles stuck into the creek bed marked the rise of the waters during flooding rains.

At various spots beside the road, often near the creek, scrubby trees offered shade, and picnic tables and benches had been placed beneath them. They reached the end of the road and turned back, pulling off the road at one of the picnic spots.

Leaving behind the picnic tables—and the family that was already sitting at one of them—they hiked farther up the trail. Finally they came to a secluded spot beside the creek bed—all dry now except for a shallow ribbon of water running down the middle. Here a large slab of stone rose in a wavelike fashion, like icing that had melted and dripped down from a cake into an undulating puddle, then had frozen in place. A mesquite tree's feathery leaves cast a shadow over one portion of the rock ledge, creating a pleasant spot to spread out their blanket and sit down to enjoy their picnic.

"What's the creek?" Jack asked, taking one of the soft drink bottles from the cooler and prying off the top.

"Oh, it's a fork of the Red River," Claire explained. "Prairie Dog Fork."

"Colorful name." His mouth quirked in amusement.

"Colorful place." She smiled back at him, taking out the food and spreading it out in front of them.

"It is that," he agreed, taking a long look around them. "I never imagined there was anything like this here. It's so different from East Texas—so stark and flat and treeless, and then this huge hole opening up right in front of you. But it's beautiful, too. Not like anyplace else."

Claire nodded. "I love Austin, but I love Amarillo, too." She glanced over at him as she said carefully, "Where will your work be taking you? You said you'd gotten a job with Hammond…"

"Yeah. They have an office in Austin, and I've worked there while I was in school, sometimes rough-necking in the summer. But now I'll be starting out in their west Texas fields, the Odessa area."

Claire made a face. "Talk about flat and treeless."

Jack laughed. "Yeah. Well, I could have stayed in Austin, but this is a better opportunity. They also have offices in Corpus and Houston, so I imagine I'll have a chance to live a few other places in the future. It'll all be good experience for going out on my own."

"Is that what you want to do? Be a wildcatter?"

"Yeah. I can't see working for a company forever. I got enough of taking orders in the Army."

"Murphy Oil Company," Claire said. "Sounds good."

He grinned. "Sounds even better when you say it."

They settled down to eating and soon polished off the sandwiches Claire had made, topping them off with Bonnie's apricot tarts, which Jack agreed were the best he'd ever tasted. Afterward they strolled along the creek bed, and Jack reached out and took Claire's hand. Her heart sped up a little at his touch, and she was suddenly warmer. She hoped he couldn't feel the abrupt flush of heat in her hand.

Her mind went to their kiss last night, and she couldn't help but wonder if he intended to kiss her again. She knew that she wanted him to. If nothing else, she wanted to find out if their kiss had really been as special as it had seemed at the time. She had told herself that it had simply been more exciting because she barely knew Jack; that had made it a little daring and reckless. Or perhaps it was the aftermath of the tension and excitement from the scene Harlan had created at the nightclub. Surely this man's kiss was not *that* different from any other man's.

Claire sneaked a sideways glance at Jack. He was looking ahead, his profile to her, and she could not help but think what a clean, strong face he had. Angular as it was, he might have looked stern if it were not for the softening effects of his thick dark eyelashes and the fullness of his lower lip. Though slender, he was wiry. He had rolled up the sleeves of his shirt against the warmth of the afternoon, and she could see the muscles coiled beneath his skin. His skin was brown from years spent in the harsh Texas sun. The tanned column of his throat rose from the unbuttoned collar of his shirt, and Claire was aware of a startling desire to press her lips to the smooth flesh.

She remembered the smell of him as she had danced in his embrace last night, the heat and hardness of his body against hers, and her whole body tingled in response, as if it were happening to her now instead of being just a memory. Claire swallowed and quickly looked away. She did not dare look at him now. If he should turn and read her thoughts on her face…

Claire tried frantically to think of something to say, but her thoughts were as scattered as the wispy clouds above them. So intent was she on her thoughts that she did not even notice that Jack had stopped until his hand, linked with hers, pulled her to a stop, as well. Turning, she looked back at him.

He was watching her, his eyes glass-green in the sunlight, his face still and unreadable. Then his gaze dropped to her mouth, and she saw the subtle change in his face, and she was certain that he was remembering their kiss, as well.

Holding her gaze with his own, he tugged her forward. Claire went easily toward him, and he looped his arm around her back, pulling her to him. She could feel the hard line of his legs against hers, and she had to lean back a little to look up into his face. What she saw there made her tremble.

For a moment their gazes were locked, the silence charged with unspoken desire. His head lowered a fraction; she sensed the question in him, the opportunity he was giving her to turn her head or pull back. She did not move, simply looked into his eyes.

He bent his head and kissed her.

CHAPTER FIVE

HIS OTHER ARM came around her, too, and he pressed her tightly against him. Claire was glad, for she was not entirely certain that she would have been able to stand if he had not. She melted into him. She could feel the hard strength of his bones and muscle digging into her, and the touch excited her. Her blood thrummed in her veins, roared in her ears. She looped her arms around his neck, holding on to her only support in a suddenly unstable world.

His mouth was hard and insistent on hers, opening her lips to his questing tongue. She responded eagerly, all shyness and uncertainty fleeing in the rushing sweep of her desire.

Claire had dated frequently, but her heart had never been engaged, and she had never gone out with a young man for any length of time. Nor had she possessed the boldly experimental nature of some other girls. There had been a few girls in her sorority who had, as they said, "gone all the way," but Claire had not been one of them. Brought up with firm, if not prudish moral standards, she had never felt the inclination to discover the delights of the lust that society had warned her about.

But here and now, she was suddenly, astonishingly eager. Passion rolled through her, hot and heavy, igniting her nerves like a flash fire. Her breasts swelled and tingled, the nipples tightening, sensitive now to the merest touch of her clothes upon them. Her loins turned liquid, and she felt herself loosening, opening up, her whole body more fluid.

Jack swept his hand down her body, caressing the curve of her hips, then moved back up to stroke her back. His mouth left hers to trail down her throat and onto the tender skin of her chest. Claire let out a little sigh of pleasure, arching back her head in a silent invitation. With one arm hard against her back, holding her up, he moved his other hand between them, gliding up her body until it curved beneath her breast.

Claire gasped as a tremor ran through her, and her hand dug into his shoulders. Jack's mouth clamped down on hers again, hungry and urgent. Heat poured from his body, surrounding her, and Claire wrapped her arms around his neck, clinging to him, returning his kisses with an equal hunger.

At last he raised his head and gazed down at her. His face was flushed, his eyes blazing with desire, his lips damp and slightly swollen from their kisses. Claire could feel the tension in his body, the effort it cost him to stand still, the struggle that raged within him to regain his composure.

Finally he loosened his hold, and Claire went back flat on her feet. His arm was still around her shoulders, and she leaned her forehead against his chest for a moment, taking a deep breath as she waited for the trembling excitement to leave her body.

Jack bent his head, and she felt his lips brush her hair, and a tiny sigh escaped her. It was better that they stopped, she knew, yet she could not help but feel a whisper of regret. If only they weren't so responsible, she thought.

Claire straightened, shaking that momentary weakness aside, and moved a little away from him. "Do you— would you like to go farther back into the canyon?"

"Sure." He took her hand, and they left the winding path of the water.

They made their way back through the scrubby mesquite bushes and yucca plants, carefully avoiding the clumps of prickly pear cactus. When they reached a formation of rocks, they clambered up it—though Claire found her climbing was hampered somewhat by her skirts—for a better view of the colored canyon walls.

There was no mention of the embrace they had shared earlier, but the memory of it lay just beneath the surface for both of them, casting a shimmering glow of desire over the whole afternoon. The feel of his hand clasping hers was a constant reminder of the way it had felt gliding over her body, and every time she looked at him, her eyes were drawn to his supple mouth. Whatever commonplace thing either one of them said, underneath it hummed the knowledge of their passion.

Standing on the rocks, Jack kissed her again, and though the kiss was soft and brief, desire flamed up in Claire with all the force of before. They left the rocks after that and walked back to their picnic spot, his arm curled loosely around her shoulders.

They sat down once again on the bank, watching the shadowed stream. Claire hated for the moment to end. She didn't want to even think about the fact that Jack would be leaving town tomorrow and after that she would not see him again. It seemed so unfair that he had come into her life so briefly, but she could think of nothing to stop the inevitable from happening.

Her mood as they drove out of the park was pensive, and as they once again neared the outskirts of the city, she turned to him, saying quietly, "Would you like to visit Denny's grave? The cemetery's just down that road."

He glanced at her. "Yeah. I'd like that."

He took the turn she indicated, and soon they were driving into the tree-shaded cemetery. She directed him toward her family plot, and when he stopped the car on the narrow dirt road, they got out and walked through the graves.

It was quiet and peaceful here. They were in an older part of the cemetery, and trees planted long ago cast wide shadows over the graves. Claire stopped in front of a plot marked off by a low wrought-iron fence. A tree stood at the back of the small area, and beneath its branches lay the graves of Emily Winters's parents. In front of them was a grave marked by a simple military tombstone.

"My parents had his body brought back after the war," Claire said softly. "It felt better, somehow, to have him close to us."

Jack nodded and squatted down beside the grave of

his friend. Claire left him alone for a moment with his grief and went over to the tree, sitting down at the base of it, her legs curled up under her. After a while Jack stood and came over to sit down beside her. They were silent, but it did not feel uncomfortable, only peaceful.

"This is a special place for you, isn't it?" he asked.

Claire nodded. "Den and I were close. I mean, there was a three-year difference between us, but we were friends. He'd talk to me, tell me things." She let out a little sigh. "He always wanted to do something extraordinary. I guess he did, really."

"Yeah."

"Could you tell me about it—when Denny died?"

"It was December—and so cold. The Germans attacked, tried to push through. It was their last-ditch effort—the Battle of the Bulge. I guess you know that. I was there when Den got shot." Jack paused, then went on, his voice roughened by unshed tears. "I grabbed him and pulled him back behind cover and...I tried to stop the bleeding. I remember yelling for the medic. And yelling. It seemed like it took forever for them to get there. I sat and held my hand against his wound, but I couldn't stop the bleeding. He was still alive when the medics got there, and they carried him off. I didn't see him again."

Claire slipped her hand into Jack's, and his fingers closed around hers. He gave her a small smile. "I think Dennis knew he wasn't coming back. A couple of weeks before he died, he gave me something. But I think that you should have it."

Jack reached into his pocket and pulled out an old-fashioned pocket watch, which he handed to Claire.

She stared at the object in surprise. "That's our grandfather's watch." A smile lit up her face. "The one he gave to Dennis. Den loved it. He carried it everywhere."

She opened it, glancing at the engraving inside, then closed it again and smoothed her thumb over the case. "No." She shook her head and held out the watch to him. "You should keep it. He gave it to you. He wanted you to have it."

He looked at her, surprised. "But it was your grandfather's. I shouldn't keep it."

"No." Her voice was firm. "It belongs to you. I'm sure Den would have wanted you to keep it."

When he hesitated, she took his hand and placed the watch in his palm, folding his fingers over it. "Really. It's fitting that you should have it."

He looked at her for a long moment, then finally he nodded. "All right. If you're sure."

"I am." She smiled at him. "I know how much you meant to Dennis if he gave you that watch. You probably understood him better, knew him better, than most people in his family. My parents loved him terribly, but they could never understand why he didn't want to go to law school and be a lawyer, like my father. I remember he and Daddy used to have some thundering arguments about what Den planned to do with his life. And Den would say that that was just it— he didn't want to *plan* his life. He just wanted to live it as it came up."

"That sounds like Dennis." A brief grin flickered over Jack's face.

"It's strange…my father always complained about

how unfocused Den was. And now he tells me that I'm too focused."

Jack shrugged. "All parents are odd like that. I remember how my father used to gripe about working in the oil fields and how hard it was. He always told me that I should make something out of myself, not be a roughneck all my life like he was. Then, when I got out of the Army and decided to go to college, he accused me of thinking I was better than him. He said I was 'acting above myself.'"

"I guess there's no pleasing people," Claire said lightly.

"Sometimes there is. Sometimes not. So there's not much point in trying to live your life to please somebody else. You have to live it to suit yourself in the end."

They continued to sit for a while in the tranquil spot, but finally they left, getting back into Jack's car and driving into town. Claire could feel her heart growing heavier with every passing block. She hated to think about never seeing Jack Murphy again.

He pulled to a stop in front of her house, and she turned toward him, putting on a smile that was happier than she felt. "Thank you. It was a lovely afternoon."

"I'm glad you enjoyed it. But I'm hoping that maybe you'd be willing to extend it into the evening. We could go out to dinner. Or maybe to a movie."

Claire felt her smile turn into something far more real. "I'd like that."

"Claire…I want to see you again. Not just tonight. But tomorrow and the day after, too."

She looked at him in surprise. "But what about California? I thought you were leaving for your vacation."

"Well, I've been thinking about that. California will be there for a long time. It can wait. I'd rather spend the next couple of weeks with you. I think I could spend my vacation just fine here in Amarillo."

"Really?" She knew that her face must have lit up, but she realized she didn't care about trying to conceal her feelings from him. "You're sure?"

He nodded. "The thing is, during the war, when guys were talking…what everyone always regretted were the things they didn't do. The girl they didn't ask out, the trip they didn't take, the places they never went to, the baby they'd never seen. I made a vow back then that when I got back here, I wasn't going to put things off. I wasn't going to spend my life regretting what I'd missed. I was going to seize every opportunity—do the things I really wanted to do." He paused. "And staying here, seeing you—that's what I want."

Claire felt tears suddenly pricking at her eyelids, and she had to clear her throat before she could speak. "Good. Because that's what I want, too."

OVER THE COURSE of the next two weeks, Claire and Jack spent every moment they could together. He came again to have dinner with her family. They swam at the country club pool; they went to movies and restaurants; they danced again at the Nat. They took long, lazy walks through Elwood Park. Often, they simply spent their time together in her family's game room, desultorily playing cards or listening to the radio. And all the time, they talked. Their pasts, their dreams, their failures, their families, their old friends and romantic interests—all were grist for the mill of their conversations. Only one subject seemed to be off-limits for them: What would happen when Jack left the city.

There was more than words. There were quiet moments, when his arm curled around her, cradling her against his chest, and Claire laid her head upon Jack's shoulder, breathing in the scent of him, luxuriating in the feel of his hard strength beneath her head. And there were times of passion, when they met in almost desperate embrace, their lips sealed together, their hearts pounding furiously inside them. They wanted more, far more, and yet they held back, aware of the deadline that loomed before them and the void that lay after that.

Claire tried not to think about Jack's departure, which she knew was rolling toward them with frightening swiftness. Instead she focused on the summer dance at the club, scheduled for the first Friday in June. Jack would still be here then, though she knew he must leave the city soon thereafter. This, then, would be one of their last evenings together, probably the last time they would dance with each other. She wanted to look her best.

None of her dresses would do, she decided after an extensive search of her closet, and on Friday morning, she went shopping. Normally her mother would have accompanied her. Clothes were one of the few interests she and Emily had in common. But her mother had been distinctly chilly toward Claire since Jack Murphy had arrived on the scene, and Claire was frankly relieved when Emily declined to accompany her, saying that she had already scheduled a bridge game at the country club with her friends.

It took her several hours, but Claire finally came upon the perfect dress—a long off-the-shoulder peach-colored gown with a close-fitted bodice fastened by a row of decorative buttons down the back. The skirt was full, but without underlying petticoats so that it fell straight to the floor in graceful folds.

Claire returned to the house, tired and hungry, but pleased with her efforts. She headed for the stairs to take her dress up to her room, but her mother's voice stopped her.

"Claire, come here. I want to talk to you."

Claire turned slowly toward the den, from which Emily's words had come. She knew that tone of voice, and it rarely boded well. With a sigh, she walked into the room where her mother was standing at the window, worrying a scarf in her hands.

"Yes, Mama?"

Emily turned to her, still wrapping and unwrapping the filmy scarf. She hesitated for a moment, then started in a rush, "Claire, this has to stop."

"What has to stop? What are you talking about?"

"That young man you've been seeing. The way you two have been together constantly for almost two weeks now. People are beginning to talk. Mary Montgomery was quizzing me about him this morning at bridge. Even Cecilia, who is the most oblivious woman I know, had heard that you have been seeing him."

"Oh, really, Mama, I can scarcely believe people are bored enough that they're talking about my dating Jack Murphy."

"It's not a question of boredom, Claire. It's a question of...of propriety."

Claire couldn't keep one eyebrow from quirking up. "Propriety? You sound like something from a British play."

"I sound like a concerned mother," Emily shot back. "This won't do your reputation any good. Dropping Harlan Ames to spend all your time with this...stranger."

"He's not a stranger. I know him quite well."

"Well, no one else does."

"No one else is dating him," Claire pointed out. "I shouldn't think it would matter whether or not they knew him."

"Don't be obtuse. You know good and well that seeing him so much is the sort of thing that sets tongues to wagging."

"I don't know why it should! I've done nothing wrong. And I cannot see that it is anyone's business, anyway, who I date or how much I date him."

"That's all well and good to say, but you know that it's the way the world works. A woman simply cannot afford to get a reputation as 'fast.'"

"How does seeing one man several times make me 'fast'? This is ridiculous."

"It's not ridiculous. Everyone is watching you throw yourself away on this young man. You could have any man you want, and you choose this...this Murphy fellow, who has no family, no prospects."

"Of course he has family. You just don't know them."

"No, I don't. No one does. That is what I'm talking about. His father worked in the oil fields, for goodness' sake."

Claire rolled her eyes. "So? That scarcely makes Jack a pariah. He has a college degree, and he's got a job. He's reliable, responsible and hardworking. How can you act as if he were a…a drifter or something?"

"Well, he's hardly husband material, not for a girl like you. Honestly, Claire, I don't know what's gotten into you. A couple of weeks ago, you were dead set on going to law school, and now you're about to marry this stranger."

"Marry!" Claire stared at her mother, shocked. "What are you talking about? I'm not about to marry anyone."

Mrs. Winters cast a scornful look at her daughter, "Oh, really, Claire, where else would you think this is all headed? Well, the only good thing about it is that at least you found out early enough that you didn't make the mistake of going to law school."

"I'm still going to law school."

"Claire, make up your mind."

"Why? I have no plans to marry anyone, including Jack Murphy, but if I did, why would I have to make a choice between marriage and law school?"

"Jack Murphy is a young man just starting his life. He will want a wife, not a girl off at law school for three years. And I certainly hope you don't think that if you get married, we're going to support you through law school."

"You needn't worry," Claire responded tightly. "I'm going to law school. I'm not marrying Jack or anyone else. And if someone feels the need to question what I'm doing, tell them to address their concerns to *me* instead of gossiping behind my back."

Claire turned on her heel and stalked out of the room.

CHAPTER SIX

CLAIRE HURRIED up the stairs to her bedroom and closed the door behind her. It took an effort not to slam it shut. This was all so maddening! What right did anyone have to poke around in her life? And exactly what was so awful about seeing a man several times over the course of a week or two?

Claire flung her dress down on the bed. She began to pace, rearguing her talk with her mother. Her righteous indignation took her through several minutes of pacing around her room before she began to lose steam. Finally, heaving a huge sigh, she flopped down in her chair.

Maddening as it was that people were watching her and judging her, Claire knew that was not really what made her feel so jittery and upset. Nor was it even the fact that she had argued again with her mother, much as she disliked doing so. No, the real problem, the thing that ate at her, was what her mother had said at the end of their argument—that Jack's courtship was a headlong rush toward marriage.

Was it? Was Jack Murphy thinking of marrying her? She would have liked to be able to dismiss her mother's words as simply an example of her mother's old-fashioned beliefs, but Claire knew that she could not. She and Jack were not high school kids in the first throes of love. They were mature adults, both of them out of college, and Jack had spent over three years in the war, an experience that would age a man beyond his years. He was starting his career, setting out on the road of his life. He wasn't the sort of man who would be playing around when he dated a woman, particularly not when he dated one with such intensity and frequency.

Yes, of course, a lot of that rush he'd been giving her had been because he was going to be here for only a limited time and after that they would be parting ways. But, remembering the feel of his lips on hers, the way his skin seared with heat when they kissed, the touch of his hands on her, she knew that he felt a great deal more for her than just an urgency because of time constraints.

He burned with passion for her, and Claire knew that she felt the same way about him. He had only to look at her a certain way, and she went all soft and warm inside, like chocolate melting in the sun. She wanted him in a way she had never felt for any other man, and there had been more than one time these past two weeks when she had almost let go of all restraint and given into her desire. Once, in fact, she was not at all sure that she would have stopped if Jack himself had not pulled back.

Did she love him? The thought filled her with a kind of terror. She did not want to love him; that way lay disaster.

Claire was certain that she wanted him. Everything seemed to light up the moment he walked into the room, and when she wasn't with him, life was far grayer and emptier. Jack was the first thing she thought of in the morning when she woke up and the last thing she thought of before she went to sleep. And the past two weeks had been the happiest of her life.

Did all of that mean she loved him? Claire had not examined her feelings—indeed, she had assiduously avoided looking at them in any depth. She had concentrated simply on feeling, pushing aside all thought of what might lie ahead. Even now she cringed away from the possibility that she might be in love.

It was too soon, she told herself; what she felt was attraction, certainly. But surely it required more time than this to fall in love. What she felt was at most infatuation. It was fun while it lasted, but when he left town and she never saw him again, the feeling would gradually die.

Wouldn't it? Claire's heart sank as she thought of Jack's leaving. That was, she knew, the last thing she wanted. But what if he wanted to part from her as little as she wanted to part from him? What if he managed to stay in town longer? She wasn't sure when he had to report for his job. It might not be for a few more weeks, even the whole summer. And if and when he did leave, he might come back now and then, drive up from Odessa. Mightn't he? The trip was several hours, but they could see each other on the weekends. What if they managed to keep their relationship going? What if he wanted to marry her?

She couldn't deny that her heart leaped at the thought. She knew that there was a crazy romantic part of her that wanted to marry Jack, that would be thrilled if he told her that he felt the same.

But it was impossible. She had wanted to be a lawyer for years. She could not imagine throwing aside her dream. And her mother was right. No man was going to want to wait for three years while she finished law school. She could not help but remember her father's words on the matter, too—a man wanted a wife, not a lawyer. Jack would doubtless want to have kids, and he would expect her to stay at home and raise them. Everyone would.

Claire sighed, feeling perilously close to tears. Why had her mother had to bring this up now? She had been so happy about her dress, so looking forward to the dance. Now, she realized, as she looked at her beautiful peach gown spread out over the bed in a shimmer of satin, all her excitement had turned into something bittersweet. This night would be lovely, one she would remember always, but one reason it would be so memorable was that she suspected it would be her last night with Jack.

THE COUNTRY CLUB blazed with lights, a welcoming sight as Claire and Jack drove up the long driveway. Couples of various ages were strolling into the building, the women in long brightly colored dresses, their beauty accented by the stark black and white of the men's suits. A table in the foyer held an arrangement of delicate white gardenias, giving off a heady scent.

The ballroom was decorated in more prosaic artificial flowers, with Japanese lanterns strung across the ceiling to provide a low, exotic glow. Tables were scattered around the perimeter of the room, leaving the floor open in the center for dancing. A slightly raised stage held a few chairs and music stands for the small dance band. At the far end of the room were the bar and refreshment table.

Claire smiled at Jack as they made their way to a small table for two near the back of the room. She noticed some of her friends at a couple of larger tables near the bandstand, but she merely waved at them. Tonight she did not want to be with anyone but Jack. She was doubly glad that she had avoided them a few minutes later when Harlan Ames entered the ballroom and went over to sit with them.

Jack, following the direction of her gaze, raised his eyebrows a little and murmured, "Think we'll have the pleasure of his company tonight?"

"I sincerely hope not." She turned a little in her seat so that Harlan was no longer in her line of sight.

With Jack looking into her eyes, the subject of Harlan Ames was quickly forgotten. They talked of other things, enjoying simply sitting together, and when the band started, they got up to dance. The next hour passed quickly, their dances interspersed with talking, heads close together over their little table.

They were rapt in conversation, so intent on one another that at first they didn't notice when a man approached their table. He reached Claire's side and stood there, unmoving, until at last they were forced to look up at him.

As soon as she felt his presence, Claire had suspected who it was. When she glanced up, her suspicion was confirmed. Harlan Ames loomed over their table, swaying a little. She could smell the odor of bourbon on him even at this distance.

"Hello, Harlan," she said evenly. "How are you?"

Harlan had avoided her since that unpleasant scene at the Nat. Claire knew that he probably thought he was punishing her for her waywardness, but she had been happy not to have to talk to him. She had figured that the situation was too good to last, however; once Harlan realized that his absence did not bother her, she knew he would have to make an impression on her some other way.

"Oh, I'm fine, Claire. Just fine." His gaze flickered from her to Jack. "I'm not the one who's been providing everybody with gossip."

"No? Well, that's certainly nice for you."

Harlan blinked, obviously not sure how to respond to Claire's answer. Claire, looking at him, wondered how she had managed to remain friends with Harlan for as long as she had. If she had not been away at college most of the last four years, she thought, she would have realized much sooner how little there was to like about Harlan. He had been growing steadily more sarcastic and arrogant, but, taken in small doses, it had been fairly easy to overlook his lapses, just as it had taken longer to notice how much more he drank.

"I came over to ask you for a dance," Harlan went on after a moment. He cast a sneering glance at Jack. "If your boyfriend doesn't mind, of course."

If it had not been for his contemptuous look at Jack, Claire might have gone out on the floor with Harlan just to get rid of him. But his attitude made her bristle. "I don't think so, Harlan. Not tonight. Why don't you go back and sit down with Bob and the others?"

"What? Now you won't even dance with me?" He swung toward Jack. "You jealous? Afraid I'll steal her back from you?"

"Not really." Jack's voice was cool and lazy. "I'd be more afraid you'd fall over and knock her down."

"What do you mean?" Harlan glowered at him.

"He means you're drunk again, Harlan," Claire spoke up. "Please, just go sit down. If you create a scene here, it's going to embarrass your parents."

"I'm not creating a scene," Harlan retorted, his voice rising, and he flung out an arm expansively. "I'm not the one refusing to dance with an old friend." He glared at Claire. "What are you doing, Claire? Why are you hanging around with this…this cracker?"

"Harlan, stop." Claire rose to her feet, hoping that she could get through to Harlan before he disrupted the whole dance. "That's enough. Go back to your table. And you might want to slow down on the drinks."

From the corner of her eye, she saw Bob and another of Harlan's friends making their way toward them. Hopefully they would be able to steer him away.

"Don't tell me what to do!" Harlan snapped back.

Beside Claire, Jack rose to his feet, moving around the table to step between Harlan and Claire.

"Take it easy," Jack told Harlan. "Just do as the lady says and go back to your table."

"Or what?" Harlan sneered. "You gonna make me? I got news for you, buddy, you're in my territory now. You go up against me, and you're gonna lose."

"Is that so?" Jack simply looked at Harlan.

"Jack, please..." Claire laid a hand on his arm.

Jack half-turned to look at her, and Harlan seized the opportunity to take a swing at him. Harlan's movements were far too clumsy from drink, however, and Jack easily turned back before Harlan's fist reached him. He raised his left arm to knock Harlan's punch aside and followed with his right fist, planting it squarely in Harlan's jaw.

Harlan staggered backward and crashed into the table behind them, then slid to the floor, turning over a folding chair on the way down. Several women shrieked, and the band faltered. All around them voices swelled in excitement.

Jack turned to Claire. "Are you okay?"

"I'm fine." Claire glanced over at Harlan, who had sat up, nursing his jaw and looking sullen, then at the curious faces around them. "Come on. Let's go."

She grabbed her small beaded handbag from the table and took his hand. Jack hesitated, then followed her through the tables and out the door.

"I'm sorry," Jack said as they emerged from the country club into the soft June night.

"It doesn't matter," Claire assured him.

"But I ruined the dance for you," Jack continued penitently as they walked toward his car. "I didn't mean to. I told myself I wasn't going to let him get under my skin, but..."

"Well, he did try to hit you," Claire pointed out. She turned toward Jack with a grin. "Actually I'm glad you punched him. Harlan's been working up to getting knocked down for quite a while now." She let out a chuckle. "In fact, I suspect there were a few folks there who would have liked to cheer you on."

He smiled faintly. "Then you aren't mad?"

"No. I'm not mad." Claire stopped and turned to face him. She went up on tiptoes, wrapping her arms around his neck, and slowly, deliberately kissed him. When at last the kiss ended, she went back down on her heels and smiled at him archly. "There. Convinced?"

He grinned back, his eyes lighting up. "Yeah. You're pretty persuasive."

"I'd rather be alone with you anyway," Claire went on honestly. "And I've gotten to wear the pretty dress, so…"

They continued to the car, holding hands.

"Where to now?" Jack asked. "You want to grab a late dinner?"

"At the coffee shop?" Claire asked, feeling a bitter-sweet pang at the thought of revisiting the restaurant they had gone to that first night. "Sure. But we better go home first so I can change."

They drove to her house and stopped in the drive-way. Claire looked up at the dark house, and suddenly she was aware that no one was at home. Her parents were still at the country club dance. She and Jack would be alone in the house. Feeling suddenly flustered, she couldn't quite look at Jack. She turned and slid out of the car before he could get around to open her door.

Claire looked up at him, her heart suddenly thumping wildly in her chest. Jack's face was so serious as he gazed down at her, so intent and...

He kissed her, and all other thoughts left her head. Claire clung to him, her own passion rising up to meet his. Finally he broke their kiss and buried his face in her neck.

"I love you," he murmured.

"Oh, Jack!" Claire wrapped her arms even more tightly around him. Happiness surged through her, yet she felt, at the same time, as if she might burst into tears. "I love you, too."

It was true, she realized. What all her agonizing and thinking this afternoon had not made clear to her, her rushing emotions now did. She loved Jack. Loved him with all her heart. The feeling glowed in her, lighting every corner of her being with warmth and happiness.

"Good." He kissed her neck, then lifted his head and kissed her tenderly on the forehead and each cheek, then once again on her mouth.

He stepped back, linking his hand in hers, and they started up the driveway in silence. She pulled out her key from her small bag and stuck it in the lock and turned it. But when she reached out to open the door, Jack put out his hand and stopped her.

"No, wait. I want to ask you something."

Claire turned to him, her eyes going up to his face. The moon cast only a faint light, so it was hard to read his expression. But he looked, she thought, nervous. She started to speak, but he hurried on.

"Claire, I've been thinking. I want—I mean, do

you think—oh hell, I'm no good at this." He sighed, then starting over again, he took both her hands in his and gazed straight into her eyes. "Claire, will you marry me?"

Claire gasped, and her hands flew to her mouth, tearing out of his grasp. "Oh, no. No, no…"

She should have known this was coming, she thought, from the moment he said he loved her. She had let herself be lost in the happiness of the moment, however, instead of thinking.

Jack stared at her, stunned. His suddenly empty hands fell back to his sides, and he straightened. "Oh. I—I see. I'm sorry. Obviously I, uh, I mistook your feelings. Well…" He glanced around, looking everywhere but at her, and his arms came up to cross over his chest. "Maybe I'd better go."

He turned and trotted down the two steps from the porch to the sidewalk, starting toward his car. Claire stared at his retreating back, horror sweeping through her. Her heart twisted inside her; she felt as if it were being torn out of her chest.

"No!" she cried.

At the same moment, Jack turned around, his face suddenly fierce, exclaiming, "No, I'm not going to give up that easily."

He strode toward her, and Claire ran to him, throwing herself into his arms. Tears streamed down her face as she kissed him, clinging to him as if she'd never let him go. He wrapped his arms around her, pulling her even more tightly into him, and rained fervent kisses over her face.

"I love you! I do!" Claire gasped out in between kisses. "Oh, Jack, I can't bear it! Don't leave me."

"I won't. I won't. Ever," he promised, kissing her again, firmly, then setting her down. He reached up to wipe the tears from her face. "Okay. Let's go inside and sit down. And you tell me what's wrong."

She nodded, and they walked back to the front door and went inside. Claire led him into the den, and they sat down on the couch, half-turned to face each other.

"Now, then." Jack took her hands and looked at her earnestly. "Tell me what's going on. Why do you say you love me, but then you say you don't want to marry me?"

"I do!" Claire cried. "I do want to marry you. More than anything."

She realized, too, how true that was. Everything inside her ached to be with Jack. In every way. To live with him, love him, spend all the rest of her days with him. It didn't matter how much she told herself that she hadn't known him long enough or that what she felt was only infatuation and would pass. She knew it would not pass. If she lost Jack, she was certain that she would regret it every day of her life.

"Then what's the problem? Your parents? I know your mother doesn't approve of me."

"No. I mean, yes—she doesn't approve of you. But I don't care about that. It's not my mother. It's that— I want more than marriage. I want a career. I want to go to law school. I want to be a lawyer."

He looked at her expectantly. After a moment of silence, he said, "I know. You've told me about that."

He paused again. His face cleared. "And that's all that's holding you back?"

"It's a lot," Claire responded. "It's important to me."

"Well, of course it is. But those are just details. As long as we're together, we can work out that kind of stuff."

"But how? You have a job you've got to start soon—in west Texas. And at the end of the summer, I've got to go to law school in Austin. We'll be miles apart for three years."

"Okay. Yeah, I do have to start work in a week. But I don't have to live in west Texas. I'll go back to Austin and talk to the guys at Hammond. I'll explain to them that I have to live in Austin for the next three years while my wife's in school. Maybe we can work out something where I'm based in Austin and drive to west Texas some of the time. Or, if that's not feasible, I'll ask for my old job back, the one I had when I was going to college. I think they'd let me. I'll put off this job for a few years, till you're finished with law school. Then we could go wherever we want. You could set up practice anywhere. Right?"

Claire nodded, a smile starting to spread across her face. "Honestly? You'd put your career on hold like that?"

"So I could be with you? Sure." He raised his hands to cup her face, gazing down into her eyes. "Claire. I love you. That's what's important. Holding off on a better job for three years—that's not a problem. Maybe I'll even go back to school myself, get a master's. It doesn't matter. It's just a few years. We've got the rest of our lives to do all that."

"But what about children?"

He looked puzzled. "Well, I'd like children. Don't you want children?"

"Yes, I do. But I don't think I'll want to quit law to stay at home and raise them."

"Okay."

"You don't mind?" Claire searched his gaze carefully. "You won't care if I have a career?"

"Not if that's what you want. We'll hire someone to help with the kids. And you'll be your own boss if you have a private practice. You can set your own hours, work part-time or full-time, whatever you want. Before too long, I intend to be my own boss, as well. We'll manage it."

"I can't believe it's this easy," Claire marveled. "That you're okay with all this."

He shrugged. "I'm sure you'll find I'm not always so agreeable. But I am about this. It's your life. You can be a lawyer or not. Whatever you want. I just want to marry you and live with you for the rest of my life. You remember what I told you about deciding I wasn't going to ever regret not doing things?"

Claire nodded.

"Well, there is nothing I would regret as much as I would regret not marrying you. The rest of that doesn't matter."

He bent his head and their lips met in a long, lingering kiss. When at last they parted, Claire said, "Then let's do it. Let's get married right away."

He stared at her. "You mean it?"

Claire nodded. "I don't want to wait. I want to marry you now."

"Elope? To New Mexico?" He mentioned the state popular with eloping Texas couples, where there was no waiting period for a marriage license.

"Yes. Tonight. I'll go upstairs and pack a bag right now."

Jack grinned. "You won't get an argument from me."

Claire ran upstairs and made quick work out of packing two bags, then wrote a letter to her parents explaining her decision and left it on their bed. Jack carried her things out to his car and stowed the bags in the trunk. They got into the car, and Jack started the engine, but then he turned to Claire.

"Are you sure?" he asked, his eyes searching her face. "Your mother's going to be madder than a wet hen."

"I know. But I can't live my life for Mama. She'll be mad about me marrying you whether I do it now or six months from now. And I'm not going to ruin all this by staying here and arguing with her."

"But don't you want a fancy wedding?" he persisted. "The pretty dress and the church ceremony and all that?"

Claire looked back at him, her face solemn. "I don't need a fancy wedding, Jack. As long as I have you, I have everything I want."

She leaned across the seat and kissed him. He smiled and put the car in gear, and they drove off together.

EPILOGUE

Christmas
Amarillo, Texas

"GRAN!" Rebecca exclaimed when Claire finished her story. "That's so romantic! I never knew what a whirlwind courtship you and Granddad had."

"Probably because it was the perfect example of what your parents hoped you'd never do," Jackson Murphy told her.

"Yeah, but look at how it turned out," Nate put in. "You two have been married for…"

"Sixty years this coming June," Claire supplied the answer with an understandable degree of pride.

"Wow." Rebecca gazed at them in awe. In her capacity as a wedding planner, she had seen all sorts of couples, and she had to admit that she could not imagine many of their marriages lasting for even half as long as her grandparents' marriage had. "Maybe I should have you two talk to my brides and grooms."

Claire chuckled and shook her head. "I don't know that I have any answer, really. They always say that marriage is hard work—and sometimes it is. Mostly

there were times when it was hard to hold my tongue."
She smiled at Jack.

"There were some rough moments," Jack admitted.
"Especially when the kids came along and Claire was
still having to juggle law school and I was traveling a
lot. But you know…" He flashed a grin at his grandchildren. "I wouldn't trade those times for anything.
It was tough, but it was fun, too."

Claire released a little sigh, her face tenderly intro-
spective. "He's right. Every time I thought that it was
too hard or that I wanted to quit, I would just think
about spending the rest of my life without Jack. And
I'd know it was all worth it."

"So what about your mother?" Nate asked. "Did she
ever come around? Or did she stay mad at you?"

"Oh, she put up a pretty good fight," Claire admitted. "It was *months* before she'd even speak to me.
But when I had your mother, it got pretty hard for
Mama to hold out. A grandbaby is a powerful force for
reconciliation. Then when Daddy was in that wreck
and Jack drove me up to the hospital in Amarillo in the
middle of a snowstorm, well, after that Jack was the
apple of her eye. By the time she died, listening to her,
you'd have thought she had handpicked him for me."

"As I remember, she got to be pretty proud of your
being a lawyer, too," Jack put in.

"Did you ever wish you'd had the big wedding,
though?" Rebecca asked. "All the pictures and memories and all?"

For an instant, Rebecca thought she saw a faint
shadow touch her grandmother's face, but then it was

gone, and Claire smiled. "No. I mean, it would have been nice. The dress and the cake and dancing…all my family there. But I wouldn't change anything about my marriage. As long as I have Jack, I don't really wish for anything else."

"No regrets," her husband agreed with a nod. He had been holding her hand all through her story, and now he raised her fingers to his mouth to press a gentle kiss upon them. "No regrets."

Claire squeezed his hand, then said, "Now, if you young ones will excuse me, I think I am going to go up to bed."

Jackson stood up and reached down, his hand under his wife's elbow, to help her to her feet. Claire bent to pick up their cups, but Nate reached out to take the mugs from her.

"Never mind those, Gran. Rebecca and I will clean up."

"You sure?"

"Of course. You go on to bed." Rebecca stood up and gave each of her grandparents a hug and kiss on the cheek.

Nate did the same, and the two of them stood, watching the old couple make their way to the stairs.

"What a sweet story," Rebecca said and let out a little sigh. "But it's too bad she didn't get her big wedding day."

Nate shrugged. "She doesn't seem to regret it."

"No. I don't think she regrets any of it. But I think she'd have liked to have the ceremony, as well." She stood for a moment, a faraway look on her face, tapping her forefinger against her lips.

"What?" Nate asked somewhat warily. "I've seen that look before. You've got something up your sleeve."

"I was just wondering…you know, they could still have a wedding."

"Little late, isn't it?"

"Nonsense. Lots of people renew their vows—they have a whole new ceremony. I planned a renewal of vows ceremony just last year."

Nate turned to her, and a slow smile crossed his face. "Well, maybe you should do it again."

"For Gran and Granddad?"

"Why not? We could arrange it for their 60th anniversary. Have all the family here. Throw a big party."

"You're right," Rebecca answered. "I could plan it all."

"We'll do it as a surprise for them," Nate went on. "You plan it. I'll pay for it."

Rebecca stuck out her hand, and Nate shook it.

"This is going to be fun," Rebecca said with a grin.

"It will," Nate agreed. "And Claire and Jack will finally get to have the wedding they deserve."

* * * * *

ALWAYS A
GROOMSMAN

Gina Wilkins

* * *

For John—thirty-two great years and counting.

Dear Reader,

I still very clearly remember reading my first Harlequin romance. It belonged to my mother, an avid romance reader. I was in my teens and until then, I hadn't been interested in romance novels. But I read that one, and I fell in love—with the hero, with the writer's clever use of humor and emotion, with the entire genre. That book clarified for me what I wanted to write—stories about dashing men and courageous women falling in love and overcoming all the obstacles between them and a happy future together.

Harlequin Books has been providing such compelling stories for sixty years. I consider myself blessed to have been part of the Harlequin family for twenty of those years. I've had many wonderful experiences during my writing career. Interacting with other romance fans, both readers and writers, has certainly been the high point. I am always struck by the universal appeal of stories about love, about the search for a soul mate, about the priceless value of family. It was especially fun to work with Candace and Allison to craft these stories about three generations of a family created by the enduring love between a dashing hero and a courageous heroine, Jack and Claire Murphy. I hope you enjoy the results of our collaboration.

Happy anniversary, Harlequin. Thank you for all the wonderful stories that have entertained generations of readers for the past sixty years. May that tradition continue for many years in the future.

Gina Wilkins

CHAPTER ONE

WHAT WAS IT ABOUT being a bride, Rebecca Murphy wondered, that turned the most rational and pleasant young woman into a raving, unreasonable tyrant? As for what it did to a bride who wasn't the most pleasant person to begin with…

She had been a wedding coordinator for almost two years now, since shortly before her twenty-sixth birthday. As much as she enjoyed her work, the transformation that occurred in so many of her clients never ceased to amaze her. It wasn't always drastic—a few moments of selfishness, a small tantrum or two, a panic-driven attack against a caterer, florist, musician or, in some cases, the coordinator. She'd become quite skilled at deflecting those minicrises with such aplomb that she had developed a reputation for handling the most out-of-control bride-to-be.

But that was before she had starting working with Melanie Warner, the youngest child and only daughter of Rebecca's mother's first cousin, Coleen.

Rebecca hadn't spent much time with Melanie. They had grown up in different Texas towns, Rebecca in Lubbock, Melanie in Plainview. Yet she'd known that Melanie was more than a bit spoiled, somewhat impetuous, often temperamental with her adoring and indulgent parents. No worse than other challenging brides Rebecca had worked with in the past—or so she had assumed.

But as the months passed, Melanie had turned into a "Bridezilla" of reality-TV proportions. With the wedding only four days away, Rebecca would consider it a miracle if she managed to finish this job with her professional reputation—not to mention her sanity—intact.

"Now, Melanie," she said, trying to keep her voice both soothing and firm, "you know it's too late to change your theme. Besides, you love lavender and sage. They're your favorite colors."

"They're too pastel," Melanie protested tearfully, her big, blue eyes filled with tears that threatened to spill down her overly salon-tanned cheeks. "I should have chosen something bolder to better suit the tropical setting. That's what Hannah said, anyway."

"Hannah is just jealous because you're getting married before she is," Melanie's mother, Coleen, crooned to her pampered daughter. "She's been saying all these things just to shake your confidence, Mellie, you know that."

"She can be a real pain," Melanie agreed slowly.

Rebecca tried to guide the topic back to the original discussion. "The lavender and sage are perfect for an April wedding, Melanie. It will be a beautiful ceremony."

"You're sure I shouldn't have chosen tropical colors?" the bride fretted, refusing to be so easily pacified.

"Maybe a Mexican theme instead of a spring gala? We could still change the decorations... maybe find new dresses..."

The very thought made Rebecca's stomach knot. There was no way she could change the spring gala wedding into a Mexican fiesta with four days' notice, even though she had no doubt that the bride's indulgent parents would somehow find a way to foot the bill. They weren't a particularly wealthy family, but they would sacrifice everything they had to keep their daughter happy. Rebecca suspected they had already taken a second mortgage on their home just to pay for the wedding arrangements thus far.

Melanie's parents had talked her out of the Caribbean wedding she had at first demanded, but they'd managed to appease her with a painfully expensive week at the San Gabriel Hotel and Spa in Galveston, Texas, on the Gulf of Mexico. She had resisted at first, because Galveston was not exactly the glamour destination wedding she'd had in mind, but they'd finally slipped enough incentives into the offer to satisfy her. Eager to reclaim tourist business after the devastating Texas-coast hurricane a year earlier, the luxury resort had offered the family a good deal for all the wedding festivities. The resort and spa provided a full slate of amenities, and Melanie was taking advantage of all of them.

It was the third Tuesday in April and the wedding was scheduled for the following Saturday afternoon. Four of the ten bridesmaids were already at the resort, and the others would arrive during the next few days.

The groom was due later that afternoon. Rebecca had been told that some of the groomsmen were also coming early. Daytime diversions included a fishing excursion, golf and tennis tournaments, shopping and sightseeing outings, along with the amenities of the day spa. Other events were planned for the evenings, much of the work on those having fallen to Rebecca.

She had met the groom, Charlie O'Neill, only a couple of times. He seemed nice, but he had been almost entirely excluded from the wedding preparations, leaving the decisions up to Melanie and her mother.

Rebecca had asked about the mother of the groom, but she'd been informed in no uncertain terms that the groom's mother was not included in the planning. It seemed that Coleen Warner and Shelley O'Neill had taken an instant dislike of each other at an engagement party for their offspring the year before and hadn't spoken since. Which should make the occasion even more festive, Rebecca thought with an exasperated shake of her head.

It was at times like this that she sometimes wondered why she hadn't followed her father's advice and gotten a more normal job. Or at the least, listened to her mother and claimed she was too busy to coordinate her cousin's wedding. Never work with family, she'd been told. Why hadn't she listened?

She knew why, she answered herself in resignation. Because she couldn't stand to be told what to do. Especially when it was for her own good. Blame that on being the sheltered only child of parents who hadn't expected to be able to have even one baby. With only one daughter to focus on, they had micromanaged her until she had firmly asserted her independence when she went away to college in Nashville. It was a wonder, she thought, that she hadn't turned out as self-absorbed and spoiled as Melanie—not that her own parents would have allowed that.

Craving peace and quiet, she slipped away for some precious alone time on the beach at dusk. It was still a little early in the year for this first tourist season after the hurricane to be in full swing, so the beach wasn't crowded. Only a few people wandered across the sand around her, staying just out of range of the lapping waves.

It was a little chilly, but not uncomfortably so. Her hands in the pockets of the long sweater she wore with a white T-shirt and khaki pants, she turned her face into the gentle wind off the gulf and drew a deep breath of salty air, letting the soothing sounds ease her frayed nerves. The breeze caught her dark, straight, collar-length hair, tossing it around her face, forcing her to reach up occasionally and remove a strand from her mouth or eyes.

Her enjoyment of the moment was shattered when she realized that this was the first time she'd walked on a beach since she'd left Hawaii two and a half years ago. Her heart clenched. Maybe this walk hadn't been such a good idea, after all.

If she closed her eyes, she could imagine she was back on that beach in Maui with Ryan. She could almost feel his hand reaching out to brush her hair away from her face. Could almost sense his warm breath mingling with the tropical breeze on her skin, his lips hovering just above her own.

She wondered how the memories could still hurt this badly after more than two years. After all, she'd made a good life for herself since their painful goodbyes. She hadn't completely stopped loving him, and wasn't sure she ever would, but she had moved on. She had accepted that her wistful fantasies about him would never come true. She'd put her efforts into arranging weddings for other couples, and she took pride in what she had accomplished. So why was she standing here moping about Ryan? she asked herself impatiently.

She turned to retrace her steps to the resort. It was getting darker, and she still had several things to do that evening before she could go to bed. She didn't like to be away for very long, anyway. Heaven only knew what sort of crazy new ideas Melanie would come up with if Rebecca wasn't there to keep her in check.

Smiling wryly, she glanced ahead, then felt her steps falter in the damp sand when she spotted a male figure silhouetted against the bright resort lights. Something about the way he stood, the way he walked…

But no. It was ridiculous to think that Ryan would be here. It was only because she'd been thinking of him that she saw such a powerful resemblance in this shadowed figure.

The man stopped a few feet in front of her, close enough now that she could see his face. She realized even before he spoke that her imagination had not been playing tricks on her, after all.

"Hello, Rebecca. It's good to see you again."

RYAN COULDN'T TELL if the blood had drained from her face or if it was the artificial lighting that leached the color from Rebecca's cheeks. Her face looked as pale as the pearly inside of a seashell when she stared up at him. Her eyes appeared very dark this evening, but he knew them to be a clear hazel, surrounded by long, lush lashes. She'd changed her hairstyle since he'd seen her last; it had been sort of choppy and trendy then, but was now styled in a more classic bob. It looked good on her. But then, anything would.

"I just found out you're coordinating the Warner-O'Neill wedding," he said when she remained silent. "I ran into Charlie and Melanie in the lobby when I was checking in, and they mentioned your name. Melanie said she saw you leave the hotel for the beach."

He didn't tell her what a shock it had been for him to find out that she was here, or how hard it had been for him to hide that reaction from his old friend.

Her voice was only slightly husky when she finally responded, and he figured she must have silently cleared her throat before speaking. "What are you doing here, Ryan? How do you know Charlie and Melanie?"

So she hadn't known he would be here. He'd wondered if she had. "I'm one of the groomsmen. Charlie's an old friend from UT. He was my roommate for a couple of years there. Quite a coincidence, huh?"

"Yes, I guess it is," she said after a rather lengthy pause.

"You didn't know I was coming?"

"No. I haven't seen the list of groomsmen's names. I was only given a number. I've met the best man and two others, but that's all. I had no idea you were in this wedding. Or that you even knew Charlie."

He shrugged. "You know what they say. Texas is a big state, but a small world. Six degrees of separation and all that stuff."

Their mutual Texas background was one of the things that had drawn them together two and a half years ago at that big blowout of a wedding in Hawaii. One of her sorority sisters from Vanderbilt had married one of his Army buddies from Georgia, where he was stationed. Rebecca and Ryan had been in the wedding party. Ryan had been on leave, having planned all along to spend extra time in the islands after the wedding. Rebecca extended her own trip to spend time with him there. They had shared an amazing two weeks together, which had, to his enduring regret, ended with a bitter quarrel.

"Is the bride a friend of yours?" he asked to distract himself from those painful memories.

"She's a relative, actually. Her mother and my mother are first cousins."

"Oh." So he would do well to keep his too-quickly formed opinions about Melanie Warner to himself.

"My business is actually doing very well," she added as if she wasn't sure how to interpret his monosyllabic response. "I'm solidly booked for several months ahead. I even have a full-time assistant back in Lubbock to help me handle everything."

"That's great. I know you always wanted to go into business for yourself."

Nodding, she glanced at his sandy-brown hair, which he kept militarily short. "You're still in the Army?"

"Yes. I'm a captain now. Looking to make major soon."

"Should I salute?"

Ignoring the sarcasm, he answered lightly, "That's not necessary. I'm not in uniform."

She glanced at his long-sleeve, blue twill shirt and jeans, but didn't otherwise respond to his attempt at a joke.

They stood there a few moments longer, staring at each other, the memories of those other nights on a beach hanging between them. A strand of wind-whipped hair blew across her mouth, and his fingers itched to reach out and brush it away. He pushed his hands into his pockets to keep himself from giving in to that temptation.

"I'd better go in," she said, making an abrupt move to walk past him. "I have things to do this evening."

He swiveled to watch her. "I guess we'll be seeing each other around this week," he called after her.

She glanced over her shoulder. "I'll be very busy. But yes, we'll see each other in passing. That shouldn't be a problem, should it?"

It was almost a challenge. He responded in a murmur, "No, not a problem. See you, Becks."

Did she flinch in response to the nickname? If so, she hid it behind a cool nod as she turned and hurried away. Not quite running, but very close.

Seeing him had shaken her more than she'd wanted him to see, he realized. Unclenching his fists, he released a long, low, unsteady breath, a sign that she hadn't been the only one affected by that awkward reunion.

CHAPTER TWO

RYAN WAS HERE.

Curled in a chair, staring blindly at the screen of a television that wasn't even turned on, Rebecca tried to prevent her hands from shaking. They hadn't stopped since she'd closed herself into her room almost an hour earlier.

She couldn't believe he was here. What cruel and capricious quirk of fate had brought them together again, at another wedding, on another beach? What had she done to deserve going through this again?

But, no, she told herself firmly. She wouldn't be going through the same thing again. This time she knew better than to give her heart to a man who didn't want it.

That thought almost made her laugh, though with little amusement. Give her heart to Ryan? The sad truth was, she had left it with him two and a half years ago. She hadn't been even slightly interested in any other man since him.

She only hoped she had been able to conceal the fact that her first instinct upon seeing him had been to throw herself into his arms.

He had looked so much the same, she thought wistfully, calling his face so easily to her mind. His steel-blue eyes had still looked at her with an intensity that awakened every nerve ending in her body. His sandy hair was still thick, though cut short, and he was still lean and fit-looking. She remembered exactly how strong those arms had felt when wrapped around her, precisely how hard that broad chest had felt when pressed against her softer curves.

Her cell phone rang and for a moment she was afraid Ryan was calling her. Glancing at the screen, she relaxed when she saw her mother's number on the ID screen. Ryan didn't even have this number, she reminded herself with a frown.

She cleared her throat. "Hi, Mom."

"I hear the strain in your voice," her mother said. "Coleen and Melanie giving you problems?"

"Nothing I can't handle."

"Mmm." Her mom sounded skeptical, but that was because she knew Coleen so well. She had warned Rebecca that Coleen would not be easy to work with on this wedding for which both Coleen and Melanie had such unreasonably high expectations. "Is there anything I can do to help you?"

"No, really, I have everything under control. Even if Melanie did try to change her theme from spring gala to Mexican fiesta this afternoon."

"She didn't! Four days before the wedding?"

"I'm afraid so. I was able to talk her out of it."

"Well, I should think so. What on earth possessed that girl?"

"Her BFF and maid of honor has a catty streak, I'm

afraid. She seems to take great pleasure in making Melanie second-guess her choices."

Being a high school teacher, Rebecca's mom needed no explanation for the acronym for "best friend forever." She'd heard them all in the halls of her school. She sighed gustily through the phone. "I don't envy you the next few days. But I'll come early if you need me. I can take off tomorrow and be there by tomorrow evening if you think it would help."

"No, thanks, Mom. I've got everything under control." She didn't tell her mother that Ryan had shown up; she wasn't ready to talk about that just yet. Her mother knew about Ryan, but had never met him. That was going to change when her parents arrived Thursday evening. They were making the ten-hour drive from Lubbock to Galveston a day early to enjoy a few hours of walking on the beach and eating fresh seafood before the all-day wedding festivities on Saturday.

"What about your grandparents' vow renewal ceremony?" her mother asked, oblivious to Rebecca's dilemma. "Is everything going well with that?"

Rebecca was relieved to change the subject to the surprise ceremony she and her cousin, Nate, were putting together for their grandparents' sixtieth wedding anniversary in June. Her father's parents set the standard for long, happy marriages, as far as Rebecca was concerned. She had always hoped to have a strong, loving relationship like theirs for herself someday. For two glorious weeks, she had thought she'd found her soul mate in Ryan Fuller....

"There are a few details to work out, but the most

important arrangements have been made," she said, pushing Ryan to the back of her mind again. "We're still looking for Great-grandmother Winters's veil, and the caterer has been giving me a few hassles, but other than that it's falling into place. I hope Gran and Granddad will be pleased with their big surprise."

"They're going to be thrilled. More than once since I married your dad, his mother has told me she didn't regret one thing about her marriage to your grandfather, but she still sometimes imagined what it might have been like to have the fancy ceremony with all the trimmings." Having lost her own mother while still in her teens, Angela Murphy had always been very close to her mother-in-law. She was eager to do anything she could to help with the upcoming momentous celebration.

Rebecca was happy that she was going to have a part in giving her beloved grandmother that fancy ceremony she'd missed out on so long ago. She was doing the planning and Nate was financing a large portion of the affair. They had recruited other family members to help with details, but everyone was under strict orders to keep the secret from Grandmother Claire and Grandfather Jack Murphy. It was going to be a very special day for the entire family, she mused, crossing her fingers that nothing would go wrong on her end.

"Oh, and I have an idea about your great-grandmother's veil," her mother added. "I remembered today that Claire and Jack gave us some things to store for them back when they had that storm damage to their roof a dozen years ago. As far as I know, there are a couple of old trunks still in our attic. One of them may very well contain some of Claire's mother's things."

"Will you look?" Rebecca asked eagerly.

"I'll get your father to help me. We'll do it tomorrow after work."

"It would be great if you could find it. Gran has shown me her parents' wedding photo several times, and she always mentions how pretty that lace mantilla was on her mother. I know she didn't throw it out, but when I 'casually' asked about it a few weeks ago, she said she didn't know what had happened to it. Maybe she forgot it was in one of those old trunks she asked you to store."

"Don't get your hopes too high. It might not be there. But we'll look."

"Thanks, Mom."

"You're sure you're okay? You still sound a little stressed."

"Just the usual prewedding pandemonium," she prevaricated, recognizing the tone that meant her mother was starting to get all overprotective and overly concerned. "You know Melanie and Coleen expect perfection from me and everyone else. They won't accept anything less. But don't worry. I can handle it."

It was the truth, of course, even if not the whole story. She *was* stressed about the wedding—though not nearly as stressed as she was about spending time with Ryan again.

The only way she was going to get through the rest of this week, she decided as she completed the call with her mother and closed her phone, was to concentrate fully on her work. She would keep telling herself that Ryan was just another groomsman. They would both be so busy they would hardly see each other.

That was her plan for now, anyway.

"WHAT DO YOU MEAN, you've lost your dress? Are you *trying* to ruin my wedding?"

The outraged shriek ended in a note so high-pitched that Rebecca winced as if she were hearing fingernails on a blackboard. Had there been any dogs in the room, with their sensitive hearing, they'd have been howling in pain. She was close to that point, herself.

"What's going on?" she demanded, studying the scene she'd walked into Wednesday morning. Melanie and three of her bridesmaids were gathered in the spacious sitting room of the luxurious suite in which Melanie and her fiancé were staying as the wedding approached, the base of operations for all the organizing and finalizing. Red-faced with anger, Melanie stood in front of the dainty little chair where one of the bridesmaids sat sobbing.

"How could you lose your bridesmaid's dress?" Melanie shouted, ignoring Rebecca.

"I don't know. I just can't find it. I've looked everywhere. I know I had it when we arrived, but…"

"You did this on purpose, didn't you? You want my wedding to be a disaster, you—"

"Melanie!" Rebecca cut in rather loudly to get her cousin's attention. "What is going on?"

Melanie turned and promptly burst into tears. "My wedding is ruined!"

"Your wedding is not ruined. Whatever it is, we can fix it." She looked at the only bridesmaid who didn't seem to be on the verge of a meltdown. "You. Abby, isn't it? Tell me what happened."

It turned out that sometime in the bustle of arriving and checking in the day before, Cassie—the crying bridesmaid—had misplaced her dress. "I swear I had it when I arrived," Cassie insisted. "It was in the back of the SUV with the other luggage, wasn't it, Abby? And Nicki, you saw it when you put your bags in, right? The three of us came in the same car and I know there were three bridesmaids' dresses, but now mine's gone."

"When did you notice it was missing?"

"Just a few minutes ago. I thought I'd better make sure it wasn't getting wrinkled, but when I looked in the closet I couldn't find it. The closet's pretty full because I maybe brought a few more clothes than I really needed, but I looked through everything and the dress isn't there. And it's not like it would be hard to miss, because it has that big poufy skirt and all—"

Melanie whirled furiously. "Are you making fun of the dresses I picked out? Are you saying they're ugly? Is that why you 'lost' yours? Because you hate it?"

"No, Melanie, I swear. I think the dresses are beautiful," Cassie insisted. "I don't know what happened to it. Maybe someone stole it. One of the maids, maybe."

Having seen the godawful lavender dresses—and "poufy" hardly did justice to the overly embellished design—Rebecca doubted sincerely that anyone had stolen the garment. "Have you looked in Nicki and Abby's closets?"

The three bridesmaids stared at each other blankly.

"Why would Nicki or Abby steal my dress?" Cassie sniffled. "They have dresses of their own."

Swallowing a sigh, Rebecca motioned toward Abby. "Why don't you all go look? It's possible that the dresses got mixed up in the confusion of settling in."

"My closet's pretty full," Abby admitted. "There could be an extra dress in there I didn't notice."

"Mine, too," Nicki chimed in. "I'll go check."

"I'll go with you." Eager to have an excuse to get away from the baleful bride, Cassie jumped to her feet and followed the other two out of the suite.

Confident the dress would be found, Rebecca got busy settling her client. She fetched a cold washcloth, poured Melanie a glass of juice from the minifridge and assured her everything would be fine, even though Melanie seemed to be enjoying her tearful assertions that everything was going wrong, and her wedding was ruined.

A few minutes later, Melanie's cell phone rang and the happy news was relayed that the dress had, indeed, been found, stuffed into Nicki's closet.

"Make sure you put it someplace where it won't get more wrinkled," Melanie snapped into the phone. "All of the dresses are going to be steamed and pressed on Friday, but I expect you to take care of them until then."

She snapped her phone closed and looked to Rebecca for sympathy. "It's like wrangling cats."

"I know the feeling," Rebecca murmured beneath her breath. In her normal voice she continued, "The van is reserved to take you and your mother and your four bridesmaids to the mall in Houston this afternoon. It's about an hour's drive, so you'll arrive in plenty of time for a nice lunch and then several hours of shopping before coming back here for the dinner and dance tonight."

She expected Melanie to brighten at the reminders of her entertainment for the rest of the day, but instead Melanie merely sniffled again. "If Daddy doesn't cancel everything while I'm gone. He's just looking for an excuse to ruin my week."

Now what? "What are you talking about, Melanie? Your father dotes on you."

"He keeps talking about how expensive everything is. I just happened to mention at breakfast this morning that I hope to find a new outfit for tonight and I said if I did I'd put it on my credit card, like always, and then he got all stiff and he said—"

She changed her voice to mock her father's tone, "'What's wrong with the hundred dresses you brought with you this week?' So I was like, Daddy, you know I didn't bring a hundred dresses. Don't exaggerate. And he goes, 'Well, you might as well have. Surely there's something you can wear tonight.' So I was all, Fine. If you don't want me to enjoy my wedding week, I'll just stay in my room. Or maybe you'd like me to do some janitorial work or something to repay you for giving me the wedding I've dreamed about my whole life."

Rebecca could picture that scene. She had no doubt that the quarrel had ended with Melanie's father apologizing and assuring his cherished child that he wanted her to have anything her heart desired. No matter what it cost him—and since she had little doubt that he was the one who paid for Melanie's credit card, it was costing him dearly.

"Well, I have a few things to do this morning," she said, inching toward the door. "I just wanted to remind you to be ready for the shopping excursion. I've sent text messages to all the bridesmaids to remind them of the time and place to meet. Let me know if any more problems crop up and I'll take care of them."

She escaped before Melanie had a chance to come up with a list.

Fortunately the elevator doors opened almost immediately after she pressed the button. She jumped in with a sense of relief. And then she saw who was already standing in the elevator.

Out of the frying pan and into the fire.

"Good morning, Rebecca," Ryan said, watching her from the back corner of the wood-paneled car.

"Good morning," she replied, trying to keep her tone light and friendly while studiously avoiding his eyes. Just in case hers gave away too much.

"Problems?"

"Nothing major." She eyed his neatly pressed green shirt and khaki slacks. "Aren't you supposed to be leaving for a fishing trip?"

"I'm not much of a fisherman. I sent the other guys on without me."

"Oh. So, what are you going to do today?" she asked, because it seemed the polite thing to do.

He shrugged. "Just hang. What about you?"

"I have a few errands to run."

"For the wedding?"

"Not exactly. It's for the party tonight."

"Ah, yes. The 'Island Luau,' officially kicking off the wedding festivities. Followed by tomorrow night's 'Eighties Bash,' celebrating the decade of the bride's birth, and the formal rehearsal dinner Friday night." He made little effort to hide his wry feelings about the week's entertainments. "I didn't realize you were also organizing the activities."

Rebecca rolled her eyes. "I've organized everything but the bridesmaids' closets. And I guess I should have done that."

The elevator door opened at the lobby and Ryan followed her out. "Are there problems with the party tonight?"

"Just some things I thought had been taken care of and it turns out they weren't. I'm going to be spending part of the day rushing around trying to find party favors and game prizes."

"Want some company? Maybe I could help."

Startled that he'd even made the suggestion, she stammered, "Oh, um, that isn't necessary. But thanks for the offer."

He stayed right at her heels as she crossed the lobby toward the parking deck. "Come on, Becks. It's not like I have anything else to do all day. And maybe I could be of assistance to you."

"No, I—"

He stopped. "Okay, fine. I understand."

Something about his tone made her stop, too, and turn toward him with a frown. "What do you understand?"

"You're still upset about what happened the last time we were together. Sorry." He started to turn away.

Even knowing she was being played like an Army bugle, her ego smarted in response to the implication that she was afraid to spend time with him. That she couldn't control her emotions around him. "You'd be bored."

He shrugged. "I'm going to be bored here, anyway."

"Fine. But don't blame me when you find yourself hauling shopping bags as I tow you from one store to another."

He smiled and moved toward her again. "I won't blame you."

What was she doing? Watching him climb into the passenger seat of her car, she asked herself if she'd lost her mind. Why had she let him manipulate her into accompanying her today? She had a sneaking suspicion she had let herself be talked into it much too easily.

"Are you sure you want to do this?" she asked again, one hand resting on the key in the ignition. "Because I'm going to spend the next few hours shopping. Running from one souvenir store to another trying to find kitschy items to hand out at the party tonight. As I remember, you weren't too crazy about shopping."

"Not particularly," he agreed equably, fastening his seat belt. "But we usually managed to have a good time no matter what we were doing."

Remembering some of those good times, she felt her cheeks go warm. She focused intently on backing out of the parking space in an attempt to mask her reaction.

CHAPTER THREE

IF ANYONE HAD ASKED, Ryan would have been hard-pressed to explain why he'd been so determined to accompany Rebecca on this shopping excursion. If he had a lick of sense, he'd be out on the fishing boat with his buddy, Charlie, and the other groomsmen, despite his lack of enthusiasm for the sport. Still, wouldn't risking a few hours of boredom be smarter than risking his heart again?

He hadn't been pining for Rebecca since they'd parted two and a half years ago, he assured himself. After all, he still thought the reasons for doing so were legitimate ones. He'd been headed for a war zone, and he didn't want to leave anyone behind to worry about his safety, so he'd suggested to Rebecca that, for her own good, they part as friends. It had seemed perfectly reasonable to him; after all, they'd known each other only a couple of weeks. Even if they had been the most amazing two weeks he had ever experienced.

Something he'd said—or maybe the way he'd said it—had really set her off. She'd informed him in no uncertain terms that she didn't need him, or anyone, telling her what was best for her. Or implying that she was incapable of looking out for her own best interests. Yet, beneath her anger, he could sense that he had hurt her badly. Something he had never wanted to do.

The more he'd tried to explain, the more heated the conversation had become. Regrettably, they had parted angrily.

Which didn't mean he hadn't missed her like crazy after they'd gone their own ways. Or that he hadn't thought of her almost every day since. Or that seeing her again hadn't made him feel like he'd been kicked—hard—right smack in the middle of his chest.

So, here he was, walking into a souvenir shop on Seawall Boulevard just so he could watch Rebecca comb through buckets of shells and numerous shelves filled with made-in-China Gulf Coast souvenirs. She carried a small black notebook. Looking over her shoulder, he could see that it was filled with lists and stick-on notes in a variety of colors, all covered with her handwriting.

"What, exactly, are you looking for?" he asked when she had picked up, examined and then replaced the sixth—or was it seventh?—item.

"I'm hoping to know it when I see it," she said, moving to the next row of shelves and picking up a clear, fat candle filled with seashells.

"You said this is for the party tonight? Favors?"

"Favors and game prizes."

"Game prizes?" He frowned. He'd missed that part earlier, probably because he'd been too intent on convincing her to let him accompany her. "They're having games?"

"Melanie thought it would be so much fun."

Her wry tone didn't escape him. Apparently she'd been having her share of disagreements with her cousin/client. "What kind of games?"

"Trust me, you'll feel better about going tonight if you don't ask too many questions."

He doubted that. But since he had no choice but to attend, he decided to take her advice. "So, how did you end up doing the shopping?"

"Because the person who was supposed to do it didn't."

"Don't you have any minions?"

She handed him the candle. "I do now."

He chuckled. Without smiling back, she made a note in her book, then moved on with him following obediently down the rows of gift items.

She handed him a grass-skirted hula girl with swiveling hips. When he lifted an eyebrow at her, she shrugged and made another mark in her notebook. "Yes, I know it's a ridiculous souvenir of an island in Texas rather than one in Hawaii, but gag gifts are always good for a laugh."

"You might have better luck with nice gifts at one of the shops in The Strand," he suggested, mentioning the island's historic Victorian-era tourist and shopping district.

"Oh, we'll be going there," she agreed. "After I've checked some more of the souvenir shops along the seawall."

"So," he asked as they stashed her purchases from the first store in the back of her car, "are you and Melanie close?"

"We've never been close. After this week, it will be a miracle if we're even still talking."

He smiled, not at all surprised by the candid answer. "Yeah. I got the feeling she can be a little…difficult."

As if she were concerned that she'd sounded both unprofessional and disloyal to her family, Rebecca said quickly, "I've dealt with other brides who went a little overboard with their expectations. Melanie isn't the first, and certainly won't be the last."

"So, you like this job?"

Walking up the steps to the doorway of the second shop, she gave him a rather tight smile. "I love it."

"O-kay." He followed her in, snagging a shopping basket inside the door.

He couldn't help noticing that she didn't seem to be taking a lot of pleasure in her shopping. Even when she selected the silly gag gifts, she rarely smiled, just looked satisfied to have another item marked off her list. Her Internet-connected phone buzzed and blipped regularly to announce a call or text message. She let most of the calls go to voice mail, and answered only a couple of the texts, but she made several notes in her little book. Probably calls she intended to return later, he decided.

When they had exhausted the souvenir shops, they climbed back into her car to head inland toward The Strand. Like the rest of the island, the historic district had been devastated by the hurricane, but every effort was being made to restore the heavily damaged old buildings. Rebecca commented that she was happy to be doing her part to help the recovery by patronizing the shops that had reopened in the past months.

"I didn't realize quite how much goes into planning a wedding," he commented, snapping his seat belt.

"Some are more difficult than others, of course. Melanie's is one of the complicated ones."

He'd been watching her profile as she drove, finding himself so intrigued by the very slight tip at the end of her nose that he was having a hard time concentrating on their small talk. He remembered that little tilt, of course. He'd just never thought he would have the chance to see it again.

"It really was a bizarre coincidence that you happen to know Melanie's fiancé," she commented. "I was so surprised when I saw you on the beach the other night."

He wondered if she'd been half as surprised as he'd been when Charlie had made an offhand comment about their organizer, Rebecca Murphy. Somehow it had felt at that moment as if the universe was laughing at him—or maybe offering him a second chance. He still wasn't sure which. "Like we said, it's a small world," he said blandly, keeping those other thoughts to himself.

"Charlie seems very nice," she remarked after an awkward moment of silence.

"Yeah, he's a great guy."

"I hope he and Melanie will be happy."

Because of something he heard in her voice, he asked curiously, "You see a lot of weddings, I guess. What odds do you give Charlie and Melanie of staying together? Honestly."

"Honestly?" She gave him a wry smile. "Maybe

twenty-five percent chance that they'll last a year. As spoiled as Melanie is, she'll run home to her mama and daddy the first time poor Charlie doesn't give her exactly what she wants."

Ryan laughed. So she wasn't quite the orange-blossom optimist she pretended to be in her job. "That's kind of what I thought."

Rebecca grimaced. "I shouldn't have said that. It was completely unprofessional, not to mention disloyal toward family."

"Don't worry. I won't tell anyone what you said."

"It's just that she's been driving me crazy this week," she said, still looking annoyed with herself for the indiscretion. "It's no excuse, but I spoke without thinking."

"Rebecca. It's okay. I know you're a professional, and I'm sure you never say a disparaging word about any of your clients to anyone else. You and I have always been in the habit of saying what we think to each other. You know you can trust me not to repeat you."

"Always?" She gave him a quizzical look as she parked in a convenient spot on Strand. "We spent two weeks together, Ryan. It's hardly as if we've known each other for years."

"I'd say we got to know each other pretty well in those two weeks," he replied evenly.

Turning her head away, she reached for her door handle. "Not as well as I thought," she muttered, sliding out of the car.

Contemplating her words, he opened his door to follow her.

HER SHOPPING FINISHED, Rebecca stowed the last of the gifts in the car with a sense of relief. One chore accomplished for the day. Another dozen or so to go.

Ryan caught her arm when she started to reach for her car door. "Wait."

She glanced at his hand on her forearm then up at his face. "What?"

Motioning toward a restaurant behind her, he gave her a faint smile. "I'm starving. You've got time for a quick lunch, don't you?"

Glancing at her watch, she thought about making an excuse. But because that made her feel cowardly again, she changed her mind. Ryan had been on his best behavior all morning. She still wasn't quite sure why he'd wanted to follow her around and watch her shop, but he'd given her no reason to be uncomfortable around him. Nothing, that was, except the bittersweet memories she couldn't quite suppress.

"I guess I can take time for lunch," she agreed after a moment. "I don't know when I'll have another chance to eat today."

"Great. You know anything about this place?"

"No, but it looks fine."

"And the best thing? It's close."

Glancing over her shoulder as she walked through the door, she smiled. "Are you saying you're tired of walking?"

"We've pretty much covered every inch of this island, I think."

A hostess in a brightly colored top with jeans greeted them and escorted them to a table for two beside a big window where they could watch pedestrians passing on the busy sidewalks.

"I would have thought an Army man was used to long hikes," Rebecca said over her menu, continuing the conversation.

"An infantryman, maybe," he drawled. "Us Rangers tire easily."

She snorted. "Yeah. Right."

She might not know much about the military, but she'd read enough to recognize baloney when she heard it. Maybe she'd looked up information about the Army Rangers a few times after she'd left Hawaii. She didn't have to tell him that.

She set her menu aside.

"You've decided?" he asked.

"Yes. I'm having the shrimp po' boy."

"You always loved shrimp," he said, laying his menu on top of hers.

There was that word again. Always.

"Why are you here, Ryan?"

He lifted an eyebrow. "I told you. Charlie and I were roommates in college. He asked me to be a groomsman because, frankly, he doesn't have ten close, current friends."

She shook her head impatiently. "I didn't mean why are you in Galveston. I meant here. In this restaurant."

"I was hungry." He held up a hand before she could express her exasperation with his obtuseness. "I know what you mean. Why did I want to come with you today?"

She nodded.

He shrugged. "I thought we should clear the air a little between us if we're going to be spending the rest of the week together."

She shifted a little in her seat. "We aren't exactly spending the week together. We're both going to be busy with our respective wedding responsibilities from here on out. And I don't know what you mean by clearing the air. I think we said everything we needed to say in Hawaii."

"I didn't like the way things ended between us there," he said with a frown. "It wasn't…"

"Are you two ready to order?" a perky server inquired, popping up beside their table.

Dragging her attention from Ryan, Rebecca ordered her sandwich with a glass of iced tea. Requesting coconut shrimp for himself, Ryan handed the menus to the server, then waited until she had left before finishing what he'd started to say earlier. "It wasn't the way I wanted our time together to end."

She hadn't wanted their time together to end at all. She still didn't agree with the reasons he had given her then for breaking it off. She still thought he'd been high-handed and stubborn—and when he'd added that it was "for her own good," she had *really* lost control.

"Yes, well, there are no hard feelings on my part," she fibbed, toying with her napkin to avoid looking at his eyes. "So you needn't worry about this week being awkward between us. As I said, I'll be extremely busy."

As if to prove her point, her phone buzzed. She read the texted question from her assistant in Lubbock, answered with a couple of quick words, then dropped the phone back into its holder.

"I'm glad to hear you aren't still angry with me," he said when she glanced up at him again. "Those two weeks were very special to me. I'd hate to think I'd left you with bad memories when all I wanted to do was protect you from—"

"Would you mind if we don't talk about the past right now?"

Though he looked a bit surprised by her forceful interruption, he hesitated only a moment before changing the subject by asking questions about her business.

That had been a narrow escape, she told herself in relief, even as she replied to his seemingly sincerely curious questions. Because, honestly, if he had started talking about protecting her from herself or some such nonsense, she might have embarrassed them both by dumping a pitcher of ice water over his head.

She had made a name for herself as a wedding organizer by being cool, calm and collected. But something about Ryan tempted her to throw all of those fine qualities right out the window. It had been that way from the first moment they had met. He had ignited previously unlit passions within her, and those sparks had extended to her usually controlled temper, as well.

She was not going to risk her professional reputation this week by letting him get to her again.

Even as she made the silent vow, she found herself crossing her fingers beneath the table.

BACK AT THE HOTEL, Ryan helped Rebecca carry the purchases to her room. He'd made no further effort to talk about Hawaii during their lunch or the drive back, to her relief. Nor had he wanted to talk about his time in the Middle East, as he'd made it clear when she had tried to ask about his tour of duty there.

They had talked, instead, about her business. He'd seemed to enjoy some of her humorous anecdotes about weddings she had coordinated and he'd asked quite a few insightful questions.

"I guess I'll see you at the party tonight," he said at her door.

She nodded. "I'll be there. Making sure everything goes smoothly."

"You're sure there's nothing else I can do for you?"

"No, thanks. I have everything under control. Thanks for being my pack mule today."

He chuckled. "Believe it or not, I enjoyed it. So— we're friends again?"

That was the way he'd wanted to leave things between them when they'd parted in Maui, she remembered. Just friends. It was all he'd had to offer at the time, he had explained regretfully. Those words had cut her to the quick, since she had been prepared to offer him so much more of herself.

"Friends?" she repeated, trying to convey just the right amount of nonchalance in her tone. Hoping she hadn't let him see that she was as dissatisfied with that status now as she had been when they'd parted, she said, "Sure, I guess so. Now, if you'll excuse me, I have about a dozen calls to return."

He didn't look particularly satisfied by her answer, but he nodded. "Okay. I'll see you this evening, Becks."

She all but shut the door in his face. Then sagged against it, her heart beating a little too fast in her chest, her eyes burning with the memory of old tears she had shed over him.

CHAPTER FOUR

RESTLESS and vaguely dissatisfied, Ryan wandered down to the lobby of the resort. He didn't know quite what to do with himself for the remainder of the day, but maybe he could find a decent book in the gift shop. He could always kill a couple of hours sitting on the little balcony outside his room overlooking the gulf with a canned soda and a paperback thriller.

He was just about to step into the gift shop when he caught sight of Charlie sitting alone on one of the low couches in the sunken bar centered in the lobby. Making a detour, he rounded the brass railing that lined the bar, descended the three marble steps down and approached his friend. "Charlie?"

"Oh. Hey, Ryan." Charlie set his beer on the low table in front of the couch and motioned toward one of the comfortable-looking chairs grouped invitingly around the table. "Have a seat. Let me buy you a drink."

"I'm surprised to see you here. I didn't think you'd be back from the fishing trip yet."

Motioning for a server, Charlie laughed wryly. "The water was extremely rough this morning. Most of the guys started throwing up. We voted to come back early. They're all up in their rooms recovering."

"I can't say I'm sorry I missed that."

"I don't blame you. Think you'd have been hanging over the railing, too?"

"Nah. I just don't like the smell of bait."

Charlie chuckled and took another sip of his beer. "So what did you do all morning?"

"A little shopping."

"Shopping." Charlie eyed him quizzically. "You?"

"I went with Rebecca. She had to pick up some stuff for the party tonight and I offered to be her pack mule."

"Rebecca Murphy?" Charlie looked startled. "The wedding coordinator?"

"Yeah. Turns out she and I know each other. We met at another wedding in Hawaii a couple years ago."

"No kidding? That's quite a coincidence."

"Yeah. That's what she and I said." He still wasn't sure Rebecca considered it a happy twist of fate.

"Rebecca seems really nice. She's got the patience of a saint, I can tell you that. I mean, Melanie's not exactly easy to work with when it comes to this wedding."

Because he didn't quite know what to say in response to that understatement, Ryan murmured something noncommittal as he took a sip of his beer.

"It's just that Melanie wants our wedding to be perfect," Charlie explained earnestly, looking concerned that Ryan was getting a less than favorable impression of his bride-to-be. "She gets a little carried away. She's even yelled at me a couple of times in the last few days, because she's so nervous about everything."

"Mmm." Ryan figured Charlie had better get used to that.

Charlie took another long swig of his beer, then motioned for the server to bring him another. Ryan shook his head when asked if he'd like a second.

"I really appreciate you being here for me this week, buddy," Charlie confided after draining his first mug. "I mean, when Melanie told me I needed ten attendants—well, I told her that wasn't going to happen. I didn't think I could come up with ten guys who could spend several days here in Galveston for my wedding. She got pretty stressed and threatened to find friends of her own to fill in, but I came up with eight, counting you, and we're using two husbands of bridesmaids to fill out the number."

He made a face. "It was a little easier to convince some of my friends when I told them almost everything was paid for, so they could look at it as a mostly paid vacation."

Ryan wondered how much this wedding was setting his old pal back. Charlie made good money as an orthodontist, but he wasn't exactly wealthy. Not to mention whatever Melanie's family was spending for this blowout. None of his business, of course.

"So, anyway, this party tonight," Charlie said, already well into his second beer. "There's one of the bridesmaids I want you to meet. Her name's Abby. She's hot. Red hair, green eyes, built. Nice girl, too. Laughs a lot. I think you'll like her."

Ryan was surprisingly uninterested in meeting Abby. He was, however, already anticipating seeing Rebecca again.

REBECCA CLIPPED a bright pink hibiscus flower into her hair above her right ear, studied it a moment, then took it back out. And then clipped it in again.

She didn't know why she was taking so long to get ready for this party. It wasn't as if anyone would be taking much notice of the coordinator. The bride and groom would be the focus of everyone's attention, and the rest of the wedding party would be busy drinking and dancing and socializing. She would stay in the background, keeping an eye on things, making sure the festivities proceeded as the bride desired.

Standing in front of the full-length mirror in her room's dressing area, she turned to check the back of the bright pink and purple print sundress she'd selected for the night's festivities. Everything was straight. Nothing showing that wasn't supposed to be. Bra straps were tucked neatly beneath the wide straps that supported the rather deeply square cut bodice of the dress. She supposed she was as ready as she was going to be. Even though, after the nonstop busy day she'd had, she would have liked to have crawled into bed for a half hour or so.

She had just slid her feet into her sandals when her phone rang. Glancing at the caller ID screen, she smiled and lifted it to her ear. "Hi, Nate."

"Hey, Rebecca. Sorry it's taken me so long to return your call. It's been crazy here."

"I know the feeling."

"Is anything wrong?"

"Oh, no, it's nothing like that. Everything seems to be on track for Gran and Granddad's ceremony. I just wanted to tell you that my assistant put down a deposit on flowers today. We've also paid deposits for the caterer and the videographer."

"You charged it all to the credit card I gave you, right?"

"Yes. As you instructed."

"And you didn't stint on anything? You're getting the best for Gran and Granddad, aren't you?"

"I'm ordering exactly what I think they would like. You're sure you want to pay for all of this, Nate? I mean, the rest of us could pitch in… "

"You're already pitching in," he reminded her. "You're doing all this planning and ordering free of charge, when I know it must be interfering with your other jobs."

"Oh, I don't mind that. I'd do anything for them."

"Exactly. Everyone in the family is contributing in their own way to the big event. Footing the bill for the ceremony is what I want to do."

She knew he could afford the gesture. A successful corporate raider, her cousin had done very well for himself. Still, it was incredibly generous of him to pay for this surprise vow renewal ceremony, considering that the whole idea had been a spur-of-the-moment impulse. "Okay, then. If you insist. But when you look at your credit card statement, remember I asked."

He chuckled. "I won't blame you. I promise."

"I hope we can pull this off, Nate. I hope Gran and Granddad are as thrilled as we think they'll be. And I hope…"

He laughed again. "It'll work out, Rebecca. You do this all the time, remember?"

"I know. It's just…this one's more important than any of the others."

"I know," he answered gently. "This one's family."

Melanie was family, too, she thought a few minutes later, after she and Nate had concluded the brief call. But she couldn't say she was nearly as invested in Melanie's wedding as she was in her grandparents' renewal ceremony. Professionally, yes. She would do everything she could to make sure Melanie got the wedding she—or rather, her parents—had paid for. But, to be honest, Melanie's wedding was just another job, as far as Rebecca was concerned. The renewal ceremony was so much more—the most important assignment she had ever taken on. She couldn't help but obsess about it a little.

She was giving her grandmother the wedding she might have wanted for herself, she acknowledged, had things turned out differently between her and Ryan.

Trying to concentrate on the job at hand, she added one last touch of lip gloss and headed out of her room, ready to get this first party behind her.

TO REBECCA'S exasperation, Melanie had insisted on a tropical island theme for the party, complete with silk leis and fake tiki torches. Though Galveston had a colorful and interesting history of its own, which Rebecca would have used as a backdrop had it been her choice, Melanie was still pining for a more exotic location. She had insisted that Rebecca help her create that illusion at tonight's party.

Rebecca had done her best, as always. The party

room was filled with silk orchids, palm fronds, fishing nets, shells and glass balls. Hawaiian music drifted from discreetly hidden speakers. Drinks garnished with paper parasols and pineapple slices were being served at a bar draped in raffia and net. And the food tables almost sagged beneath the weight of the tasty offerings.

A good-size crowd attended the event. Taking a four-day weekend from their jobs, most of the wedding party had arrived late that afternoon, several bringing guests. Other special friends and family members of the bride and groom had also made plans to spend the next three days at the resort and had been invited to the luau, so Rebecca assumed Melanie was pleased with the turnout.

Melanie certainly seemed to be making the most of her position as the guest of honor. Wearing the vividly printed silk sheath she'd purchased in Houston that afternoon, she reigned like royalty in the center of the room, graciously dividing her time among her guests, her recent bad mood masked now by beaming smiles.

All dressed in bright tropical colors, her bridesmaids fluttered around her, each trying to share as much of the spotlight as possible. They giggled and gossiped and hula-ed, checked out each other and the others' significant others, generally acted like a bunch of sorority sisters who'd had too many umbrella-topped drinks.

"Oh, there you are, Rebecca. I've been looking for you." Coleen spoke as if Rebecca had been hiding in a corner during the party rather than bustling from one end of the room to the other making sure everything was going smoothly, freeing everyone else to simply enjoy the festivities.

"I've been right here, Aunt Coleen. What can I do for you?"

"I was looking through a wedding magazine today while the girls were shopping and I found a fascinating article that gave me an idea."

Rebecca swallowed a groan. This could not be good.

"Anyway, the article was all about the meaning of flowers. Did you know that yellow poppies bring wealth and success? So I thought," she continued before Rebecca had a chance to respond, "we could incorporate yellow poppies into Melanie's bouquet. I mean, the other flowers she's carrying are all about love and happiness and such, but it wouldn't hurt to add a little good-luck symbol for wealth, would it?"

"She can put a penny in her shoe. It's really too late to change the bouquet. Melanie chose her design of cascading lavender roses, sweet peas and parrot tulips months ago, and it really is lovely. I don't think yellow poppies would work in it at all."

"It will look fine," Coleen assured her somewhat imperiously.

"The florist needs more than two days' notice for something like this. Yellow poppies would completely change the design of the bouquet. I don't even know if she could order them and get them in time for the wedding."

"Oh, I'm sure she could work it out somehow."

"Have you even discussed this with Melanie?"

"Well…no. I thought it would be a nice little surprise for her."

"Aunt Coleen, has Melanie been open to *any* surprises so far when it comes to the details of her wedding?"

Coleen bit her lower lip for a moment, then sighed. "It did seem like a good idea at the time."

"It was a very sweet thought," Rebecca responded gently, allowing herself to relax just a little. "But I think we'd better stick with the penny in her shoe."

"All right. I'd better get back to my guests. We're going to start the games soon, now that it looks like everyone has had something to eat. I'll give you a signal when I'm ready for you to get them started."

Oh, joy, Rebecca thought, but kept the sarcasm hidden behind a bland smile.

She turned to come face-to-face with Ryan. Judging by his expression, he'd been there long enough to overhear at least part of her conversation with her aunt.

"Has that been going on all week? Them wanting to change things at the last minute, I mean?"

She shrugged. "Part of the job. Almost all brides have last minute inspirations or change their minds about something."

"You handled that very well. "

"Like I said, it's what I do."

"Have you had anything to eat?"

She glanced at the food tables, where the crowds had thinned, though a few guests were still stuffing their faces. "No, I haven't had time. I'll get something later."

"Have you eaten anything at all since lunch?"

"No, but—"

He nodded grimly. "I thought you looked kind of pale. Come on. Let's get you some food."

"But I need to bring the game prizes out—"

"I'll help you with that, after you've eaten." He had a hand on her arm now, nudging her toward the tables.

It was the second time that day he'd been determined to feed her. And it was another reminder of how bossy Ryan could be, a trait that never failed to activate her stubborn side. She dug in her heels and spoke from between teeth set in a bright, fake smile. "I said I'll eat in a minute, Ryan."

He stopped in his tracks, giving her a searching look. "I'm only trying to make sure you're taking care of yourself while you're taking care of your cousin's wedding."

"I can take care of myself, thank you."

Sighing, he lifted both hands, palm outward, a sign of surrender. "Sorry. I didn't mean to offend you."

"I just don't like being told what to do," she muttered.

Her aunt chose that moment to motion demandingly toward Rebecca, the promised signal that it was time for the games to begin. Sighing, Rebecca thought fleetingly that she really should have taken the brief chance to get some food while she'd had it. Even Aunt Coleen might have waited a few moments if she'd seen Rebecca eating. Or maybe not.

"Excuse me," she said to Ryan with as much dignity as possible. "I have to go lead the games now."

He nodded with an expression that made her tempted to step on his foot as she passed him. The man could certainly push her buttons, she thought grumpily.

All her buttons, unfortunately, she added, realizing that her fingers were twitching to straighten the collar of the rather muted Hawaiian shirt he wore with jeans and sneakers, his only concession to the tropical theme of the party. The collar was a little crumpled on the right side, probably from when he'd removed the silk lei that had been placed around everyone's neck as they'd entered the room. The crumple was very close to the strong line of his jaw. Which led her eyes inevitably to his firm, beautifully shaped mouth.

Feeling even crankier now—not to mention a bit overheated—she forced herself to concentrate on her job. She would deal with her Ryan obsessions later.

CHAPTER FIVE

REBECCA had just walked away when Ryan felt a hand fall heavily on his shoulder. He turned to find Charlie standing right behind him, grinning a bit foolishly. Charlie's blue eyes were a little too bright and his ruddy cheeks even redder than usual. He'd obviously had a few drinks since those beers in the lobby earlier.

"Ryan! I've been looking for you. There's someone here I want you to meet."

Ryan nodded toward the rather embarrassed-looking redhead Charlie held in a death grip on her arm. "Hello."

"Abby Coleman, this is Captain Ryan Fuller of the United States Army Rangers," Charlie intoned, then ruined the solemn tone with a laugh. "What do you think, Ryan? Is she as beautiful as I told you?"

Abby blushed rosily. "Honestly, Charlie."

Giving her a sympathetic smile, Ryan said, "It's nice to meet you, Abby. You're one of the bridesmaids, aren't you?"

"Yes. Melanie and I were in the same sorority at SMU. I understand you and Charlie know each other from UT."

"That's right."

"If everyone will take a seat at one of the tables, we have some entertainment planned now," Rebecca announced from the front of the room. She stood by a table that had been covered with a cloth until that point, now uncovered to reveal the eclectic selection of prizes he'd watched her select that very morning. She used a small microphone to make her voice carry throughout the room, and the beautifully modulated tones had their usual effect on him, making it difficult to concentrate on anyone else at hand.

Forcing himself to try, he spoke to Charlie. "Melanie's looking around this way. I think she's hunting for you."

"Guess I'd better get over there, then. I'll leave you two to get to know each other," he added with a leer that looked more comical than suggestive.

"I think my friend has had a little too much celebration today," Ryan commented, watching Charlie make his way somewhat unsteadily toward his bride-to-be at the table closest to the front of the room.

"I think you might be right," Abby agreed with a giggle. "I hope he didn't embarrass you. He insisted on dragging me over here."

"No, of course not. I guess we'd better take a seat for the games. Melanie's mother is starting to glare at us."

"Come sit at our table," she invited him. "There's an extra seat."

Because there was no polite way to decline, he accepted graciously, following her across the room to a table for eight where three other bridesmaids and their guests were already seated. She introduced him quickly to the others, whose names he forgot almost as soon as he heard them, then motioned him to take the seat beside her.

Pulling his chair beneath the table, he glanced toward Rebecca again. Their gazes collided, but then she looked quickly away, as if she hadn't wanted him to know that she'd been watching him.

He wondered if it bothered her even a little to see him sitting with Abby. He'd hate like hell for some guy to be flirting with Rebecca this evening. But maybe that was just his problem.

Not being much of a party game player, he wasn't thrilled to hear that the first game was something called "matrimonial bingo." Melanie's parents distributed laminated bingo cards along with little baskets of purple plastic hearts to use as chips. Each card had a free space in the center, like a traditional bingo card, but the other twenty-four squares were filled with words.

He noted that the other guests at the party prepared to play with varying degrees of enthusiasm, some looking about as delighted as he felt, others eagerly memorizing their cards. Abby and her friends at the table seemed to be among the latter group.

"I love bingo," Abby confided to him. "I hope I win a prize."

Not wanting to put a damper on her fun, he smiled and assured her that she had a good chance of doing so.

Rebecca served as caller. She looked so pretty standing up there smiling at the guests that he had a hard time taking his eyes off her. The overhead lights gleamed in her hair, and the yellow silk lei she wore around her neck brushed her cheek when she looked down to read the words on the printed tiles she drew out of a little bingo cage. He remembered exactly how soft that cheek felt against his own. How sweet her skin tasted on his lips and tongue. How smooth—

"Ryan." Abby tapped his hand as it hovered over his game card. "You have the word she just called. 'Rice.' See, it's here in this corner. Only one more word and you'll have a bingo."

Dragging his attention from Rebecca, he laid a purple heart on top of the word. "Thanks, Abby. I didn't see that one."

Fortunately someone at another table called, "Bingo!" after the next word. Amid laughter, applause and groans of disappointment, the winner was invited to select a prize from the "goodies table."

Abby leaned flirtatiously against Ryan's arm while the winner dithered over her choice. "I saw the relief on your face," she accused him. "You didn't want to win, did you? Don't try to tell me you're the shy type who would be embarrassed to call out bingo and have everyone look at you."

He smiled wryly. "Yeah, that's me. A real wallflower."

She laughed musically, drawing attention their way. "I don't believe that for one minute. I bet you can be the life of the party when you want to be."

Fortunately Rebecca started the next bingo game before Ryan had to come up with a response.

They played several more games of bingo. To Abby's delight, she won the final game. She squealed, "Bingo!" and then hugged Ryan's arm in her excitement. He congratulated her warmly, then watched her hurry to the shrinking prize selection. His eyes caught Rebecca's again, and the expression on her face made him thoughtful. He didn't think he was imagining this time that she wasn't pleased with the way things appeared to be progressing between him and Abby.

Once Abby had returned to her seat with her prize, Rebecca introduced the next game. This one, she said, was called a "bouquet relay." She invited everyone who wanted to play to come to the dance floor between where she stood and the tables.

"Oh, this is going to be fun." Abby stood, along with everyone else at the table, smiling down at Ryan. "Come on. We can be on the same team. I bet an Army Ranger is really fast at this sort of thing."

"I've got news for you. Bouquet relays are not part of our basic training."

She laughed and tugged at his arm. "Come on. Play with us."

"Yeah, come on, Ryan," someone else urged.

"Hey, Ry," Charlie called from where everyone was gathering at the starting point. "You're playing, aren't you?"

He swallowed a sigh and exchanged a look with one of the other groomsmen who looked like he'd rather be sitting in a dentist chair than playing this game. Ryan identified with that feeling all too well, even as he said, "Sure, Charlie. I'm playing."

Rebecca separated them into two equal-numbered teams, then lined them up on one end of the dance floor. The first person in each line had to run to a tape mark some six feet in front of the next person, pick up a silk flower bouquet and throw it over the shoulder to the next person in line. That player had to catch the bouquet, run to the line, and throw it over the shoulder to the next team member. If they missed, and the bouquet touched the floor, the thrower had to toss it again until it was successfully caught. The hilarity would continue until the last person of each team had caught the bouquet, and the first team finished would all win prizes.

All in all, it was pretty silly. But Ryan found himself laughing along with the other players as bouquets flew through the air. The other team won by seconds. They collected their prizes—key chains shaped like flip-flops—which they showed off smugly.

The final game was a trivia challenge. Returning to their tables, the guests were instructed to hold up a hand if they knew the answer to several obscure questions about the bride and groom, contributed, apparently, by the couple, themselves. The first contestants to answer each question correctly won their choice of the remaining prizes.

Ryan sat back in his seat and watched Rebecca during the trivia game. He didn't even try to play, since he didn't know Melanie's favorite flavor of ice cream or the first song she and Charlie had danced to, or where they'd gone on their first date. But since Rebecca was asking all the questions, it was only polite to look at her, he assured himself wryly. As if that were a hardship.

"Okay, one final question," she announced. "To be

followed immediately by dancing until we wrap up at eleven," she added, motioning toward the corner of the room where a small band was setting up.

Still smiling, she read from the paper in her hand, "What did Charlie do to celebrate his twenty-first birthday?"

"Got drunk!" someone shouted.

Rebecca shook her head. "No, that's not right."

"Got a tattoo?" Abby ventured.

"No. That's not it, either. Does anyone know?"

A few other suggestions were made, some of them colorful enough to make Melanie's mother blush. Charlie's mother wouldn't arrive until Friday, fortunately. Realizing that no one else in the room knew the answer, Ryan sighed and raised his hand.

"You know what he did, Ryan?" Rebecca asked.

Glancing at Charlie, who was laughing at his table, probably having planted this question just for Ryan's sake, Ryan nodded. "He jumped out of an airplane. And I know that because I jumped with him."

There were laughing cries of "cheaters," "no fair" and "it's rigged!" Abby giggled and hugged Ryan's arm again, something that was becoming a habit with her. One he would just as soon she'd break.

Charlie would probably think he was crazy. After all, Abby was pretty, amusing, flirtatious and—as Charlie had pointed out—built. She appeared to be unattached, and Ryan certainly was. But he just didn't feel anything when she leaned against him except a perfunctorily masculine appreciation for a woman's soft curves.

He forgot all about Abby as he moved toward Rebecca, their eyes locking again. She was smiling, as she had been throughout the games, but her smile changed a little as he moved closer. Still, she kept up the cheery, professional tone she'd used for all the games.

"Well, Ryan," she said, "you have your choice of prizes. What's your pick?"

He glanced at the almost empty prize table, then looked at her again. "Any prize I want?"

She motioned toward the table. "Absolutely."

"I'd like a dance with the wedding organizer."

"I DIDN'T REALIZE I was one of the prizes," Rebecca commented dryly a few minutes later as Ryan took her into his arms on the dance floor.

He grinned, looking rather proud of himself. "Anyone would consider you a prize, Becks."

She groaned. "Gee, thanks."

Laughing, he pulled her a little closer and matched his steps to hers as the band played the slow song that Melanie had requested to start the set. She tried to concentrate on the music. The steps. Anything except the feel of him against her. Though she couldn't help noticing that he had kept himself in excellent shape. His arms and chest were still firmly muscled, his abs lean and hard, his legs long and taut.

She wondered if it was getting warmer in the room, or if that was just her. She strongly suspected the latter.

Everyone seemed to have been amused by Ryan's choice of "prize." Everyone except Abby, maybe, Rebecca mused, glancing toward the pretty redhead who was dancing with one of the other groomsmen now, but kept sneaking peeks toward her and Ryan. It had been obvious that Abby had been flirting with Ryan during the games. She probably wasn't used to having men wander away from her when she worked the hugging-his-arm tactic.

Rebecca couldn't help wondering why Ryan hadn't displayed more interest.

"Your party seems to be going well," he said, smiling down at her. "Even the games weren't as bad as I expected."

She gave a little shrug, glad that he'd broken the silence between them. If she could concentrate on conversation, maybe she wouldn't be quite so aware of him on a physical level, she thought without much optimism. "Melanie chose the games. My job was simply to organize them."

"Well, you did a great job."

"Thanks. Um, you and Abby seemed quite friendly."

What might have been a flash of amusement appeared in his eyes, as if he were pleased that she'd noticed and hadn't particularly liked what she'd seen, but he masked the expression too quickly for her to be certain. She was already mentally kicking herself for letting the remark slip out after she'd promised herself she wasn't going to mention Abby.

"Charlie introduced us. For some reason, he thought she was my type. He was wrong, of course."

Deciding not to follow up on that intriguing comment, she changed the subject quickly. "Did you really jump out of an airplane with him on his twenty-first birthday?"

"I did. Charlie's mom would have killed us if she'd known. She was always the overprotective type. Which was probably why he was so determined to try it."

She knew all about overprotective parents. "What about your mom? Did she know about it?"

He shrugged, his eyes going distant. "She wouldn't have cared."

They hadn't talked about his family much when they'd spent time together in Maui. He'd told her he had a younger brother who traveled a lot with his job, and that he rarely saw either of his divorced parents, but other than that he'd shared little of his childhood with her. She'd gotten the impression that it had been far from ideal. But since a dance floor was no place to discuss anything that personal, she simply asked, "Were you scared?"

"If I was, I didn't let anyone know it."

Tilting her head back, she studied his face, noting that he was smiling again. "But were you?"

His grin widened, making her pulse rate jump a bit. "Petrified."

Unable to resist smiling back, she asked, "Did you enjoy it?"

"Oh, yeah, it was great. I couldn't wait to do it again."

"Have you?"

"Many times."

"What about Charlie?"

"He kissed the ground when he landed, and said he was never doing anything like that again. As far as I know, he never has."

"That would probably be my reaction," she conceded.

"Nah. You'd love it."

Surprised, she asked, "What makes you think that?"

"Because you like a challenge. You like proving yourself. And because someone would probably tell you that you shouldn't do it—for your own good. Which would be all it would take to get you to jump."

With that too-close-for-comfort observation, the music ended. As if he were reluctant to let go, Ryan held her just a moment longer before letting his arms fall. "Thank you for the dance."

"You won it, remember?" she asked lightly, trying to hide her own disappointment that the dance was over.

His left eyebrow cocked into a wicked expression she remembered very well. "Any other games planned? Because there are a few other prizes I wouldn't mind winning…"

"The games are over," she replied firmly, taking a quick step back. "I'm going to find something to eat now."

"I could eat a little more," he said, moving to accompany her.

But another song had begun, and Abby popped up in front of him with an enticing smile. "How about a dance, Captain?"

"You two go ahead," Rebecca said to them, forcing a cheery tone. "I'm going to eat and then I have some things to check on."

Ryan gave her a look over Abby's head, but Rebecca pretended not to notice as she moved toward the tables, leaving him to politely lead the bridesmaid onto the dance floor. Rebecca kept her back turned to the dancers while she filled a plate and then carried it to a quiet corner to enjoy. She had no desire to watch Ryan dancing with anyone else.

CHAPTER SIX

THE PARTY ENDED promptly at eleven, when Rebecca announced to the guests who remained that the staff was waiting to clean the ballroom. "Don't forget about the tennis and golf tournaments tomorrow," she reminded everyone. "And the Eighties Bash begins tomorrow night at eight in this same room. Good night, everyone."

She was relieved to see the last guest straggle out of the room. Glancing around to make sure she wasn't forgetting anything, she followed them out.

Ryan waited by the elevator, his shoulder propped against the wall, his arms crossed over his chest. Though her heart tripped at the sight of him, she realized she wasn't particularly surprised to see him there.

She pushed the button for the elevator. "Are you going up?"

"I thought I'd go out for a walk on the beach. To decompress from the party. Will you join me?"

She moistened her lips. "It's getting pretty late."

"Yeah."

He continued to watch her, making no effort to pressure her into accepting.

She should tell him good-night. Go to her room. Get

some sleep. And yet she knew she wouldn't sleep a wink for thinking about him walking on that beach, his face silvered by moonlight, his shirt plastered against him by the ever present Gulf breeze.

She sighed. "I'll change and meet you in the lobby."

He nodded, his expression giving her no clue to his feelings about her acquiescence.

When she joined him in the lobby ten minutes later, she noted that he'd donned a light jacket. She had changed into jeans and a T-shirt and sweater, replacing her sandals with sneakers.

As she had predicted, it was cool out. A stiff breeze kicked the waves into white peaks that splashed against the sand near where they walked. Clumps of seaweed washed in by the waves covered the beach, and she had to watch her steps to keep from being tangled in it. The moon lit their path, supplemented by the lights from the resort behind them and a few businesses on the other side of the boulevard.

As tired as she had been at the end of the party, the walk was more refreshing than she had expected. She could almost feel the residual tension float away on the wind that tossed her hair and chilled her skin. Turning her face upward, she closed her eyes for a moment and let the sounds and smells of the water surround her.

When she opened her eyes again, Ryan was standing in front of her, looking down at her. She could almost feel time rewind, taking her back to another beach, another moonlit night. The night she realized that she had fallen completely in love with him, despite having known him only a matter of days.

She blinked hard and forced herself to return to the present. On this beach, this night, they weren't two young people in the giddy early throes of love. They were former lovers who had split painfully, and there were two and a half years of distance between them now. Years in which she had established her own business, her own life in Lubbock. In which he had gone to war.

Though she had been too busy with her work to get involved with anyone since Ryan—or so she'd told herself—she didn't know anything about his life since Maui. Was there someone special now? Had he thought of her at all during those two and a half years?

"Have I told you I like your hair like this?" he asked in a murmur, reaching up to catch the fluttering ends of her bob with his fingertips.

Her heart beating faster, she moistened her lips, tasting the faintest hint of salt from the breeze. "Thank you."

He slipped his hand more deeply into her hair, cupping the back of her head. "Do you know how many times I've thought of you like this? Standing on a beach in the moonlight?"

"How could I know that?" she asked, hearing the husky edge to her own voice. "I haven't heard a word from you since we left Maui."

"I wasn't sure you wanted to hear from me. You were pretty angry when we parted."

"I was angry," she admitted. "And I was hurt. I thought we were getting very close. And then you basically told me it had been fun, but it was over. So long."

"That's not exactly the way it happened," he protested with a frown.

"So I paraphrased. It's been a while. I don't remember the exact words."

"Rebecca, I told you why I didn't think we should get too serious. I was leaving for a war zone."

She pulled away from his hand. "And you didn't think I could handle that. Or so you said."

Shoving his hands in his pocket, he scowled. "What's that supposed to mean?"

"It means that maybe you simply didn't want to keep it going. I could understand that you weren't interested in a long-distance relationship, if you'd been honest about that. But to make it all about my best interests…"

"Why does it make you so angry for someone to try to take care of you?" he demanded, throwing his hands in the air in a gesture of frustration. "What is so bad about that?"

"Because I am not a child," she shot back. "I spent my whole life being sheltered and overprotected by my parents. It took me until I was out of college to convince them I was capable of making my own decisions. I never thought I would have to deal with the same thing from the man I—"

She stopped herself from saying "loved." That was an admission she had never made to him.

"The man I had a vacation fling with," she substituted, instead.

His scowl deepened. "It was more than a vacation fling, damn it."

She looked away, staring blindly at the waves breaking close by. "That's certainly the way it felt when you gave me that rehearsed brush-off speech."

She thought his cheeks might have darkened, though there wasn't enough light to be sure. "It wasn't rehearsed. And it wasn't a brush-off. I said I wanted to part as friends."

Pushing a hand through her hair, she sighed, the weariness from earlier returning full force. "Why are we rehashing all of this? It's too late."

She wasn't only talking about the time, and she figured he knew that.

"Rebecca—"

Huddling into her sweater, she nodded toward the Gulf behind him, wanting to change the subject. "Look at that man. He's obviously intoxicated. He's not one of the groomsmen, is he?"

Ryan hesitated for a long moment, as if he knew very well what she was trying to do. And then he turned his head reluctantly in the direction she had indicated. Both of them watched as a man in a short sleeved tropical print shirt and jeans staggered barefoot into the surf, seemingly oblivious to the chilly temperatures. He almost fell headfirst into the water, but he managed to right himself just in time. He stood, weaving and gazing out over the water, the waves lapping at his ankles.

Ryan muttered a curse beneath his breath and started that way. "It's Charlie."

"Charlie?" Startled, she hurried after him, wondering how he knew for sure just by seeing the guy's silhouette in the deep shadows. But obviously he knew Charlie much better than she did. When they were close enough to see the man's face, she realized that Ryan had been correct.

Standing just out of reach of the waves, Ryan spoke. "Charlie? Whatcha' doing?"

Spinning, Charlie toppled and almost fell again. His arms flailed and he staggered, but remained on his feet. Ryan had started toward him, but he paused when Charlie regained his shaky balance.

"Hey, Ry," Charlie said cheerfully. "What are you doing out here this late? Is that Abby with you?"

"No," Ryan said, a frown in his voice. "It's Rebecca. You need to come out of the water, Charlie. It's too cool for wading. You don't want to catch pneumonia before your wedding."

"Wouldn't *that* get Melanie's panties in a twist?" Charlie asked with a laugh that was a shade too hearty. "Think she would expect you to fix that, too, Rebecca?"

"Probably. And since I have no medical training, I think you should follow Ryan's advice and come out of the water."

She was aware of the irony of her advising someone else to listen to Ryan's well-intentioned recommendation, but this time she happened to agree with him.

"You're a saint, you know that, Rebecca? No matter what Melanie and her mother throw at you, you just smile and handle it. Or smoothly talk them out of it."

"That's my job. Would you like to walk back to the resort with us now? I'm sure Melanie wonders where you are."

"Very likely," he agreed gravely, then staggered again.

Ryan moved forward, splashing into the water to put an arm around his friend's shoulders. "Come on,

Charlie, let's get you back inside. It's late. You're wet and you've had too much to drink."

"You're absolutely right," Charlie agreed gravely. "You're a good friend, Ry."

"Yeah, I know. Where are your shoes?"

"Don't know. I think I might have left them in the room. Maybe."

Rebecca moved forward to take Charlie's other side once they were out of range of the waves. Charlie wrapped his left arm around her neck, moving unsteadily between them as she and Ryan started toward the hotel.

Fortunately it was late enough that there weren't many people in the hotel lobby. They were able to get Charlie into the elevator relatively unnoticed. Ryan pushed the button for Charlie's floor.

"You remember that time we jumped out of the airplane, Ry?"

"I remember. I answered the question in the game tonight, didn't I?"

"Yeah. I put that question in there for you. I never jumped again, you know."

"I know."

"I was scared spitless."

"You did great, Charlie. Jumped like a pro."

Charlie shook his head so vehemently that he caused Rebecca to stumble a little at his side. She braced herself as Charlie sagged against her.

"You were the pro," he told Ryan. "Everyone said you looked like you'd been jumping all your life. Then you went off and joined the Rangers and went to war and won a bunch of medals. I became an orthodontist."

"The world needs orthodontists. Kids need braces."

"This guy's a hero," Charlie confided to Rebecca. "Ask him to show you his Purple Heart sometime."

Purple Heart? Trying not to recoil visibly from Charlie's boozy breath, she eyed Ryan curiously. Weren't Purple Hearts given only to soldiers who were wounded in service? Had Ryan been injured? If so, she had seen no evidence of it since he'd arrived.

The elevator bumped to a stop and the doors swooshed open. "We'll talk tomorrow, Charlie," Ryan promised as he and Rebecca walked him to his door. "If there's something bothering you, you can tell me about it when you're thinking a little more clearly."

"When I'm not drunk as a skunk, you mean." Charlie laughed at his own wit, sending another wave of alcohol-laced breath into Rebecca's face. She wondered if it was possible to become intoxicated just from secondhand fumes.

Because Charlie didn't have his key, Ryan tapped on the door. Melanie opened it, wearing a slinky black gown and robe set and a sullen scowl. "What on earth is going on?" she demanded, looking from Charlie to Rebecca to Ryan.

"Charlie's been celebrating a little too much," Ryan said smoothly, helping his friend inside. "Rebecca and I just gave him a lift home, so to speak."

"That's right, honey. I was celebratin'," Charlie assured her. "Because in just three more days, you're going to be my wife. I'm one lucky man, right, Ry?"

Rebecca didn't think he was looking very lucky at that moment. Melanie appeared mad enough to tear a good-size strip off his hide as soon as they were alone.

"You're a great guy," Ryan assured him, neatly side-stepping the question. "Now get some sleep. I'll see you tomorrow. Good night, Melanie."

"Good night, Ryan. Rebecca, I'll want to see you early tomorrow," Melanie added. "We need to go over a few things before the party tomorrow night."

"Of course. I'll see you in the morning."

Rebecca and Ryan made a hasty escape. Though she couldn't make out words, she heard Melanie's raised voice through the door Ryan closed behind them. It didn't take much imagination to fill in the blanks.

"Well," Ryan said when they stepped back into the elevator. "That was awkward."

She nodded and pushed the button for her floor. "Very."

"I've seen Charlie drunk maybe three or four times since I've known him. It's not like him to get plastered and wander off that way."

"I wouldn't have thought so."

"You think he's having second thoughts about this marriage?"

The question had certainly occurred to her. "I suppose it's possible. It isn't uncommon for grooms—or brides, for that matter—to get cold feet before the wedding. I've seen a few last-minute panic attacks."

"So you don't think Charlie's making a mistake? Going through with this, I mean?"

"I think that's a decision Charlie's going to have to make for himself," she answered firmly.

"Yeah, but maybe I should talk to him tomorrow."

"He's your friend, of course. You should know whether he'd consider it intrusive if you ask any questions about his true feelings for Melanie."

"You think I'm trying to tell someone else what to do, don't you?"

The elevator stopped as she said, "You do seem to think you know what's best for everyone else."

He followed her out of the elevator car. "I don't think that's a fair thing to say."

Her door was only three doors down the hall from the elevators. She threw a look over her shoulder as she dug her key card out of her pocket. "It seems pretty apparent to me. Maybe it's the military thing. You've gotten in the habit of looking out for the people who report to you. Or maybe it's something from your childhood, I don't know. But not everyone appreciates it."

The mention of his childhood made him scowl. Which only reminded her how little she really knew about him, despite what they had shared in Maui.

Somewhat sadly, she shook her head. "I'm sorry. I shouldn't be criticizing you for worrying about your friend. I guess I'm still a little too sensitive about that sort of thing. Maybe you *should* ask him if he wants to talk."

He put a hand on her arm when she opened her door and moved to step inside. "Wait."

She couldn't look at him as she asked in a whisper, "What do you want from me, Ryan?"

"I—" The question seemed to have caught him off guard.

"It's getting late, and I have a lot to do tomorrow. I really need to get some sleep."

"Just one more thing first."

She looked up at him. "What?"

"This." Cupping the back of her head with one hand, he drew her closer, covering her mouth with his.

The kiss lasted a very long time. His mouth moved slowly, skillfully against hers and after a mere heartbeat, she leaned into him, letting her lips part slightly. He accepted the invitation hungrily. She clutched his jacket as the kiss deepened, heated.

It felt so familiar to be in his arms. As if the years that had passed since the last time simply melted away. Her lips fit against his as if they'd been made to do so. Her body settled against his with a memory of its own. And her heart ached with the love that she had tried to convince herself must not have been real.

She drew her mouth from his, still holding on to his jacket as she looked down for a moment to collect herself. And perhaps to hide the expression in her eyes. When she felt she had herself a bit more under control, she loosened her fingers, dropped her arms and took a step back before looking at him. "If that was to prove that I'm still attracted to you, I guess you were successful."

She didn't give him a chance to respond. She closed herself into her room and then leaned her forehead against the door, sensing that he stood on the other side for several long moments before he turned and walked away.

CHAPTER SEVEN

WHAT DO YOU WANT from me, Ryan? Rebecca's words echoed in his head the next day as Ryan lined up a putt in the four-man scramble golf tournament. The other three members of his team, one of them Charlie, high-fived in celebration when the ball circled and then dropped into the cup, cinching the win.

"Way to go, Ry."

Ryan shared knuckle bumps with Charlie and then the other two groomsmen on their team. He and Charlie climbed into the cart they shared, Ryan behind the wheel. He turned toward the clubhouse, falling into line behind the others.

"Great game, wasn't it?"

Ryan nodded. "Yeah. It was fun."

Charlie cleared his throat. "Uh—about last night."

"You were pretty plastered."

"Yeah. Felt awful this morning. Don't know what the hell I was doing out on the beach. Kind of embarrassing, to be honest."

"You don't have to be embarrassed about it."

"Oh, not with you," Charlie said, waving a hand. "I meant Rebecca. I hope she didn't get the wrong impression."

"That you're a drunk? Or that you're so conflicted about getting married Saturday that you escaped into a bottle?"

"Now, don't go getting all psychoanalytical on me," Charlie said with a short laugh. "It's normal to get nervous at a time like this. Every guy does."

"I wouldn't know, of course."

"Nope. You're Captain Unshackled. But you know, some of us like the thought of settling down. Having someone to come home to at night. Having kids, maybe."

"And you want all of that with Melanie."

After a barely perceptible pause, Charlie replied heartily, "Of course I do. I love her."

Ryan didn't know what to say, so he said nothing.

"I really do love her," his friend added more quietly. "That doesn't mean I'm oblivious to her flaws. I'm not exactly perfect, myself, you know."

"Nobody is. But—well, I just hope you know exactly what you're getting into."

"That's my old friend," Charlie muttered. "Always looking out for everyone else."

Because that was too close to the things Rebecca had said to him—and not in a complimentary way— Ryan frowned. "I was just trying to—"

"Help," Charlie chimed in. "I know."

"Look, forget I said anything, okay?" Somewhat crossly, Ryan parked the golf cart. And then relented enough to add, "But if you need to talk, you know where to find me."

"Thanks, Ry. Same goes, you know. I'm not blind. I saw the way you were looking at Rebecca last night.

I think you two were more than just acquaintances before this weekend."

"We had a—" He didn't know what to call it. Whatever Rebecca said, it had been more to him than a vacation fling. "Thing."

"A thing."

Feeling a little foolish, Ryan nodded.

"So you're not crazy in love with her?"

"I, uh—"

"Yeah, that's what I thought."

Grabbing his clubs out of the back of the cart, Ryan scowled. "Look, there were good reasons why Rebecca and I went our separate ways before. I was on my way to a war zone. She was making plans to start her business, had a lot of dreams she wanted to fulfill. I couldn't complicate her life that way."

"And she agreed with that?" Slinging his own bag over his shoulder, Charlie followed Ryan toward the clubhouse.

Ryan didn't answer.

"Ah. You made the call—for her own good."

Throwing a look over his shoulder, Ryan said, "We were talking about you, not me."

Charlie ignored him. "Are you going to try making a go of it this time? Because it's pretty obvious that she isn't over you, either."

Ryan wasn't as sure about that as Charlie seemed to be, despite what she'd said after he'd given in to the increasingly fierce need to kiss her last night. Still… "Nothing has changed. She's busy with her business in Lubbock and I'm stationed in Georgia. And I'll be serving at least one more tour of duty in the Middle East. I expect to receive orders sometime this summer."

"So all the guys in your regiment are single and unattached, huh?"

"Well, no, of course not, but—"

"Oh. So they can manage it, but you can't."

"Look, we were talking about you, not me."

"Right." Charlie smiled. "You can dish out the advice, but you can't take it."

Ryan was relieved when the other men surrounded them then to talk about the game and to make plans for later. He made a vow to himself right then to keep his well-intentioned advice to himself for the remainder of the weekend.

MELANIE WAS HAVING another crisis of indecision, and her mother wasn't helping with her dithering and hand-wringing. Rebecca's jaw ached from gritting her teeth as she tried to deal with the latest crisis.

"But Hannah said eighties parties are completely passé," Melanie said tearfully. "She said everyone's going to be bored."

Rebecca shook her head. This was one of the most shallow and spiteful group of "friends" she'd ever dealt with. They seemed to relish tears and drama, and went out of their way to create them. Melanie was as bad as the rest of them; she seemed to thrive on the attention she received when she cried and fretted. The term "drama queen" didn't even begin to describe her cousin, Rebecca thought privately.

"Your party won't be boring, sweetie," Coleen

assured her anxiously. "Remember how much fun last night was? This one will be, too."

Melanie looked at Rebecca. "Maybe we should come up with some new ideas for tonight. Something more original."

"Melanie, your guests came prepared for an eighties party. They brought costumes. It would be rude to change the plans at this late hour," Rebecca said firmly.

Though she pouted, Melanie couldn't really argue with that. "Well, then maybe we should rethink the entertainment. You could go out and get some cooler favors and maybe we could make the menu a little more avant-garde, you know? Something that would make everyone really remember this night."

Rebecca had had enough. Yes, Melanie was a client, but she was also her cousin. And sometimes family simply required more candor. "Would you just stop it, Mel?" she said in exasperation. "The party starts in less than four hours. I am not going to go buy more supplies, when we have a perfectly good selection already. And the menu is set. It's too late to change it. So just concentrate on making this a pleasant event for yourself and everyone else, okay?"

Melanie blinked rapidly a few times. It was the first time all week that "the princess bride," as Rebecca's assistant had dubbed her, had been spoken to so firmly. "I only want everything to be perfect."

"It won't be perfect," Rebecca replied flatly. "Nothing's perfect. Get over it."

Melanie spun on one heel. "Mother!"

"Rebecca, honey—"

"Really, this is getting out of hand. We've been planning this week for months, and I've spent hours organizing every detail, yet both of you keep expecting me to change everything at the last minute. I might remind you that I'm giving you a significant discount for my services because you're family, but I'm going to draw the line at any more changes—or even suggested changes—between now and the wedding. If something unexpected occurs, we'll deal with it, but everything that's already on schedule is going to remain that way."

Coleen looked as though she was about to launch into another lecture about how her precious child deserved to have everything exactly the way she wanted it this week, but fortunately she was forestalled when her husband stuck his head in the door. "Coleen, the Gerhardts just arrived. They're down in the bar and want to know if we can join them for a cocktail."

"Oh. Of course. Melanie, why don't you come with us?"

Melanie shook her head. "All the girls are coming up to the suite at six so we can start getting ready for the party. I want to take a nap and a shower first."

"That's a good idea," her mother approved. "You need to get some rest so you'll be all fresh and pretty for the party. Call me if you need me," she added, moving to join her husband. She gave Rebecca a frown as she passed her, as if to warn her not to upset Melanie again.

When her aunt Coleen and uncle Mick had left, Rebecca picked up her bag. "I'll go downstairs and make sure the decorations are underway."

"Rebecca, wait."

Suppressing a sigh, Rebecca turned back to her cousin. "What is it?"

"You've been spending a lot of time with Charlie's friend, Ryan, the last couple of days. Charlie told me you and Ryan already knew each other."

Rebecca nodded, dreading where this might be headed. "We knew each other briefly a couple of years ago. Why?"

"Well, Abby wanted me to ask if there's anything going on with you two. I mean, she and Ryan sat together at the party last night and they danced a couple of times and she really likes him, but she isn't sure if she has a chance with him."

Feeling as if they were back in high school, Rebecca muttered, "I don't know. I'll ask him after class and then pass her a note in gym."

Melanie sighed gustily. Without her mother there as an audience, she'd abandoned some of the dramatics, knowing they would get no reaction from her cousin. "It's not that strange a question, Rebecca. He does seem taken with you. And the two of you were out walking on the beach later when you found Charlie."

"How is Charlie today?" Rebecca asked, deliberately changing the subject. "Did he feel okay this morning?"

"He said his head hurt like crazy, but I didn't feel sorry for him. He should have known better than to drink that much when he hardly drinks at all back home. I told him it was embarrassing, and that people were going to think he's getting cold feet about the wedding. You and Ryan didn't think that, did you?"

"Charlie said he was celebrating your upcoming marriage," Rebecca answered, sidestepping the question a little.

"If one of us should have second thoughts, it would be me. Charlie can be a real pain sometimes. Like this morning, when I was trying to tell him how mean Hannah has been to me, he just shrugged and said Hannah's always like that, and I knew it when I asked her to be my maid of honor. So I tried to tell him how stressed I've been and how I don't think he's being very supportive, and he said I shouldn't have turned our wedding into such a circus if I couldn't handle the stress. A circus! Can you believe he said that?"

Rebecca tried to answer diplomatically. "I'm sure it's a stressful week for Charlie, too. And you just said he was suffering from a hangover this morning."

She glanced pointedly at her watch. "I really have to go down and check on the party room. If you're going to have a nap and a shower before your friends show up, you'd better take advantage of the opportunity while you still can."

"Okay. But keep your cell phone on in case I need you, will you?"

Rebecca was already at the door. "My cell phone is always on."

"Oh, wait. You never answered me about Ryan—"

She closed the door quickly, almost running toward the elevators, greatly relieved that Melanie didn't bother to follow her.

Ten minutes later, she stood in the same room in which the party had been held the night before. The tropical decorations had disappeared, to be replaced by memorabilia from the 1980s. Movie posters hung on the walls; she recognized *The Breakfast Club, Pretty in Pink, E.T.* and *Flashdance* among the dozen or so on display. Pink and purple crepe paper streamers and hanging colored lights added to the party atmosphere.

Kitschy eighties icons had been used in table decorations. A DJ would play eighties music all evening, and a couple of games had been planned to continue the theme. Baskets of party favors and prizes waited to be distributed—among them cheap plastic Ray-Ban-style sunglasses, mini Rubik's Cubes, "jelly" bracelets and CDs of eighties music. Granted, Rebecca didn't remember much of the decade, and neither did Melanie or most of the rest of the wedding party, but she thought the decorations were just campy enough to work.

"Looks like a kids' party," Ryan commented from behind her.

She turned to find him standing behind her, studying one of the tables. "It's whimsical," she corrected him. "It's supposed to encourage everyone to loosen up and have fun."

"I know. You're giving the client what she wants."

"Exactly."

"It looks good, I guess."

"Well, thanks for that high praise."

Smiling, he reached out to toy with the ends of her hair. "Sorry. Didn't mean to offend your professional pride."

"I'll survive," she said dryly. "How was the golf tournament?"

"My team won. I sank the winning putt."

"Congratulations."

"Thanks. Do I get a prize?"

She wasn't sure how her hand ended up on his chest. She didn't remember deliberately placing it there. But she appreciated the feel of his muscled chest beneath her palm, the warmth that radiated through the fabric of his shirt into her skin. "You get the satisfaction of winning."

"Not exactly what I was hoping for," he murmured, his gaze on her lips. Feeling the tingle there, she resisted the impulse to moisten them with her tongue.

"How did you know where to find me?"

His eyes lifted to hers again. "I think you must have magnetic qualities. I just seem to be drawn to where you are."

Her fingers twitched reflexively against his chest. A funny feeling started deep inside her in response to his words. "Ryan—"

He lifted his hands to cup her face. "I tell myself the reasons I should stay away from you. All the logical, sensible excuses I gave you in Maui, all of which are still true. But even after the time that has passed since we saw each other last, I took one look at you on the beach the other night, and I knew nothing had changed when it came to the way I feel about you."

"I felt the same way," she whispered around a lump in her throat. "But—"

It wasn't necessary for her to elaborate.

"I know," he murmured, his head lowering.

Sighing in surrender, she lifted her mouth to his.

How could she still be so in love with him, after all this time, all this pain? How could it be so hard for her to resist him, even when she knew that being with him would only lead to heartache again? Even knowing that, she still found herself wanting to spend every remaining moment with him, to soak up more memories of him to savor in the days to come.

The kiss was so very tender, yet so very thorough. By the time it ended, Rebecca felt warm and tingly. And a little sad, a feeling she didn't want to dwell on just then.

He gazed down at her. "There's still a couple of hours before the party. Do you have anything more to do here?"

She shook her head. "No. Everything's under control."

"Will you have a drink with me? I've got bottled fruit juices in the minifridge in my room."

She hesitated.

"Just a drink," he added. "Maybe talk a little."

"I have a little time free before I have to get ready," she said after a brief mental battle.

He turned with her toward the doorway.

CHAPTER EIGHT

RYAN'S ROOM looked much like Rebecca's—airy, plush and comfortable. Though it wasn't a suite, it had a small sitting area at one end with a couch and chair, a small writing desk and a television cabinet. Studiously avoiding looking at the bed, Rebecca took a seat on the couch while Ryan opened the minifridge. He read off the types of juices he had available, and she tried to pay attention, though she kept getting distracted by the bulge of his thighs as he knelt in front of the fridge.

"I'll have the pomegranate," she said, and he nodded.

He poured the cold juice into a glass before handing it to her and taking one for himself. Sitting beside her, he took a sip, looking as if he were doing so more to have something to do than because he was actually thirsty. She did the same—for much the same reason.

"Has Melanie been giving you any more problems today?" he asked, setting his glass on a coaster on the low coffee table.

"No more than usual. Trying to make some last minute changes, that sort of thing."

"I suppose you'll be glad when this wedding is behind you."

"There's still the party tonight, the rehearsal and dinner tomorrow night and the ceremony and reception to go," she said with a wry shrug. "I suspect that most of the guests will be glad to go back to their everyday lives after that schedule. I'm sure you will be."

He looked down at his hands. "You'd think so, wouldn't you?"

She wasn't sure what he meant by that. "You'll be going back to Georgia?"

He nodded. "For the next three months. And then I'll be overseas again on another deployment."

She swallowed a sip of juice that almost stuck in her throat before she asked, "For how long?"

"Fifteen months, most likely."

"Fifteen months." She tightened her fingers around her juice glass. "How badly were you hurt last time?"

He frowned. "What do you mean?"

"Charlie said you got a Purple Heart. Those are for being wounded in battle, aren't they?"

"Oh. Yeah, that. I took a little shrapnel in my side. It wasn't life-threatening, but I spent a couple of days in the hospital."

"That must have been frightening," she said, struggling to keep her voice uninflected. "Did your family come to see you?"

"I was treated in a field hospital. The injury wasn't bad enough to send me back to the States, so I asked to stay. I was back on patrol in just over a week."

"Dedication."

He shrugged. "It's my job."

He would see it that way. Ryan didn't view himself as a hero, she realized. He was career Army. Wherever he was sent, he would go willingly, despite the risks. And he had made the decision to leave no one behind to worry about him.

"Tell me about your family," she said, wondering if that would make her understand better. "What was your childhood like?"

"Why?"

Setting her glass on the table beside his, she turned to face him. "Humor me."

His mouth twisted a little. "Let's just say I didn't grow up in one of those happy families you see on TV."

She only looked at him, waiting for him to elaborate.

After a long moment, he conceded. "My parents drank a lot and fought even more. They rarely attended parents' day events, and when they did, I wished they hadn't, since they were argumentative with each other and with people around them. They split up for the last time when I was twelve. Things were better after that."

"Who did you live with?"

"My mother. She still wasn't much of a parent, but at least the fighting stopped. To tell you the truth, she wasn't home much. She hung out with her drinking buddies most nights while Danny and I took care of ourselves. Dad took off after the divorce, and I've seen him maybe three times since."

"Since you were twelve?" she asked, startled.

He nodded. "Last time I saw him was at my kid brother's wedding four years ago. We didn't think he would show up, and when he got drunk and started a fight with our mom at the reception, we were sorry he did. As usual."

"How much younger is your brother?"

"Three years."

"You took care of him, didn't you?" Which would explain a bit more about Ryan's habit of looking out for other people, she mused, saddened by his story.

He shrugged. "Until he was old enough to take care of himself. Both of us grew up early. He got married when he was twenty-three. It lasted just over a year. They split up not long before I met you. They were too young, I guess, and Danny—my brother—traveled so much in his job that they just drifted apart."

"What does Danny do?"

"He's a sales rep for a business software corporation. He travels all over the world demonstrating their software to international businesses. I see him maybe four times a year. We exchange e-mails sometimes."

"And your mother?"

He spread his hands. "I don't see her much at all. Once I left for college, paying my own way with student loans and scholarships, what little connection I had with her pretty much ended."

It was a wonder, she thought, that he'd turned out as well as he had. Still, a childhood that painful and chaotic had to leave scars. Was that the real reason Danny's marriage hadn't lasted? Did it explain why Ryan was so skittish about getting too serious? He had seen his parents' and brother's marriages break up, and probably his share of Army marriages. He was highly skeptical about the future success of his friend Charlie's marriage.

Would he spend the rest of his life alone to avoid any chance of failure for himself?

"You've had a difficult time," she said quietly.

"Nah. It's not like I was physically abused or lived on the streets or anything. I ended up okay, I think."

She smiled tremulously. "Better than okay. You're a decorated officer in the elite Army Rangers. And you got there on your own."

His eyes darkened. "Don't start making me out a hero, Rebecca. I'm not."

"I guess that depends on your definition of hero."

She watched his throat move with a hard swallow. "Becks—"

Leaning forward, she took his face in her hands. "You know what I think, Ryan?"

Frowning a little, he searched her eyes. "What?"

"I think you're afraid of getting hurt again. Not by bullets or shrapnel, but by people you care about. Have you ever even been in love?"

He hesitated a long time before answering a bit roughly, "Once."

"What happened?" she asked in a whisper.

His gaze still locked with hers, he replied, "I had to tell her goodbye. And yeah, it hurt like hell. And even worse, I hurt her, too. I don't want to do that again."

Her heart twisting, she pressed her lips to his. Her arms locked around his neck, and she nestled into him until he groaned deep in his throat and crushed her against him, returning the kiss with an intensity that demonstrated how much he had been holding back.

He loved her, she thought dazedly, opening her mouth

to deepen the kiss. He'd as much as said so. Maybe it was as close as he would ever come to telling her.

Maybe he would never let her tell him how she felt about him. But she could show him that she had not stopped loving him just because he had hurt her. She could prove to him that time and distance had not changed her feelings.

Sliding one hand between them, she started to unbutton his shirt.

Ryan caught her hand. "Rebecca—"

She lifted an eyebrow. "You don't want this?"

"More than I want my next breath," he admitted raggedly. "But—"

Smiling a little, she unfastened another button as she said, "You know, maybe it's time for you to let someone else look out for you, for a change. Maybe for once you should just let someone love you without worrying about when or how or if it's going to end."

"I don't—"

Whatever he might have said, she forestalled him by kissing him again, her hand sliding into his open shirt to glide across his lightly furred chest. When her thumb circled his nipple, he inhaled sharply and buried his hands in her hair, tilting her head to give him better access to her mouth.

She found the scar on his side when she dropped his shirt on the floor beside the bed. Her heart clenched as she traced her fingertips very lightly over the puckered, reddened skin on the right side of his back, just above his waist. She could see where the stitches had been placed to close the jagged tear.

"It wasn't that bad," he said again, reading her expression.

"It was bad enough," she murmured, thinking of how badly it must have hurt. "Has anyone kissed it to make it better?"

His mouth quirked into a very faint smile. "No. That isn't the way the Army treats wounds."

She wondered if anyone had ever kissed his hurts to make them better. Even when he was a troubled little boy. And because the possibility that no one had ever cared enough saddened her, she lowered her head to place a tender kiss on the scar.

He made a low sound and rolled her beneath him, holding her head still for a kiss that rocked her all the way to her bare toes.

"I didn't like the way things ended between us last time," he muttered against her throat. "I don't want to part that way this time. I don't want to hurt you again."

"It won't end that way this time," she assured him, wrapping herself around him. "We have an hour alone, Ryan. Let's not waste it."

She had no doubt that he was going to try to tell her goodbye again when this week ended. For her own good.

At least this time she knew it was coming, and she could brace herself.

What Ryan didn't know was that she just might not make it so easy for him to walk away from her this time.

CHAPTER NINE

THE EIGHTIES BASH seemed to be going well. Most of the wedding party had arrived by the time it started, so there was an even larger crowd than there had been at last night's luau. Surrounded by Madonna and Cyndi Lauper and Don Johnson lookalikes, Ryan watched as Rebecca checked the food tables to make sure there was no shortage of sushi and buffalo wings and the other foods Melanie had decided suited the theme.

Rebecca had done something to her hair for the party, fluffing it up so that it looked bigger, somehow, than her usual sleek bob. She must have scoured vintage stores for her outfit, a clingy red dress with big shoulders, long, tapered sleeves, a deep V front she'd filled with beads and chains, and a wide, shiny white belt. Her shoes were red pumps with high heels. Her earrings were red and white plastic circles, so big he wondered if they hurt her ears. She'd gone heavy on the blue eye shadow and vivid red lipstick. She looked like she could have stepped out of an episode of *Dynasty,* he thought with a smile.

She looked beautiful.

He'd opted for the preppie look, himself. A pale

blue polo shirt with the collar popped, tucked into belted khakis worn with white sneakers.

He'd been tempted to skip the party altogether. Claim a headache, maybe, or a sore throat. But because he'd figured that Charlie's feelings would be hurt and Melanie would probably have the vapors at the thought of one of the groomsmen possibly being ill, he'd forced himself to get dressed and come down, though he'd been a little late.

Sitting in one corner of the frivolously decorated room with a drink in his hand and an untouched plate of food beside him, he watched Rebecca move from table to table, looking as if she didn't have a care in the world other than this party she had organized. No one watching her could have known that she'd left his bed barely in time to transform herself into Crystal Carrington and be in the ballroom five minutes before the party began.

He wasn't sure he was doing such a good job of disguising his own feelings. He couldn't stop staring at her, couldn't stop reliving that hour they'd spent together. Couldn't stop dreading saying goodbye to her again.

She'd said she would have no regrets. That she wouldn't be hurt this time. And looking at her now, smiling and chatting and working that vintage dress, he couldn't help thinking that maybe she'd been completely honest. Maybe she would be just fine with him leaving this time, since she had her own busy life to return to afterward.

Maybe he would be the only one left aching and empty.

Wearing what appeared to be a lacy petticoat and a

sparkly bustier—another Cyndi Lauper clone, or was she going for early Madonna?—Abby appeared in front of his chair. "Hi, Ryan. You look great."

"Thanks. So do you."

She fluffed her massively teased and sprayed red hair self-consciously, batting her purple-and-green shadowed eyes. "It's hard to imagine people seriously dressed this way, isn't it? But it's sort of fun, I guess."

"Yeah. I guess."

"And I love the eighties music," she added.

"I'm more of a nineties rock fan, myself," he replied.

"Oh. Yeah." She switched her weight from one foot to another, visibly searching for something else to say. "Well...I'll see you around."

"Yeah. Sure."

Watching her flounce away, he suspected that Abby was annoyed with him for not asking her to dance, but he wasn't in the mood to guide her around the floor and make small talk. He'd rather brood, he thought, toying with his food.

A flash of red caught his attention and he looked up to see Rebecca standing in the spot Abby had just vacated, smiling at him. "Why are you sitting back here by yourself? Don't you want to join the fun? They're starting the air guitar contest in a few minutes."

"I think I'll pass on that, thanks."

"I don't blame you," she admitted. "So, how about a dance with the wedding organizer?"

This time he didn't even hesitate. He stood and walked with her to the dance floor, carefully avoiding Abby's glance their way.

He recognized the song that was beginning just as he took Rebecca into his arms. "Never Gonna Let You Go." He heard it on the oldies channels sometimes. It was ironic that he was dancing with Rebecca to the plaintive strains of a singer promising to hold his love in his arms forever, never to be parted again.

"My mother loves this song," Rebecca said, smiling up at him. "I think she has all of Sergio Mendes's recordings."

"Yeah? Mine listened to country. The twangier and the more references to boozing, the better, as far as she was concerned."

"I like some country. But I prefer heartbroken cowboys to boozing songs."

"The party seems to be going well."

She glanced around with a nod, though she frowned a little when she looked toward the engaged couple's table of honor. "Melanie and Charlie don't seem to be enjoying it too much."

He followed her gaze. "Yeah, I noticed that. They're smiling a lot, but they're hardly looking at each other. Think she's still mad about last night?"

"I don't know. But I have seen other brides and grooms squabble before the wedding, due to the pressure. I warned Melanie when she started all this planning that I thought she was trying to do too much. It seemed more logical to me to have the festivities start today, with this party, followed by the rehearsal tomorrow and the wedding and reception Saturday. That would have cut out two extra days of running around and socializing and significantly cut down on both expenses and stress."

"But she wouldn't listen." It wasn't a question.

"No."

Ryan shook his head. "Seems like a waste of time and money to me. All these parties and flowers and food and bands and whatever else goes into a big wedding. Isn't the couple just as married if they stand in front of a justice of the peace in a courthouse? Or gather on a beach or in a chapel with their closest friends and family instead of putting on a big show to try to impress everyone they've ever met?"

"Hey," she said with a quick laugh. "That kind of talk is not good for my business."

He grimaced. "I'm sorry. I didn't mean to sound dismissive of what you do. It's just that I—well…" His words trailed off as he tried to think of a way to extricate himself without making the gaffe worse.

"Don't worry, I didn't take offense. I'm sure a big spectacle like this would be a nightmare for you. To be honest, some of the most beautiful weddings I've coordinated have been very simple and understated, yet they still had enough frills to mark the occasion as very special. That's what I'm trying to put together for my grandparents."

"Your grandparents?" he asked quizzically, wondering if he'd misunderstood.

"Sorry. I thought I'd mentioned it. My paternal grandparents are celebrating their sixtieth anniversary in June, and my cousin, Nate, and I are arranging a surprise vow renewal ceremony for them. They weren't able to afford a fancy ceremony when they married, and my grandmother has always fantasized about what it would have been like."

"After sixty years?"

She nodded with a smile. "That's why I don't see a big wedding as necessarily a waste of time and money, if it's kept in perspective to what the couple can afford and if it's about what they really want as opposed to who they're trying to impress. Most couples hope the wedding will be their only one—or at least, their last one—and they want the happy memories to last the rest of their lives."

He had to admit that he hadn't looked at it quite that way. But then, he hadn't spent much time thinking about weddings. His family's marital history hardly encouraged him to expect success in that area for himself, especially when combined with the career he had chosen.

The song ended, and the DJ segued into a more upbeat eighties number, "Dancing in the Dark."

"All right. The Boss," Ryan muttered, pleased to hear one of his favorite artists among all the pop and valley girl tunes that had been played so far. This wasn't his favorite Springsteen tune, but it didn't make him want to put cotton in his ears, either. "Now we can dance."

All around them couples were already starting to jerk and clap to the music, some of their moves obviously inspired by the wine coolers being served as part of the period refreshments. Though she began to swing her hips in time to the driving rhythm, Rebecca smiled ruefully. "I'm not exactly dressed for this style of dancing," she said. "I should be wearing a T-shirt and tight jeans and sneakers, like Courteney Cox in the video."

"You look damned good to me," he answered, giving the form-fitting dress a slow once-over. He caught her hands and pulled her into a modified swing dance. Laughing, she participated gamely. She was flushed and breathless when the song ended and he spun her in his arms. He was grinning and half aroused just to be holding her again, even in a mob of people. He wanted very much to kiss her, but restrained himself because he didn't think she would appreciate that public display of affection.

As if she'd sensed his thoughts, she drew away and straightened her dress, looking around a bit self-consciously. She froze when her gaze fell on the doorway into the ballroom. "Oh."

Following her glance, he noted the couple in the doorway, who looked to be in their mid-fifties, perhaps. The woman, he noted abruptly, bore a strong resemblance to Rebecca. And they were looking directly at him.

He looked at Rebecca again. She moistened her lips, then motioned toward the newcomers. "My parents have arrived."

"SO THAT'S RYAN FULLER." Angela Murphy looked across the room to where Ryan was talking with a couple of the other groomsmen near the dessert table. "And you say it's just coincidence that he ended up in Melanie's wedding?"

Rebecca nodded. Leaving her father chatting with

Uncle Mick, she had pulled her mother to a relatively quiet corner of the room to explain Ryan's presence. Her parents had heard all about Ryan two and a half years ago through excited phone calls from Maui. And then they'd comforted Rebecca when she'd returned to Texas with her heart broken and her pride bruised. "He was Charlie's college roommate."

"Looked like the two of you were getting along pretty well when we got here," her mom murmured. "I take it you've forgiven him for the way things ended between you before?"

"I understand better why he felt the need to send me away," she answered carefully.

"I saw the way you were looking at him just now on the dance floor." Her mother looked worried as she searched Rebecca's face. "I've never seen you look at anyone else that way. You still have feelings for him, don't you?"

"I've never stopped loving him," Rebecca confessed in a low voice, responding to her mother's concern. "And Ryan still cares for me, too. But nothing has changed as far as he'd concerned. He's still in the Army. He's going to be deployed again in a few months, and he doesn't want to leave anyone behind to worry about him. He thinks being committed to him would disrupt my life too much, because of the uncertainty of where his career will take him."

"Being an Army wife isn't easy," her protective mother agreed. "Your father was in Vietnam while we were engaged, you know. I worried about him every minute that he was over there."

"I'm going to worry about Ryan, anyway," Rebecca said, pushing wearily at her overly teased and sprayed hair. "But does that mean I should miss out on all the time I could spend with him before he goes? Or when he returns?"

"You're willing to make those sacrifices for him? What about your business?"

"I'm a wedding coordinator. People get married everywhere," she replied simply. "I'm not naive enough to think it would be easy, but I've never met anyone else who makes me feel the way Ryan does. I can't imagine that I ever will. I don't know if I can walk away from that again. Not if I have a choice, anyway."

Her mother gave her a sad smile and touched her cheek in a familiar gesture. "I'd hate to see you get hurt again, Rebecca. You tried so hard to be brave last time, but I know it took you a long time to put it behind you."

"That's the thing, Mom," she murmured. "I never did put it behind me. I've missed Ryan ever since. I don't see that changing this time."

A sound from behind them made Rebecca look around to find her father standing there, watching her with somber eyes. He forced a smile when her gaze met his. "I came to ask your mother if she wants a drink and dessert," he explained. "We had dinner, but it's been a couple of hours."

"Yes, you two go help yourselves," Rebecca encouraged them. "I have to check on a few things, anyway."

Feeling their anxious looks following her, she moved away to go back to work.

The party came to an abrupt and painful end barely

an hour later. Bonnie Tyler's gritty voice streamed from the speakers as she sang about holding out for a hero. The beer and wine coolers still flowed, and tipsy partiers still gyrated on the small dance floor. The noise level was fairly loud, but everyone heard Melanie shriek, "That's it! The wedding is *off!*"

Though Bonnie kept singing, everyone else went silent.

Groaning, Rebecca hurried to the table where Charlie sat scowling as Melanie hovered over him. Her anxious parents flanked her, and her avidly gawking bridesmaids began to gather around. Beneath her rainbow-hued makeup, Melanie was white-faced with anger, her stiffened bangs almost quivering with the force of her emotions.

"Melanie," Rebecca said, "you don't—"

"No! You can't talk me into changing my mind," Melanie shouted. "None of you can. Charlie doesn't appreciate my soul. There's no way we can be married now. I'm sorry, Rebecca, but you're just going to have to cancel everything."

With that, she turned and ran out of the room, trailed by her parents and her gaggle of Madonnas and Cyndis.

CHAPTER TEN

IT WAS WELL AFTER midnight when Rebecca and Ryan met up again.

"You look exhausted," Ryan commented, studying her face.

"Thanks a lot," she answered wearily, pushing at her hair. She had changed into jeans and a light sweater, washed her face and combed out as much of the hairspray as she could before coming downstairs to make sure everything was cleared away in the party room. That was where Ryan had found her. She suspected he'd been waiting for her.

"You still look good," he assured her. "Just tired."

"I guess that's because I am. Melanie wears me out."

"Were you just with her?"

"I went by her parents' suite. That's where she's staying tonight."

"Is she still hysterical?"

"No, she's relatively calm now. She's being very tragic and pathetic, of course, but she's stopped ranting, anyway."

"That's good, I guess. How are your parents?"

"Tired. They drove ten hours today, then had to deal

with their niece's breakdown. I sent them on to bed about an hour ago."

"Shouldn't you be doing that, yourself?"

"I'm still too wired to sleep," she admitted.

"How about a walk on the beach?"

Glancing around the room, where hotel staff were clearing away the now sad-looking remains of the party, she nodded. "That sounds nice."

"It's cool out. Do you need a jacket?"

"No, this sweater's warm enough."

He had changed, too, swapping the polo shirt and khakis for an Army sweatshirt and jeans. He motioned for her to precede him to the lobby. "Let's go, then."

It was chilly, but not so much that Rebecca couldn't enjoy the walk. After the pandemonium earlier, the quiet, nearly deserted beach was a welcome retreat. Ryan wrapped an arm around her waist, and she nestled into his warmth as they matched their steps, the wind and waves providing a soothing soundtrack.

"Did you talk to Charlie?" she asked.

"Yeah. He'll be fine. He's upset, of course, because he wanted this to work out, but deep down, I think he's secretly relieved."

"They aren't ready to get married," Rebecca said flatly. "Melanie was more excited about the wedding than the marriage, and Charlie just wants to settle down and start a family. I think once she started really thinking about what it was going to be like when the wedding was over and she would be expected to do her part to make a marriage work, Melanie realized that she didn't want to make that commitment. She seemed to be just waiting for him to say something she could use as an excuse to break it off. When he did, she jumped on him with both feet."

"I'm sorry it ended that way for them. Were you able to get everything canceled this late?"

"There are still a few things I have to take care of tomorrow morning. Poor Uncle Mick is out a lot of money that can't be refunded, not to mention the costs of the parties and entertainment so far this week, but maybe he can get a little back from the canceled rehearsal dinner and reception."

"Charlie's leaving first thing in the morning."

"So are Melanie and her parents. My folks have decided to stay through Saturday. A little vacation."

"What about you?"

"I'm not sure how long it will take me to get everything settled here." She almost asked when he was leaving, but she found she didn't really want to know.

"Your dad and I had a little talk while you and your mother were with your aunt and Melanie."

Rebecca stumbled a little, then turned to stare up at him. "My dad? What did he say?"

"We talked about his military service. He told me about when he was in Vietnam, just before the troops pulled out for good. How it felt to leave your mom behind. How hard it was for her while he was gone."

Rebecca nodded, having heard all those stories many times. "He signed up after his high school graduation to honor his dad, who served in World War II. After Dad's enlistment ended, he went to college on the G.I. Bill and then to law school, like his mother."

"Yes, he told me. He said when he was in college and law school, he hardly ever saw your mother. He said they learned to keep their marriage strong despite their different schedules."

"They've had a good marriage. They'd hoped to have more children, but because of a physical problem, they were lucky to finally conceive once. That's why they focused so intently on me while I was growing up. And why my dad still tends to get overinvolved sometimes," she added ruefully. "I hope he didn't say anything that made you uncomfortable."

"The whole conversation was uncomfortable," he said wryly.

"Yes, it must have been. I'm sorry."

"It did make me understand a little why you're so resistant to being told what to do. I'm sure your parents have been extremely involved in your life."

"They have," she agreed. "I love them dearly, of course, and I know they only want what's best for me but... well, there were times I wished for a couple of siblings to share the concern."

"Funny how our childhood shapes us, isn't it?" he mused. "I probably chose to go into the military because I needed the structure and discipline that I didn't get from my parents. You went into business for yourself because you didn't want to be told what to do."

She nodded.

"You'd think we'd be too different to be together, wouldn't you?" he said musingly.

She murmured, "Maybe it's a case of opposites attract."

"Maybe. Or maybe we're enough alike in other ways that the differences don't really matter all that much."

"Maybe." Where was he going with this? And why was her heart suddenly beating so fast?

Ryan drew a deep breath. "I'm committed to going back overseas, Rebecca. There's a shortage of leadership right now and I have an obligation to go."

"I know. I wouldn't expect anything less of you."

"Eighteen months," he said. "Max. And then I can get out."

She stared at him in bewilderment. "Get out? Quit the Army, you mean?"

He nodded. "Yeah. That's what I mean."

"But you wanted to be career. You're—what?—ten years away from retirement?"

"More like twelve. Too long to ask you to make that sacrifice with me. But I was thinking maybe eighteen months wouldn't be too bad. We could make that work, couldn't we?"

Her heart was beating so quickly now that she could hardly breathe. "Are you—?"

"We've spent two and a half years apart, and I still can't imagine spending the rest of my life with anyone but you," he said simply. "I didn't want to admit it, even to myself, but I've never stopped loving you. This isn't going away."

"I love you, too," she whispered, blinking rapidly. "But I don't want you to quit the Army because of me. We can make it work, Ryan. Despite the failures you've seen, other people make it last. My grandparents have. My parents. My aunts and uncles and lots of family friends. They had challenges and hardships—I'll have to tell you my grandparents' story soon. But they made it."

He caught her hands in his, and she could feel the fine tremors in his fingers. "We can work out the details later. I love you, Rebecca. Will you marry me?"

"I would have said yes if you had asked me in Maui," she answered unsteadily. "I haven't changed my mind. Yes."

His fingers tightened. "Do you want to wait? Until I get back from the Middle East, I mean?"

She laughed, pulling her hands from his to throw her arms around his neck. "I would marry you this minute, here on this beach in the middle of the night."

Catching her against him, he spun her off her feet, and the happiness on his moonlight-bathed face brought tears to her eyes again. "Your parents are here," he said. "You've got an officiate lined up for Saturday. It would be a shame to waste all that planning."

"It just so happens that there's no waiting period for a marriage license in Texas for active duty military personnel," she murmured against his lips.

"Isn't that convenient." He crushed her mouth beneath his to seal the commitment they had just made.

"YOU'RE SURE you don't want to wait and have a bigger wedding?" Rebecca's mother fretted Saturday as she helped her adjust the simple, white, off-the-rack wedding dress she'd found in a Strand boutique the day before.

Picking up the spray of white roses she'd purchased

at a local florist, Rebecca smiled and shook her head. "This is exactly what I want."

"You're following in your grandmother's foot-steps, you know. A whirlwind romance and a quick, simple wedding."

"Gran always says she has no regrets. I won't, either. I hope Ryan and I get to renew our vows at our sixtieth anniversary party."

"I hope so, too, honey." Smiling tremulously, her mother kissed her cheek, careful not to smudge their makeup. "I wish I'd brought the mantilla with me. You could have worn it today. I just didn't realize you would be getting married this weekend."

"That's okay. I'm content with this spray of flowers in my hair. I'm glad you found the mantilla in time to get it cleaned for Gran to wear in June."

Her mother motioned toward the doorway. "It's time to go out. Are you ready?"

Rebecca laughed confidently. "I've been ready for two and a half years."

A white gazebo, designed especially for weddings, sat behind the resort. With her father on one side and her mother on the other, Rebecca moved down the seashell walkway. The photographer she'd hired stood discreetly out of the way, recording the moment for memories. The weather had cooperated for an outdoor beach wedding. The sky was a clear, bright blue and the air was warm, with only a light breeze to catch at the hem of her dress and flutter it around her ankles.

Looking almost unbearably sexy in his uniform, Ryan waited for her, along with the officiate and the attendants, two for each of them. Ryan's brother, Danny, had happened to be at home in Dallas that weekend. He had dropped everything to drive to Galveston when Ryan had called to ask him to serve as a groomsman. Though Rebecca had known Danny only a few hours, she liked what she'd seen. He reminded her very much of Ryan. Both the brothers had turned out fine, despite their past, she was happy to note.

Charlie O'Neill was best man. Though Melanie and her family hadn't stayed, Charlie had insisted on remaining for the ceremony when Ryan broke the news to him. To Rebecca's relief, Charlie seemed to be recovering from his own broken engagement. Though he was obviously disappointed and chagrined by his situation, he appeared to be genuinely happy for his friend.

Rebecca's attendants were her assistant, Janelle, and her best friend Kathy from Lubbock, both of whom had jumped into a car the day before when Rebecca had called them. They thought the spur-of-the-moment wedding was incredibly romantic. They'd raided a friend's bridal shop in Lubbock for similarly styled dresses in sky-blue, Rebecca's favorite color, though she'd urged them to wear whatever they wanted. She was touched that they'd made that effort for her.

Ryan took Rebecca's hand as her parents were seated to watch the ceremony. "Last chance to change your mind," he murmured, gazing intently into her eyes.

She smiled up at him. "I make my own decisions," she reminded him. "And this is what I want."

He touched her face, his eyes lit with what looked like wonder. "I love you, Rebecca."

"I love you, too. Can we get married now? I don't want to waste another minute."

Grinning, he glanced toward the patiently waiting officiate. "We're ready now," he announced, the words carrying a great deal of meaning.

Making a private vow to herself never to take a moment with him for granted, Rebecca happily took her place at Ryan's side.

* * * * *

THE DADDY TRACK

Allison Leigh

* * *

Thank you to Candace and Gina
for making this such an enjoyable "60th"
and thank you to Greg…just because.

Dear Reader,

Harlequin romances have been a part of my life since before I entered high school. There just is nothing I like more than a good love story with a wonderfully happy ending! Needless to say, being asked to help celebrate Harlequin's 60th anniversary is an incredible honor for me. So this "Dear Reader" letter is as much a "Dear Harlequin" letter as anything.

Thank you, Harlequin, for continuing to bring us wonderful, empowering, inspiring and entertaining stories of love and commitment. You've enriched our lives in more ways than can be counted.

And thank you, very dear readers, for allowing *me* to be just one small part of this wonderful family.

My very best regards,

Allison

CHAPTER ONE

NATHANIEL ALDRICH stared at the two flower-draped caskets as they slowly descended into the ground. He was vaguely aware of his grandfather's hand closing over his shoulder.

Mostly he was aware of the squeak of the mechanism that lowered the caskets. It seemed to softly hiss "your fault, your fault, your fault," until the caskets finally reached bottom and the hissing stopped.

The graveside service was long over. The minister had said his piece. The hymns had been sung.

But the tears hadn't stopped.

His were just inside.

His grandfather, Jack Murphy, squeezed his shoulder a little, then slowly dropped his hand. "Whenever you're ready, Nate," he said quietly.

Nate nodded. He knew he needed to follow his grandparents and go over to the other side of the grave where Drew Chelsey and what remained of his family were sitting beneath the awning that shaded their folding seats from the Amarillo sun. Where the only remaining people who'd attended the service—Nate's grandparents—were talking with the Chelseys, expressing their condolences before walking back across the green, green grass toward the line of cars slowly exiting the quiet, curving driveway.

But he couldn't seem to look away from the caskets, laying there together in the earth.

Luke Chelsey had been his best friend. His business partner. Luke's wife, Jess, had been almost like a sister. With no other family of her own besides her husband, she'd been closer in some ways to Nate than even his own sisters were. It was Jess who'd nagged him about taking vitamins and cutting back on the long hours he kept at the office of Aldrich-Chelsey Financial Corp.

But it was Nate who'd nagged Luke and Jess into meeting him for a business dinner exactly nine days ago. Luke hadn't wanted to go. Hadn't wanted to touch the deal that Nate was working, for that matter.

But in the end, he'd agreed. And so Luke and Jess were on the Los Angeles freeway that night when a jackknifed semi sent them crashing.

Your fault. Your fault.

Nate finally dragged his eyes from the sprays of flowers atop the caskets. The faint breeze that had lifted the delicate white blossoms throughout the graveside service could no longer reach them.

Even they were now still.

His chest felt heavy and the only thing he really wanted was to go somewhere alone, tilt an icy bottle of beer to his lips and pretend that he was somewhere— anywhere—other than here in Amarillo because he couldn't stand to let one business deal go.

Instead he forced himself to walk around the fresh graves and the well-tended headstone beside them that belonged to the wife Drew Chelsey had lost ten years earlier, and approached Luke's father.

The last time he'd seen Drew Chelsey, the older man had looked fit and vital. Now, Luke's father just looked old; his face lined and nearly as gray as the thinning hair on top of his head.

"Mr. Chelsey." He pushed out his hand. "I don't know what to say. I'm sorry." It wasn't anywhere near good enough, he knew, but it was the only thing that came out.

Ironic, when he was supposed to be the guy with the golden touch. The golden words.

But Drew just stared through him, his pale gray gaze numb.

His daughter, Jordan, though, looked up at Nate over the blond head of the little girl sitting on her lap. Jordan had the same color eyes as her father, and though they were pained, they were still sharp.

She also seemed able to respond when her father couldn't. "Thank you for coming, Nate." She pressed her lips to her daughter's head and slipped the girl off her knee to stand. The hem of Jordan's slender black dress slid down around her knees and the ends of her honey-colored hair flitted in the breeze. "I know it was probably hard to find time in your schedule."

He nearly winced. But her gaze was steady, seemingly unaware of the wound she'd inflicted. "I wouldn't be anywhere else." He looked down at the two kids standing at her side, managing a semblance of a smile because that just seemed to be what he should do. Lydia and Henry, he knew, only because Luke was often talking about his niece and nephew.

Had often talked, he mentally corrected himself.

It was like slashing at himself with a knife.

Lydia looked like Jordan. Henry looked like Luke had probably looked at that age.

He focused again on Jordan, which had never been the easiest of tasks. Not since the first time he'd met her at some shindig of Luke and Jess's. Jordan had been heavily pregnant with her twins and plainly devoted to her husband—who hadn't seen a need to accompany his pregnant wife to California.

And now…now, Jordan was more beautiful than ever. Which was hardly the thing that he should be noticing at this particular moment in time. But not noticing Jordan Chelsey's beauty was like not noticing the warmth of the May sun overhead or the sweet smell of freshly mown grass.

For another thing, she was now a single mom, having divested herself of the "useless jerk"—Luke's term—of a husband. She ran a home-style restaurant on the outskirts of town. She was the kind of woman a decent guy married. The kind of woman who deserved a decent guy.

She was *not* the kind of woman that Nate let into his world. The kind of woman that Jess had rolled her eyes over more times than he could count while nagging him to once, just once, date someone who had more thoughts in her head than when her next appointment

was with her personal trainer and who was more interested in him than his bank balance.

"If you need anything," he told Jordan now, "just
say the word."

"Thank you." Her gaze flitted past him, probably
taking in the graves behind him.

"Mom," Henry whispered. "When can we *go?*"

"Soon." She brushed her palm over his cowlicked
blond head, but she didn't take her gaze from Nate's
face. "There is something," she said.

"Anything," he assured. His entire wealth would
never be enough to replace the big brother she'd lost
and he knew it.

She sank her teeth into her soft lower lip, glancing
down at her father. "Could we, um, meet later, perhaps?"

"I'm in town until tomorrow afternoon."

Her lips pressed together for a moment, her disapproval seeming plain. "I don't think I can manage it
today. So could we meet in the morning, then?
Anytime will do. Luke's always telling me—" her face
fell a little "—told me how early you start your day."

*In the office by 5:00 a.m. Out of the office by 10:00
p.m. Trying to make the rest of us mortals look bad, bud?*

He could practically hear Luke's mocking voice.

"How about nine?" he suggested, pushing past the
constriction in his throat.

She nodded and tucked a gleaming sheaf of hair
behind a pearl-studded ear. "That'd be fine. The
children will be at school. They only have another
week before summer vacation or I'd keep them out for
a few days." Her lashes fell for a moment. "More for

me, than for them, I guess," she admitted. "Can you, um, come by the restaurant?"

J's, he knew. Again, courtesy of Luke. "The restaurant is fine," he answered.

"It's located out on Tobias—"

"I know where it is."

"Oh. Okay." Her lips pressed together a moment. "Your grandfather comes in occasionally."

He nodded, though a response hardly seemed necessary.

Her hands fluttered for a moment before she seemed to deliberately get them under control, tucking them together at her slender waist. "I'd better get Dad back home. I'm afraid all of this has been a lot for him to take."

It had been a lot for *all* of them to take.

Because of Nate.

Jordan leaned over, tucking her hand beneath her father's arm. "Come on, Daddy. It's time to go home now."

Drew rose, shaking off her hold, though. "I don't need help." His querulous gaze was still on the gravesite. "Everything I need is gone."

Jordan didn't tilt her head away quickly enough for her swinging hair to hide the way her face tightened, or the way her dove-gray eyes turned to shadow as she pulled her hand away from her father. But her voice was still soothing, still gentle, when she spoke. "I know. But I want to get the children home, too. Will you come?"

Drew barely looked at Nate as he turned away and

headed toward the long black limousine waiting at the head of that dwindling line of cars.

Nate couldn't help but notice that Drew had barely looked at Jordan, either.

She pressed her hands together, giving him an awkward look. "He's obviously not himself right now."

"None of us are."

Her soft lips stretched into a faint smile. "No. None of us are." Then she looked away, as if she couldn't quite bear to meet his eyes for one second longer.

Who could blame her?

He couldn't look at himself in the mirror, either.

"So, nine tomorrow morning?" she repeated, holding out her hands to her children.

"Nine tomorrow morning," he echoed.

She nodded, ducked her chin a little, and with her children by the hand, followed after her father.

Leaving Nate alone with the graves.

He turned around and looked down into the hole. "I'm sorry," he murmured.

But of course there was no one there to hear him.

Particularly Luke and Jess.

"I'M WORRIED about him," Claire Murphy murmured to her husband as they sat in their car waiting for Nate to join them.

Jack closed his hand over hers. "He'll come through," he assured.

"Luke was like a brother to him."

And they both knew what it was like to lose a brother. Claire had lost her only brother, Denny, during the war. And it was that which had led Jack to Claire in the first place. He'd served with Denny. They had been good friends.

"He'll come through," Jack said again. He lifted her knuckles to his lips.

She sent him a faint smile, squeezing his fingers in hers. "It would be easier if he weren't alone."

"He's not alone. He has us. His parents. His sisters. Cousins and aunts and uncles."

"You know what I mean."

Jack gave her a look. Because he did know exactly what she meant. "Then find him a girl who's as perfect as you are. That's what he said when he was here for Christmas, remember?"

"He wasn't serious."

"That doesn't mean the idea doesn't have merit."

She shook her head, vaguely amused despite herself. Despite the situation. "Nate is a very eligible young man," she reminded him. "He needs no help from his old grandparents to find himself a good woman."

"Not just *good*," Jack murmured. He squeezed her fingers. "Perfect."

She sighed a little at the way her heart jumped.

Sixty years hadn't dimmed Jack's power where she was concerned.

Not one little bit.

"He's coming back," Jack said after a moment and Claire focused out the window, watching their grandson cross the green, well-manicured lawn. "He'll be all right. It's just going to take some time."

But when Nate reached the car and pulled open the door to the rear seat and folded his tall length inside without a single word, Claire couldn't help sending up yet another small prayer for everyone.

CHAPTER TWO

THERE WASN'T A PARKING spot to be found in the paved lot next to J's Eatery when Nate drove there in his grandfather's truck the next morning shortly before nine. So he joined the several vehicles that were parked on the dirt lot adjacent to the parking lot and climbed out of the vehicle.

It was about as perfect a morning as anyone could ask for. A slight breeze. An azure sky studded by puffy white clouds, unmarred by layers of smog or haze.

The kind of day that Luke had been rhapsodic over in the months before the accident. As if he wanted to convince Nate that his desire to leave ACFC and return to Amarillo had anything to do with the weather when they'd both known the real reason had more to do with Luke's father's failing oil refinery.

Now, Nate ignored the perfection of the weather and crossed to the whitewashed stucco building.

Inside, the restaurant was as busy as it had looked from outside.

Every table seemed full; every padded stool at the L-shaped counter occupied. George Strait was playing in the background but it was hardly noticeable given the decibel level of the voices and the clatter of silverware hitting sturdy white plates as the diners enthusiastically consumed the food.

The parking lot and the crowd showed just how popular J's was, even at nine on a Tuesday morning. The heady aroma of the food that filled the restaurant gave a clue for the reason for that popularity.

Or maybe it was the proprietress, herself, he thought, spotting Jordan as she came through a swinging door, leading with her hip since her hands were occupied with balancing a half-dozen laden breakfast plates.

Her shining hair was smoothed back from her lovely face in a high ponytail that reached past her shoulders. She wore blue jeans over legs that seemed to go on forever, with a white towel tugged snugly around her hips like an apron and a black T-shirt with short sleeves that probably hadn't been designed to show off the toned muscles that it took to bear those heavy trays, but did so anyway. On the front of the shirt curving over her breasts was "J's" in pink, stylized script.

He managed to lift his gaze, annoyed with himself.

You'd think he was a twelve-year-old kid who'd just discovered the wonders of a shapely woman in a T-shirt.

He could tell when she noticed him because the plate she was setting in front of a bald guy with a tattoo snaking down his arm from beneath his straining white T-shirt hovered a moment too long before finding contact with the table.

Even the tattoo noticed, and glanced at Nate before turning back to his meal.

A girl who looked no more than sixteen despite the pregnant belly visible beneath her snug black T-shirt stopped next to him at the front counter. "Just one?" She pulled a menu from behind the counter.

"Yeah. But I'm here to see—"

"I've got it, Lulu," Jordan told the waitress, hurrying over. She didn't look at Nate. "Would you mind covering my tables for a few minutes? Maria will help you."

Lulu didn't have any problem looking at Nate. Her gaze traveled back and forth between him and her boss. Nate couldn't help but wonder about the speculation in the teenager's eyes. "Sure," Lulu said to Jordan, and headed toward the counter.

"Hey, J. What about that chocolate milk?" The tattoo called out to her.

"Keep your shorts on, Dewey," Lulu answered smartly. "I'll get it for you."

The burly bald guy subsided back to his towering mountain of hash browns and eggs.

"Let's go out back," Jordan suggested. She still hadn't really looked at him.

"Whatever you say." She'd called the meeting. It was her turf.

She turned and he followed her through the swinging kitchen door where two cooks were busy at the grill. One was tall and as wide as Dewey-the-tattoo. The other was so short and skinny, she could have fit into the tall guy's apron pocket.

Neither one looked over at them as Jordan led the way around industrial-size racks to a door that opened up onto the rear of the property where he was surprised to find a fenced-in, neatly mown patch of grass. There was even a picnic table sitting beneath a trio of shady trees. It could have been a little, pretty backyard if not for the gigantic garbage Dumpster nearby.

"Nice break area," Nate told her.

"Thanks." She slid onto a picnic bench and he took the one opposite her but she popped back up. "I'm sorry. I should have asked. Would you like some coffee?"

He half expected her to ask if he wanted a menu. "Only if you're getting some for yourself."

Her eyebrows twitched a little over the fine bridge of her nose. "Be right back."

His gaze traveled over the landscape when she disappeared into the café again. Luke had grown up here in Amarillo. Nate, in Corpus Christi. They hadn't met, though, until they were both attending A&M.

"Here you go." Jordan was already back, setting a tray on the table. Not only had she brought two white mugs of steaming coffee, but she'd added a little jug of milk, a sugar dispenser, a basket of fat muffins and a small dish full of butter curls. "They're blueberry," she said, swinging her leg over the picnic bench across from him once more. "I made them fresh this morning."

Nate's grandmother had fixed breakfast that morning, but his appetite hadn't done her perfectly delicious meal justice.

Now, his stomach practically growled at the sight of Jordan's muffins. He broke one open and took a bite. Serious heaven. "Luke always bragged about your cooking."

She smiled faintly. "Jess was just as good." She didn't take a muffin, herself.

Except Jess's blueberry muffins had come out of a store package, Nate knew. More than once, she'd laughingly commented that she couldn't compete with Luke's little sister when it came to baking, so why try?

He set the rest of the muffin on a napkin.

Jordan cradled her coffee mug, lifting it near her mouth, eyeing him over the rim as she leaned her elbows on the picnic table. But he noticed that she didn't drink any. The mug was just a shield.

Against him?

Or against whatever it was she wanted to ask of him?

Under other circumstances, he would have just invited her to spit it out. Cut to the chase. Get to the bottom line. Instead he made himself finish the muffin that had turned to chalk in his mouth.

She'd get to it in time, he figured. "Looks like business is good for you."

"It is."

"You ever consider staying open for dinner, too?"

She shook her head. "It would take away too much time from the twins. If anything, I'd rather cut back on my hours here. Not the restaurant's hours. Just mine." She toyed with the edge of the cloth sticking out of the basket beneath the muffins. "I could take on some different catering jobs, then, which I usually enjoy."

"You do catering?" He didn't know why he was surprised when she nodded and he told her how he and his cousin, Rebecca, had come up with the notion of throwing a surprise vow renewal ceremony and reception for their grandparent's sixtieth anniversary while visiting them over Christmas. Since Rebecca was a wedding coordinator, she'd volunteered to do the planning and he'd been more than content just to sign the check. "Too bad Rebecca didn't know about you when she started booking people."

"Jordan." Lulu stuck her head out the back door, startling them both. "Dewey's getting all riled up again. Refusing to pay his bill."

Jordan exhaled. She set down her mug, casting Nate a resigned look as she stood again. "Sorry. This will only take a minute. I know your time is—"

He lifted his hand, cutting her off. "Don't worry about me. Take as long as you need. I won't go anywhere."

Something in her eyes flickered. She nodded and followed Lulu back inside. Her ponytail swished between her shoulder blades.

He let out a long breath when the door closed again, leaving him alone once more in the relative silence behind the busyness that was J's Eatery.

What could she want to ask him?

The trucking company—in an attempt to stave off the inevitable lawsuit—had already offered a generous settlement. Since Jess had no family of her own and she and Luke hadn't yet had children, the offer went to Drew.

Nate didn't know if it had been accepted but judging by the state Luke's father had been in at the service, he doubted the man was capable yet of making such decisions.

Maybe Jordan was handling the matter of the settlement. Maybe she just wanted some financial advice.

He didn't have to glance at his watch to know that more than a minute had passed. And though he wasn't concerned about the time, he left the picnic bench and opened the rear door.

The second he did, he could hear the commotion from out front and he strode through the kitchen where the Mutt-and-Jeff-cooks were just standing, staring openmouthed over the pass-through leading to the eating area.

"You weren't complaining about your eggs being cold when you were shoveling them down your throat, Dewey Bodine," he heard Jordan say. "Now put down that plate or—"

Nate pushed through the swinging door only to in-stinctively duck when something whizzed through the air toward him.

He wasn't quick enough, however, to elude the shrapnel when it crashed against the door behind him.

Shattered white crockery rained over his head as well as bits and specks of whatever had been on the plate in the first place.

"Dewey!" Jordan's voice was sharp and she practi-cally vaulted over a chair to reach Nate. "That's it. Out, and don't come back until I say you can!"

The last thing Nate saw was the burly tattooed man slinking toward the door, his head ducked down like a sulking child before Jordan whipped the white towel from around her waist and quickly started wiping it over Nate's face. "Are you all right?"

He brushed something off his eyebrow. A slender strip of crispy hash browned potato. "Fine." He could feel her shoulder against his chest as she dashed the towel over his head. The aromas of coffee and bacon and muffins might have been heady. But the scent of *her* was five times worse.

Or better, depending on how you looked at it.

All he knew was the scent of her, the warmth of her, was getting to him in a way that was beyond acceptable, considering everything.

He took the towel from her. "It's okay, Jordan."

She fell back a step, her hands twisting. "You have ketchup and egg yolk on your shirt," she said, looking miserable. "I'm so sorry. I—"

"It's *okay*." He leaned his head over and shook it. A few more hash browns fell to the floor, mixing with the broken crockery.

When he looked up, Jordan's mouth was finally closed.

He could see Dewey standing outside the window beside the door, staring in with a hang-dog expression. "Do you want me to get rid of him?"

Jordan followed his gaze. "No. This is the sort of thing I *can* handle."

"But—"

"No!" Her voice rang out and she grimaced. Sighed. "Thanks. But I've been dealing with Dewey for years. He doesn't really mean any harm."

Nate looked at the mess on the floor around his feet. "Could have fooled me. If he was aiming that plate at you—"

"No," she assured quickly. "He never throws anything at someone. Well, not usually. If you hadn't come through the door just then…" She lifted her shoulders. "Are you *sure* you're all right?"

"I haven't been in a food fight since I was about fifteen, but yeah. I'm all right." He plucked his shirt away from his chest. He doubted the fabric would recover, but he had dozens of others hanging in his closet back home.

"Well," Jordan sighed faintly. "I'd better go talk with him. Make sure he doesn't go off and do something really stupid." She headed toward the door. Most of the diners had already turned back to their conversations and their meals.

"None of the people here seem surprised," Nate said to Lulu, who appeared beside him with a broom and dustpan.

"Don't suppose they are," the teenager provided. "About once a month Dewey throws a fit over his bill." She swept the debris into a pile, then crouched down as gracefully as her pregnant belly would allow.

"Wait—"

"I got it, I got it." She waved off his assistance. "I need to do this stuff before I can't anymore." She rose again and dumped the contents of the dustpan into a container behind the counter.

Nate kept looking out the window. If he saw one hint that Dewey's temper was going to rise again toward Jordan, he'd be out there in a second, no matter what Jordan said. "She doesn't have to keep serving that guy."

"Jordan knows that." Lulu folded her arms atop the counter. "But Dewey's got no one and nowhere else to go. Not since they started laying off over at her dad's

oil refinery. She's always taking care of someone."
She patted her belly. "You an old friend of hers or
something?"

"Or something."

The teenager gave him an arch look and he was
damned if he didn't feel his neck get hot. "I knew her
brother," he said.

"Oh." As if that answered everything, the girl picked
up a full coffeepot and headed down the counter,
topping off mugs as she went.

Jordan came back inside and maybe it was his imagination that her shoulders seemed bowed.

"Sorry," she said. "Let's try this again."

And maybe it wasn't his imagination.

He touched her shoulder and felt her go very still.
"Why don't we talk later?"

He saw a flash of panic in her eyes. "No. I-I'd rather
not do this over the phone."

"I meant after you're closed for the day."

"But I don't close until one. And you said you're
leaving this afternoon."

"Plans can change." His had, he knew, and not just
because of Luke and Jess's accident.

He realized his hand was still on her shoulders,
as if it would be happy to stay there for about a
hundred years. He lowered it. "I'll come back after
you close."

"You'll really delay returning to California?" The
panic in her gray eyes faded, only to be replaced by a
suspicious curiosity that was almost worse.

"It seems important to you."

"It is. Everyone'll be cleared out of here by two at the latest."

"Then I'll come back then."

She pressed her soft lips together for a moment and her gaze dropped to the stains on his shirt. "I should at least get this cleaned for you. It's the least I can do."

No. The least *he* could do, was hang around in Amarillo long enough to help her with whatever was plaguing her.

It's what Luke would have done.

But as he left J's, he knew that the reasoning was only a glossing over of the truth because his interest in Jordan wasn't the least bit brotherly.

CHAPTER THREE

THE PARKING LOT was empty that afternoon when Jordan saw Nate park his grandfather's truck there later.

As she watched him walk toward the restaurant through the windows, she blamed the nervous pounding of her heart on the importance of what she had to ask him.

It *was* plausible, after all.

Saving Chelsey Oil Refinery was important. As much to her father's state of mind as it was to those employed there.

But when the door pushed open with a jangle of the bell over it and all six-plus feet of Nate Aldrich filled the doorway and his hazel gaze found hers, she was afraid the lurching inside her was owed entirely to *him*.

He'd replaced the stained short-sleeved shirt with another. The off-white button-down shirt was untucked, hanging loose past the waist of his well-washed blue jeans, looking just as casual as the shirt from that morning.

Looking just as expensive, too.

She was twisting the cleaning rag she'd been using to wipe down the counters between her hands and dropped it in the container beneath the counter. "Thanks again for coming back."

"Anytime."

"I'm not so sure you'll think that after I ask what I need to ask."

His gaze stayed as direct—and disturbing—as ever as he settled his lean body on one of the stools across from her. "Then let's find out." His voice was smooth. Easy.

And it was completely belied by the strain she could see in the lines carved into his tightly held jaw.

The accident had obviously hit him just as hard as it had the rest of them.

But he was still functioning.

Her father was not.

"Luke told you about the refinery, I suppose. What, um, what financial condition it's in."

"We talked about it."

It was decent of him not to point out that the information was freely available to anyone watching the local news. "So you know that Luke was thinking about returning. To help Dad run it."

"And to sell out his share of ACFC to me and sink everything he's made there into it," Nate added.

"You don't think that was a good idea."

His sculpted lips twisted a little. "Jordan, I'd be grateful as hell if he'd done exactly that. He and Jess would still be here even if he did end up losing his shirt on the deal."

She steeled herself to continue. "My father was counting on Luke."

"Chelsey needs a massive infusion of cash." Nate's

voice was gentle. And it didn't tell her anything she didn't already know. "You can have Luke's share to use however you want—combine it with the settlement from the trucking company, even—but it might be wiser to think long-term than to sink money into a losing concern."

She winced. "I'm not looking for Luke's share of your business. Only I'm afraid Dad won't survive if he loses the last thing that matters to him."

"The refinery? Your father still has you and your kids."

She realized she was tugging nervously on her ponytail and let go. "I'm not saying he doesn't love us. But the refinery is his life. It always has been."

"So what is it that you want to ask, exactly?"

She took a breath. "I want you to take Luke's place and help my father save Chelsey Oil Refinery."

He studied her.

She could hear the secondhand of the old clock on the wall above the door ticking. Could hear the hum of the dishwasher still running in the kitchen.

Hoped he couldn't hear her throbbing pulse as loudly as it sounded in her own ears as she waited for him to respond to what she knew in her heart was a long shot.

He finally folded his arms on the counter, which only made his wide shoulders seem even wider. "Jordan, the best thing for you—for your kids—is to sell the refinery now and get what you can out of it. I'll find the buyer. Put the right people on it so you and your dad get the best deal. *That's* what I'm good at."

"Dad won't sell. Not ever."

"Then the refinery is going to fail and none of you will be left with anything." He let out a sigh. "I'm sorry, Jordan. I wish I could tell you that there were some other quick fix, but—"

"I'm not looking for a quick fix. I'm looking for something that my father can hang on to!" Long shot or not, it was all she had. She let out a shaky breath. "You saw him yesterday. He's hardly functioning."

"It's too soon, yet. Give him time."

She closed her hands over his arm. "There *is* no time." His gaze seemed to drop to his arm and she let go, only to brush her tingling palms down her backside, tucking her fingertips into the pockets of her jeans. "For the past year, the only thing Dad has talked about was Luke coming home. Luke helping him at the refinery. Luke's fresh ideas. Luke's drive. I'm not sure that *time* is going to help."

"And I'm really sure that my walking in isn't going to help, either. I'm not your brother."

"You're the closest thing to him," she insisted. "I'm not suggesting you can replace Luke as Dad's son. A-as my brother. I'm just asking you to do this one small thing."

"Small?" He seemed to choke on the word a little. "Your dad's refinery is one of the largest independent refineries left. Running it is hardly a small matter."

How well she knew that. It had consumed her father for all of her life. "But you could help guide it back onto more solid footing. I know you could. You have expertise in gas and oil. And Luke said everything you touch turns to gold."

He looked pained. "I don't run businesses, Jordan. I acquire and sell them at the greatest possible profit for everyone concerned."

"Not everything's about money."

He went silent at that. "What does your father have to say about this?" he finally asked.

"Dad doesn't talk about business with me."

His slashing eyebrows rose just a little. "Why would you think he'd want my input at all? There are plenty of people around here who are a lot more qualified than I am."

"Right now, I don't think Dad's equipped to make any decisions. It's always been *Chelsey* Oil Refinery. First my grandfather. Now dad. It's always seemed to be against his DNA to let the reins go to anyone. But he'd been prepared to do so with Luke."

"Yeah. *Luke.*"

"But he's not here!" Her voice rose. Tears burned at the back of her eyes and tightened her throat. "If there was something else I could do, believe me, I would. I'd go work with him myself if—"

"—why don't you?"

"—I thought it would do any good," she finished. She exhaled. "I know how to run my restaurant. Not a refinery. Besides which, Dad's not interested in working with me."

"How do you know that?"

"Because he's told me so," she said evenly. What was the point of hiding it? Her father was old-school. He'd doted on his son. And though she knew he loved her, she was "just" a daughter. A daughter more comfortable in the kitchen of a small eatery than helming a multimillion-dollar business.

"If I thought there was some other solution, I wouldn't ask you. Won't you at least think about it?"

A muscle ticked in the back of his angular jaw. "Jordan—"

"Please, Nate."

He exhaled slowly. "I'll think about it."

It wasn't a commitment, but she still felt nearly weak with relief. "Thank you."

But Nate's lips only twisted as he pushed off the stool and headed toward the door. "There's nothing for you to thank me for in any of this." His voice was flat. "I'll be in touch," he said before pushing through the door.

She made her way to the stool he'd vacated and watched through the window as he got into the truck and roared out of the parking lot.

It was a long while before her shaking legs felt steady again.

It was even longer before she could stop thinking about the stark pain she'd seen in Nate's eyes before he'd left.

"NICE NIGHT."

Nate jerked at the sound of his grandfather's voice but he didn't pull his ankles off the deck railing where he'd propped them. "Suppose it is." It was dark at any rate. With a cloudless black sky studded by a million diamond-white stars.

The kind of sky you couldn't see in Los Angeles where the city lights outshone the heavenly ones.

Jack closed the sliding door behind him and joined Nate on the deck overlooking the long, sweeping lawn behind his grandparents' home. "Your grandmother wouldn't much like to see you smoking," he said after a moment. "Thought you quit."

Nate eyed the glowing tip of his burning cigarette. "I did."

What was worse?

Killing himself with a cigarette or killing himself with the tumbler of whiskey that he had balanced on his belly?

Either one wasn't going to put him under the ground quicker than the truck that had hit his best friend and his wife.

"Have you decided what to do?"

Nate had told his grandparents over the dinner table about Jordan's request. "I can't help the Chelseys," he said evenly.

His grandfather sighed faintly. "Maybe you need to help yourself, Nate. Here." He extended his hand.

Nate tucked his cigarette in the corner of his mouth and eyed the item in his grandfather's hand. "That's your pocket watch."

Jack ran his thumb over the closed case. "You remember how I came to have it?"

"Gran's brother gave it to you when you were serving together during the war."

"About five years before I met her." He held it to Nate again. "Take it."

Not really knowing why, Nate did. He flipped open the case to look at the fancy detail of the watch face. "It still works."

"Had to have it worked on a time or two," his grandfather allowed dryly. "Considering it's more of an antique than I am. I want you to keep it."

Even more surprised, Nate pulled his feet from the railing and sat up. He stubbed out his cigarette and set his drink on the deck beside his chair. "Why?"

"Not because it's pretty darn valuable at this stage," Jack allowed.

Nate grimaced. "Not everything's about money." Jordan's words.

"Glad to hear you say that." His grandfather leaned against the rail. "Read the inscription."

Nate tilted the watch so the light from the house behind him caught the faint engraving. He could barely make it out. "Fortitude and forgiveness."

"Denny—Gran's brother—gave it to me just a few weeks before he died. It was almost like he knew he wouldn't make it back home. But the inscription was on the watch when *he* got it from his grandfather. I like to think the words have stood for all of us. Generations now. They're pretty much two of the three things I think it takes to get a man through life." Jack leaned over and picked up Nate's drink, taking a sip before handing the glass back to Nate. "Just thought that might be relevant for you about now."

Nate slowly took the squat, crystal glass. He turned and watched his grandfather cross the deck and reach for the sliding door.

"What's the third thing?"

Jack paused. "You don't know?" His weathered,

lined face creased slightly in a faint smile when Nate just stared at him. "Well, now, that would be the easiest—and the hardest—thing to come by. Love, son. Love."

Then he went inside, leaving Nate alone on the deck.

CHAPTER FOUR

THE SOUND OF THE PICKUP truck door slamming shut sounded loud in the quiet neighborhood when Nate parked in front of Jordan's house the next afternoon.

He'd thought about going to the restaurant to tell her what he'd decided. Hell. He'd thought about showing what a coward he was by giving her the news by phone.

But the watch his granddad had given him had seemed to burn through his pocket for even thinking it.

The least he could do was tell Jordan face-to-face that he couldn't do what she'd asked. He couldn't fill Luke's shoes. Not even temporarily.

They were too damn big.

So, feeling like he was heading to his own guillotine, he let himself through the white gate and walked up the sidewalk bordered by mounds of colorful flowers and slightly overgrown grass.

Not surprisingly, Jordan's house looked like it belonged on a postcard. It wasn't large. The first floor alone of his L.A. condo would have swallowed her place whole. Nor was Jordan's house elaborate. But it had none of the sterility of his modern home. And when she opened the door before he could even make it up her front porch and quietly invited him inside, that particular image was complete.

Signs of her children were everywhere, from the homemade artwork that was posted on the refrigerator when she led the way back toward the kitchen, to the wooden jungle gym in the backyard that he could see through the sparkling clear windows.

But he couldn't forever focus on everything that surrounded Jordan instead of focusing *on* Jordan, and he finally looked at her.

She was still wearing her restaurant T-shirt, only this time it was a dark blue one with long sleeves and fluorescent green lettering. "I saw you drive up. I just got home from J's. Can I offer you something? Coffee? Water?"

Maybe it was in her genes to be gracious. To offer hospitality to even the likes of him. "No. Thanks."

The pearly edge of her teeth nibbled at her soft, bow-shaped lip. "Come on back." She turned toward the kitchen. "I need to take care of a few things."

He followed her, wishing like hell he'd just taken the worst of the cowards' route and phoned. "Nice place you have here." He'd known where she lived, but had never been inside. Never had reason before now. "Bet your kids love that jungle gym out there."

"They do. Particularly Henry, though lately he's decided he's not going to survive unless we add a tire swing somewhere." Her gaze slanted out the window, and her lips softened. "Dad and Luke built the jungle gym for the kids a few Christmases ago. I was always afraid they'd fall when they're climbing on it, but they never have."

He shoved his hand in his pockets, only to pull it back out again when his fingers grazed the pocket watch. "What are you fixing?"

There were several pans sitting on the scarred butcher-block counter. "Cinnamon rolls for tomorrow. Muffins on Tuesdays. Biscuits on Wednesday. Cinnamon rolls on Thursday," she told him as she flipped open the same kind of white flour-sack towel that his mom always used in the kitchen and draped it over one of the trays. "They'll rise better here in my kitchen than if I'd have left them at the restaurant." She proceeded to cover each one of the trays. "If you want one, you'll have to get to J's early. No matter how large a batch I prepare, I always sell out of them."

"What's on Friday and Monday?" He knew she was closed on the weekends.

She folded her arms and leaned her narrow hip against the counter. "Friday is kuchen. It's sort of like a pie," she added at his blank look. "Has a custard and fresh fruit—right now that'd be peaches—with a crumbly topping. It was my grandmother's recipe. And on Mondays I experiment. Try whatever happens to have sparked my fancy over the weekend." She smiled, plainly nervous. "I know. More details than you asked for. You, um, you've made up your mind, haven't you."

"Yeah. I—"

"Mom!" The front door flew open with a crash. "We're *home!*"

Jordan cast him an apologetic look and went to

catch her daughter as the girl practically vaulted into her arms. "Lydia, we have a guest."

Henry skidded to a stop inches from the counter. "Cinnamon rolls," he said, peering under the corner of one of the towels. "Are you gonna save any for us this time, huh?"

"Maybe." Jordan tapped his fingers and he dropped the towel back into place. "That depends on how well you behave. Say hello to Mr. Aldrich."

"Hello, Mr. Aldrich," both children echoed politely.

"You was at the cinematery yesterday," Henry added, eyeing him.

"Cemetery," Lydia corrected with a distinct air of superiority. "Are you my mom's boyfriend?"

"Lydia!" Jordan set her daughter on her feet. "Mr. Aldrich is a, um, a friend of…of ours."

"That's good," Henry said matter-of-factly. "I don't want mom having no boyfriend. Louis's mom has a boyfriend and they are always kissing and junk." His face screwed up, his button-brown eyes looking disgusted with the very idea of it.

Jordan's face was red. "Take your backpacks to your bedrooms, please," she told them. "And don't think you're going outside to play until you've changed out of your school clothes and done your homework."

The kids both looked put-upon, but they dragged their colorful backpacks behind them as they left the room.

"Sorry about that." Jordan shoved the sleeves of her T-shirt up her arms again. "Nothing like having two six-year-olds with ripe imaginations and an undeveloped sense of discretion."

"They're six. And they don't really have home-work, do they?"

She smiled faintly. "You'd be surprised. Spelling is our particular challenge these days. But getting this close to the end of the year, there's not as much as usual." Then her eyes glanced off his, suddenly flat. "So, you were about to give me the 'thanks but no thanks' spiel, right? Tell me that you're going back to California?"

That was exactly what he'd planned.

All he had to do was nod.

Grunt out an assenting sound.

But for some reason, he couldn't do it.

He, who'd stared down countless business rivals and brokered million-dollar deals, couldn't get out that one, simple word. He shoved his hand back in his pocket.

Her eyebrows lifted a little at his silence.

Fortitude. It felt almost as if the pocket watch was burning into his fingertip. "No," he finally said. "I've decided to stay."

Her expression went slack with surprise. Or shock. But at least there was nothing flat about her eyes now as she blinked several times. "I…I'm sorry. I'm just so surprised."

"Why? You asked me to stay. Did you never con-sider that I might agree?"

"To be blunt?" She felt for a chair at the table and sank down on it, looking up at him as if she couldn't believe what she was seeing. "Not really. I'm not trying to offend you, Nate." She let out a soft, incredu-lous laugh. "That's the last thing I need to do under the circumstances, but—"

"But Luke told you I never do anything unless there's a profit in it," he concluded. God knew he'd heard it often enough from Jordan's brother in the months before the accident when Luke had gotten more insistent about wanting to return to Texas.

"Well." She lifted her shoulders. "You pretty much said that yourself just yesterday. What, um, what made you change your mind?"

He started to answer, only to realize he *had* no answer.

What could he tell her? Those gray eyes of hers had made him reverse direction? The sight of her two kids had him switching horses midstream?

"Mo-om!" A long, drawn-out wail came from somewhere deep within the house.

Jordan let out a breath. "Excuse me, again. I'm being paged."

"Go ahead."

Not that she needed his permission, since she was already halfway out of the kitchen.

He shoved his fingers through his hair and let himself out the back door. She had a small covered patio. Nothing as spacious as the deck at his grandparents' place, but it was enough to hold a patio table and a few chairs and provide some shade when the summer was at its worst.

He avoided the chairs, though, and stepped off the patio onto the grass. It was green and thick, and like the front, due for a mowing.

He pinched the bridge of his nose.

What the hell was he doing?

"Do you know how t' hang a tire swing?"

He looked back to see that Henry had slipped soundlessly out of the back door. The boy had duly changed out of his school clothes. Now, he wore baggy cargo shorts that made him look even shorter, and a striped T-shirt easily one size too large. "Never tried," he admitted. "You don't make much noise, do you."

Henry's eyebrows shot up. "That ain't—isn't—what Mom says."

"Speaking of your mom, where is she?"

"Putting Lydia's hair in a ponytail." The little boy rolled his eyes with such exaggeration that Nate was amused, despite himself. "Girls," Henry added.

"They're not always bad," Nate murmured, catching sight of Jordan and her daughter before they came out onto the patio, too.

"Henry, Lydia tells me that you *do* have spelling to study," Jordan said when she pushed open the door.

Henry gave Lydia a glare.

"Well, you *do*," his sister defended. Her ponytail bobbed. She, too, had changed into more casual clothes, though hers were pink from top to bottom and looked more like the right size. "Same as I do."

"All right then. Back inside." Jordan held the door open. "Come on, Henry. The sooner you finish, the sooner you can come out and play."

Henry's shoulders hunched and his scuffed tennis shoes dragged. "I wish school was over *now*," he complained, heading inside.

"I know you do," Jordan said seriously, but Nate caught the sparkle in her eyes that she couldn't quite hide.

But with her children inside and focused again on

their homework, the sparkle faded as she turned, once more, to Nate. "So. You were telling me why you changed your mind."

Not exactly. He hadn't been telling her anything when they'd been interrupted. "I'll stay," he told her. "And see what I can do to help, but I can't be here indefinitely."

"Of course not," she agreed quickly. "I don't expect that. But you can help Dad and the refinery get back on track."

He was glad she seemed so certain of it, when he was anything but. "You *are* going to have to get your dad to agree, Jordan. I can't just walk in there and start asking questions and giving suggestions."

"He'll agree. I'll make certain of it."

His eyes narrowed. "How?"

The way she tugged at her ponytail belied the blithe shrug she gave. "I'll come up with something," she assured. "All I need to know is when you want to start."

"Tomorrow."

She gave him a brilliant smile.

It was almost enough to counter the dark doubts that sat like a stone inside of him.

CHAPTER FIVE

"So he's pretty hot, huh." Lulu eyed Jordan over the salt shakers they were filling that were lined up along the counter in the empty restaurant. "You could ask him to go to the school picnic with you."

"Who's pretty hot?" Jordan didn't have to ask who Lulu was referring to even though it had been a full week since Nate had come by the restaurant, but she played dumb anyway.

Lulu rolled her eyes, looking not much older than Lydia and Henry, though she was only a few months away from having a baby. *"Nate,"* she said with a decided "duh" tone. "He's working with your dad and everything just 'cause you asked him to."

"He's working with my dad because it's what my brother was going to do," she corrected. There was no point in her thinking otherwise. "And he's been very clear that it's a temporary thing." Lulu was nearly finished with the salt shakers and she began lining up the glass sugar dispensers, deftly unscrewing the metal tops.

"Well, the school picnic is the day after tomorrow. He's not leaving before that, is he?"

Jordan let out a short laugh. "Since when are you

so concerned whether or not I have a *date* for the year-end picnic, anyway?"

Lulu lifted her shoulder. "I just thought you'd have more fun, that's all. I remember the last picnic you went to, you were complaining about how all the parents were couples."

"I wasn't complaining," Jordan corrected. "It was just an observation."

"Still, it just seems to me, if anyone deserves some fun, it's you. It's been terrible about your brother. And you're always taking care of the rest of us. You never do anything for yourself."

Jordan leaned over and caught the girl's small, pointed chin in her hand. "I appreciate the thought, Lulu. But you don't have to worry about me." She let go and handed Lulu the last salt shaker. "I do plenty for myself."

"Like what? When was the last time you even *had* a date?" Lulu patted her stomach, grinning wryly. "*I've* probably had more sex than you have."

Jordan exhaled and shook her head. The last time she'd had sex had been with her husband.

Five years ago.

Which was a fact she did *not* intend sharing with her pregnant little waitress.

"And look where it's gotten you," she said instead.

"I could'a had an abortion," Lulu pointed out, typically practical. "But then the Castillos wouldn't be getting to adopt a baby. This baby."

Jordan smiled though she knew it hadn't been all that easy for her young waitress. For one thing, Lulu's foolish parents had kicked her out of the house when she'd told them she was pregnant. Now, Lulu worked full-time to pay the rent on the garage apartment she'd found and was trying to finish her high school classes at night so that she could still graduate in a year's time.

She was proud and plucky and Jordan would have had her move in with them in a second if the girl would have accepted.

"Well. The Castillos are lucky to have you and so am I. But the last thing I need is a date with anyone, much less Nate Aldrich." The man was in Amarillo only temporarily. If, and that was a *big* if, she ever wanted a man in her life again, it wouldn't be one who was just as rapidly going to leave it.

"Are you sure?"

Jordan let out an exasperated laugh. "Yes. I'm sure."

"Too bad," Lulu said with a chagrined grimace. "Because he's pulling into the parking lot, right now."

Jordan nearly dumped the entire pitcher of sugar that she was using to fill the dispensers on the floor.

"I, uh, sorta forgot to tell you that he called earlier," Lulu said with an apologetic air that wasn't entirely sincere.

"Lulu!"

"Well, you were working the grill and the tables were all full," she defended. She slid off the stool and grabbed her backpack that was loaded with textbooks. In a blink, she was headed toward the door. "See ya' tomorrow." She slid out just as Nate was coming in and Jordan heard the breezy greeting she gave him.

There wasn't even time for Jordan to dash behind

the kitchen to smooth back her hair or get rid of the dirty towel from around her waist.

And try as she might to blame the lurching skip inside her chest on Lulu's ridiculous idea when he turned his hazel gaze her way, she couldn't quite pull it off. Not when she was well aware that Nate had always had the ability to make her feel shaky inside. "Lulu just now told me you'd called," she blurted. "Or I would have called you back."

"No problem. I was out this way, anyway and saw your car in the lot." He was wearing a charcoal-gray suit, but his deep red tie was pulled loose and he'd undone the top button of his white shirt.

He was altogether mouthwatering. Particularly to a woman who'd been living in a drought.

Darn Lulu, anyway.

Thank goodness, Nate couldn't read her mind.

He held up the manila folder he was carrying. "I need to talk to you."

"That sounds ominous," she managed lightly. When she'd talked to her father about Nate signing on for a while at the refinery, he hadn't disagreed. Nor had he exactly *agreed*, for that matter. But when she called her father each afternoon, he'd told her that Nate had been there every day. All day. "What's wrong?"

"Nothing more than I suspected before I got into this." He yanked his tie even looser. "I need your signature on a few things."

"For the refinery?" Her eyebrows shot up. "I've never had anything to do with the business." Fortunately her interests had lain elsewhere, because she'd have been sadly disappointed otherwise. The oil business was for the *men* in the Chelsey family. Not the women.

"Yes, but you still own a share of it," Nate said now. He flipped open the folder and spread out several pages on the counter. The legalese looked odd sitting there next to her old-fashioned sugar dispensers. "This is an agreement for ACFC to conduct an independent audit. I've done what I can on my own, but frankly, the books are a mess."

She couldn't help the defensiveness that rose in her any more than she could help that funny, squiggly feeling she got when his gaze captured hers. "Dad should be the one signing this."

"Yes, but I can't get him to sign a memo, much less this agreement." He pulled a pen from inside his lapel and held it toward her. "He might be going to the office, Jordan, but he's not doing a thing but stare into space once he gets there, and he refuses to consider taking some time away."

"I know. He went to work the day after we got the news about Luke. I don't think he could bear to stay home."

"I'm no expert when it comes to this stuff, but I think he needs some attention."

She slowly took the pen, but didn't do anything except hold it. "I talk to him every day. I'd go out and see him if I thought it would do any good. But he doesn't want to see me."

"Medical attention," Nate corrected. "He's depressed, Jordan."

Defensiveness rose all over again. "He's grieving."

"We're all grieving. But your dad's going through something else. Something worse."

"You haven't been here that long," she pointed out. "How can you possibly think you know—"

"Gladys," he cut in gently. "Your dad's secretary has been with him for thirty years. She's the one who pointed it out to me. She said even before the accident, he's been on a decline. At least a year."

"I would have noticed." Lord. She *should* have noticed. "And why didn't Gladys tell *me* this? I talk to her every day when I call Dad."

"I think she thought you had enough on your plate. She doesn't know that I'm telling you this. But you're his daughter. You're the one in a position to get him some outside help if that's what he needs. Just think about it, at least."

"I want what's best for Dad. That's why I asked you to stay in the first place."

"I know. You've also got to do what's best for Chelsey." He nudged one of the papers toward her.

She swallowed and glanced to the bottom of the page. "My share of Chelsey is minuscule," she said as she began signing her name at the bottom of the first sheet. "I'm not really sure I have the authority to even sign this."

"It was a small share until Luke died. Now you have his share, too. And that means it's not so minuscule."

Her signature hitched to a stop.

She looked up at him, stricken by reality. "I hadn't thought of that. Luke's share should be going back to Dad. Not to me." What on earth would she do with it?

"And Luke's share of ACFC should be going to all of you, not back to me. But that was in his will," Nate said quietly. "Right now, when it comes to Chelsey, it's a good thing. When your dad is more back to himself, you can do what you want with the shares. Give them to him. Keep them for your kids, if the company survives. But right now, do what's good for the company. Do what your dad isn't able to do." He nodded toward the papers. "Starting with a complete audit."

She swallowed hard and managed to finish signing the papers. "I suppose I ought to have read through them first," she said when she handed him back his pen.

Their fingers brushed and she curled her fingers into her palm.

"I think you should sell the refinery," he reminded. "But I'm not the one in charge. You can trust me."

"I never doubted that." She wouldn't have presented her impossible case to him if she had. "So, h-how has the week gone?" She brushed a lock of hair out of her face. "I mean, other than finding Chelsey's financials in a mess. Are you getting everything you need?"

His gaze drifted over her face and she felt completely inappropriate heat curl through her.

"More or less. I have to make a run to L.A. tomorrow. I'll be back in Amarillo on Saturday or Sunday, though."

She nodded and silently bid adieu to the whisper of thought she had tried so hard not to give to him and the school picnic. "I know you still have to attend to your own business."

"Fortunately I can do a lot of it on the road. Right

now I want to get back here early enough to do something about my living situation for the duration. Staying with my grandparents has been fine for a few days, but—"

"Is it cramping your style?"

He grinned slightly. "More like I'm afraid I'm cramping *theirs*."

She laughed softly and for a moment, a very, very sweet moment, the rest of the world seemed to fall away. Luke's death. Her father's emotional state.

But all too soon, the moment passed.

She knew it by the way the amusement faded from Nate's sculpted lips and in the way his jaw tightened, making it seem even more angular.

"I know I've said it before, Nate, but I *am* grateful for what you're doing. And for being honest about how you see my father."

His lips twisted. "Save your gratitude for someone who deserves it."

His expression was so grim, she reached out and touched his hand. "But you do. I don't know who else would agree to do what you've done."

"Luke should be here. Not me." He closed the folder with a finality that she couldn't ignore, and turned toward the door. "If you need me while I'm gone, call my cell. Day or night."

"Nate—"

He stopped. Looked back at her.

She moistened her lips and tried not to lose herself in the shadows filling his eyes. "If you're really serious about wanting some space of your own, I might know a place. My neighbor is out of the country right now and he's been looking for a renter. If you're interested, he left me the keys. It's not a fancy apartment building with a gazillion amenities, I know, but you wouldn't have to worry about leases or anything."

"The yellow two-story next to you?"

The fact that he'd taken note of her neighborhood in any fashion undid her a little. "Um, no. Actually it's the house across the street. It's a three bedroom but one of the rooms is set up as an office. Joe's not looking to make money on the deal, just to keep the place from going unoccupied the entire time he's gone. Well—" she lifted her hands, wishing she could stop her tongue from running amuck when she was nervous "—not that you can't afford whatever you—"

"I'll take a look at it when I get back to town," he interrupted gently.

She closed her mouth. Nodded. "Great. I'll, um, I'll see you then."

She just wished that anticipation wasn't bubbling inside her at the prospect.

CHAPTER SIX

"HE'S HERE, he's here." Henry bounced on the couch situated beneath her front window. "Mom!"

"I heard you, Henry," Jordan said calmly. As if she weren't bouncing on the couch inside her own mind. "Now please get your tennis shoes off the couch."

It was early Saturday evening and ever since Henry had answered the phone to find Nate on the other end, letting her know that he was back and wanted to see the house across the street, her son had been bouncing to the window every time he heard a car passing.

But now her son's diligence was rewarded.

"I'm gonna go out and see him. He says he hasn't tried, but I bet he can hang a tire swing for us."

"Henry—" She was too late. Her son-the-bullet was already zooming out the front door, racing pell-mell toward the tall man climbing from the pickup he'd parked at the curb.

She supposed if she ever needed proof just how much Henry missed having a father, she was looking at it right now.

Not for the first time, she damned the twins' father for his stupidity. It was one thing to abandon her.

It was another thing altogether to pretend his own children didn't exist.

She grabbed the keys to the house across the street and reached for the screen door. "Lydia, come with us. We're going to show Mr. Aldrich around Joe's house."

Her daughter trailed out of her bedroom, her nose still buried in her book. "Do I hafta?"

"Yes." Jordan tipped down the book until Lydia looked up at her. "I don't want to leave you here alone."

Her daughter sighed mightily and closed the oversize book. It was just one of the many that they'd checked out of the library the day before. She followed Jordan outside, but she carried the book right along with her.

Jordan's heart squeezed a little and she ran her hand down Lydia's silky hair. She was so much like Jordan had been as a girl. More comfortable in the pages of the books she'd loved almost before she'd left the crib than she was anywhere else. At least until she'd begun cooking and baking alongside her mother and discovered another new world.

"Evening, ladies," Nate greeted them as they neared the sidewalk. He was dressed more casually than Jordan had ever seen him, in a Yankees T-shirt and khaki-colored cargo pants. "How are you?"

"We're well, thank you." She told her heart to get back down in her chest where it belonged. You'd think she'd never seen a good-looking man before. "Not that I'm likely to forget, but I wanted to let you know that I talked Dad into letting me take him to a doctor. We have an appointment on Tuesday."

"I hope it helps."

So did she. She was willing to try anything, but she was just as aware that her father could change his mind and insist that he needed no help from anyone, least of all her.

"We're outta school now, you know," Henry piped in, determined not to be forgotten in the conversation going on above him. "Yesterday was our last day."

"No kidding?" Nate looked down with absolute seriousness. "So you'll be going into sixth grade next year, right?"

Both Henry and Lydia dissolved into giggles.

Jordan sucked in a breath. How easily he charmed them and he wasn't even trying.

It was seductively appealing. So she took refuge in the prosaic. "How was your flight?"

His lips tilted crookedly. "Boring. Guess that'd be a good thing, though."

He had a suitcase sitting in the truck bed. "Did you come straight from the airport?"

"Yup." He looked at the house directly across from hers. "Is that the one?"

"Yes." She lifted the key ring, jingling the key. "I opened it up for a while this afternoon after you called to air the place out. Joe's been gone for a few months now." She took her kids' hands in hers and they crossed the quiet street. "It's fully furnished. I think the only things Joe took to Europe with him were his clothes and his laptop." She glanced at Nate as she fit the key in the front door lock. "He's some kind of computer expert."

"But he doesn't know nothing about tire swings," Henry said behind them.

"Doesn't know *anything*," Jordan corrected.

Henry rolled his eyes. "I *know,* Mom. That's what I said."

For about a millisecond, she debated correcting him again, but Nate's amused gaze collided with hers and she let it pass.

What she wouldn't give to see him really smile.

Or laugh.

The moment lengthened and Jordan's mouth went a little dry as the amusement slid from his hazel eyes. Only this time it wasn't replaced by somberness. By grimness.

If she wasn't mistaken—if she hadn't forgotten what such a thing looked like—it was heat.

"Are we gonna go in or not?"

She blinked a little. Looked down at Henry. "Of course." Her voice sounded a little hoarse. "The lock is sticking." A little white lie. The kind she was forever telling her children were *not* okay even when you had the best of intentions. She turned the lock and pushed open the door and her kids slipped around her hips, hurrying inside. "Don't touch anything," she warned, but Henry was already racing toward the large plasma television mounted on the wall next to the fireplace.

"Can I play the video game, Mom? Joe always lets me."

"He does," Lydia attested.

"Sounds like your kids are pretty comfortable over here with *Joe,*" Nate murmured above her ear.

She shot him a glance. He couldn't sound jealous, could he? "He's watched them a few times for me."

Nate made a low sound that she couldn't quite interpret as he passed her.

He, too, headed for the large-screen television and crouched down next to Henry in front of the sleek mahogany cabinet that held a collection of fancy electronics. "What's your favorite game," she heard him ask.

"All of 'em," Henry answered fervently.

Nate ran his hand down Henry's head and joggled him gently by the neck. "You're a man after my own heart, Hank."

Jordan could practically see rays of sunshine streaming out of her beaming son.

Then Lydia dropped her book on the couch and joined the two males. "I always beat Henry at Mario," she said, wiggling right between them.

"Do not," Henry denied, shoving back at her a little.

Nate scooped both kids up, one beneath each arm, and dumped them on the couch where they bounced and grinned up at him with besotted looks.

Jordan tucked her fingers in her pockets, torn between delight and unease. Her kids didn't need to become enamored of the man any more than she did.

No matter *how* disarming it was to see them all together.

"The master bedroom is at that end of the house," she said a little too loudly. "It's separated from the other bedrooms. And there's a screened porch off the kitchen. Other than that, it's pretty much the same layout as mine."

Nate didn't look at her. "It'll do fine." He picked up the three remote controls that were sitting on top of the cabinet. "Which one does what," he asked the kids.

They, of course, were only too eager to show him and in seconds, the television leaped to brilliant life.

"But don't you want to *see* anything more?" For heaven's sake, she was still standing in the small foyer and Nate hadn't ventured beyond the living room. "Haggle over the rent? *Something?*"

Nate glanced at her, one dark eyebrow lifting. "Why? You've already said the rent was reasonable."

She tossed up her hands and turned to the door. "Fine." It must be nice never to have to worry about the cost of something. "But I've got dinner in the oven at home that I need to check on."

The trio in front of the television didn't budge.

"Don't cross the street until I come back for you," she told the children.

"I'll bring 'em home," Nate said.

"He can have supper with us," Henry added. "Right, Mom?"

"I—"

"Joe used t' eat with us all the time, too," her little big-mouth continued to inform Nate.

"Did he, now." Nate's voice was smooth as warm molasses. Again, his gaze slid over Jordan's face and she felt herself flushing.

"Of course you're welcome to join us," she offered, feeling thoroughly on-the-spot. "But I warn you, it's just a frank and beans casserole." Hardly the kind of cuisine he'd choose, given a choice.

"It's my favorite," Lydia told him.

"Next week we get to have *my* favorite," Henry quickly put in. "Macaroni and cheese. Only Mom uses those big, *fat* kind of macaroni." He held his hands about a foot apart. "I bet she could fix your favorite, too. Right, Mom?"

Her lips parted. "I—well, I don't know what Mr. Aldrich's favorite is. We'll have to discuss it later." She hurriedly went to the door. *"Behave,"* she warned them—mostly her children—before letting herself out.

The sun was nowhere near dipping toward the horizon yet, but the warmth of the afternoon was nothing in comparison to the blood burning in her cheeks as she hurried across the lawn toward the street.

"Jordan."

Oh, so close to escape.

She exhaled and turned back to Nate, whose long legs were eating up the grassy distance between them. "Yes?"

"You don't have to worry that I'll nose in on your family dinner."

"I wasn't worried."

"Then what was that deer-in-the-headlights look on your face about when Henry suggested it?"

Her lips parted, but words failed.

The corner of his lips twisted. "Don't sweat it. Just because I might live in Joe's house for a few weeks doesn't mean I intend on taking the guy's place anywhere…else."

She blinked. "What's that supposed to mean?"

"Nothing." He went to the side of the pickup and lifted his suitcase out of the bed. "But sooner or later you're probably going to have to break the news to your kids that you've already got a boyfriend, whether they have to see any gross kissing and stuff or not."

"I'm not kissing anyone, much less Joe. He's not my boyfriend! He's old enough to be my father. But don't you worry. I wouldn't presume to think you'd want to step into those shoes, even if he were."

"Yeah, well, don't be so sure you know what I want."

Her hands went to her hips. "All right, then, Nate. What *do* you want?"

He stopped short, towering over her. His gaze seemed to burn over her face, stopping at last on her mouth. "The impossible," he said in a low, husky voice.

She pressed her lips together, but the tingling didn't go away. "And that would be—" her throat tightened oddly "—what?"

For a moment, a very long, tight moment when even the air around them seemed to still, she thought he meant to kiss her. Actually found herself waiting for it. Maybe even standing a little taller toward him; leaning a little closer toward him.

"For Luke and Jess to still be here."

The words were a douse of icy water.

The heels of her tennis shoes went back down that half-inch to the ground and her spine straightened against the grief that pelted through her.

"I wish that, too," she said carefully. Painfully. Truthfully. "But I learned a long time ago when my mother died that some wishes can never come true."

"So what do you do?" He turned his head, his profile etched sharply against the sunlight as he looked off into a distance she couldn't see. But oh, she could feel it in the waves of grief rolling off him that were as great as her own.

"You go on," she said simply. It was the only answer she had. "When my mother died, Luke was twenty-five. I was twenty. I couldn't imagine how I was going to survive it. Luke's the one who told me that life is for the living. It wasn't easy and it took a long time and even though it was ten years ago now, I still miss her. But the pain eases. The memories and the love remain. And Luke, of all people, would detest the thought of us not moving past our grief. He'd want us to remember the life he lived. The life they lived. To celebrate it." She folded her arms around her chest, wishing that her father could think clearly enough to remember that.

"I'm not sure where to even start."

She let out a slow breath, unbearably shaken by his gruff admission, as well as the stark look she caught in the hazel eyes that turned her way. "Today? You can start with franks and beans for dinner. If you're interested."

He was silent for so long she wasn't sure he'd answer. "I am."

"All right then." She exhaled and even though it was shaky, she managed a small smile. "Thirty minutes of video games and not a minute more or I'll come and hunt the three of you down. Got it?"

"Yes, ma'am."

It wasn't quite a smile on his face. But it was close. And it felt like a small victory as she headed across the street to get those franks and beans on the table.

CHAPTER SEVEN

"YOU'RE A HARD MAN to catch up to these days." Nate's cousin, Rebecca, greeted him when he answered his cell phone the next morning. "Are you in L.A. or Amarillo?"

"Amarillo." He stood near the window of Joe's master bedroom, looking through the slanted blinds at Jordan's house across the street. "I'll probably be here at least through Gran and Granddad's anniversary next month. Aren't you supposed to be on a honeymoon or something with that besotted Army Captain of yours?" His cousin had recently gotten married in nearly as rapid a fashion as had their grandparents sixty years earlier.

She laughed softly. "Let's just say we're enjoying every minute together that we can before Ryan has to ship out." Then her voice sobered a little. "I heard through the family grapevine that you're working at the refinery, now?"

Working or banging his head against a wall. He wasn't sure which. "Just for a while." He saw a light go on behind the blinds hanging in one of Jordan's windows.

Was he turning into a Peeping Tom, now?

He yanked a pair of cargo shorts out of the suitcase he had yet to unpack and pulled them on.

"Well, speaking of the anniversary," his cousin continued once again. "I have all the vendors lined up for the reception next month thanks to your trusty credit card. I still feel a little badly, though, that you're footing the bill for all of this. You know, our parents would happily chip in something."

"Paying for this is the one thing I can do. And the rest of the family's doing plenty," he assured. "It's a helluva lot easier for me to pay the bills and leave the details of figuring out how to get Gran and Granddad to the church to someone else."

"It's still pretty darn generous. I only really called, though, to see how you were doing with everything that's on your plate. Let you know that we're thinking of you."

He smiled faintly. "Thanks, Bec. Now go wake up your husband for church or whatever it is that newlyweds do on Sunday mornings."

She laughed softly. "What makes you think we haven't already done what newlyweds do?"

He was still smiling when they disconnected. Through the window, he saw Jordan's front door open and she emerged, pausing on the front step.

Even from a distance, Nate could see the shine in her tousled hair; the pink and white stripes of the loose pants that seemed to barely hang onto her hips as she went out to collect the fat Sunday paper where it was half-buried in a mound of flowers. Then, with the paper tucked beneath her arm, she straightened, seeming to look across at him.

At Joe's house, anyway.

She raked her hand through her unfettered hair,

brushing it back from her forehead as she turned toward her house. The strappy excuse of a shirt she was wearing ended at her waist and damned if he couldn't tear his attention from the narrow strip of creamy skin that was displayed between the edge of the shirt and the precariously low waist of her pants.

Before he knew what he was doing, he'd walked through the house to his own front door, and was outside, inhaling the still-cool air. "Mornin'," he said loudly enough for her to hear.

She turned, clutching the newspaper to her chest. "Good morning, Nate. I was just, um, getting the paper."

"Saw that." He'd spent a good portion of the evening before with her and her kids. He should've had his fill of their company by now.

Oddly enough, he'd realized that he hadn't. And he'd realized it when he'd had to force himself to bid them good-night after it became plainly obvious that it was the kids' bedtime and make himself go back to the solitary, rented house across the street. "Are you gonna read it?"

Her smile flashed. "Well…it *is* the Sunday paper. Isn't that what one usually does with it?"

"Some don't." His bare feet were carrying him closer to the end of Joe's lawn. Closer to the street separating him from Jordan. "Some just like looking at the ads." That's what Jess had always done whenever he'd had Sunday breakfast with her and Luke.

"Are you trying to ask if you can read my newspaper, Nate?"

"Will it get me a cup of coffee if I admit it?"

Her smile widened. "It might."

"Then can I read your newspaper? I'll even make good on the promise your son wrangled out of me last night to put up that tire swing he wants."

Her laughter was soft and lilting in the morning air. "A newspaper and coffee hardly seems to necessitate such bribery. But I'm not going to turn down the offer. Henry would disown me." She turned back toward her house. "I guess I might as well feed you breakfast, too. But put some shoes on before you cross the street."

He realized he was still standing there staring after her like a fool even after she'd disappeared through her front door.

He went inside and shoved his feet into his battered running shoes. He also yanked a wrinkled baseball jersey over his head and reminded himself all the while of every reason that Jordan Chelsey needed to remain off-limits.

None of the reasons seemed to matter in the least, though, when he crossed the street and walked in through the front door that she'd left ajar for him.

The first thing he saw was the back of her, standing at the stove. She was singing softly—and a little off-key—along with the music coming from the radio that was sitting on the counter, her hips swaying almost imperceptibly with the beat. "Someone like you…"

His feet went still, rooted in place.

He felt poleaxed by the sudden, dizzying emotion that spiraled inside him.

She turned and spotted him, her lips still rounded on the words. "Sorry. I didn't hear you come in." Her eyebrows lifted slightly when he just stood there, silent as a bump on a log. "Are you all—"

His feet moved suddenly and he crossed the kitchen in a few strides and caught her face in his hands, pressing his mouth against hers.

She inhaled so sharply he felt the soft thrust of her breasts rise against his chest. But just as quickly as she'd stiffened, she became soft.

Giving.

And she kissed him back, a low sound rising in her throat that twisted the desire inside him into an even tighter need. His fingers slid into her hair. Just as silky as he'd imagined—

A chime sounded. Twice.

She jumped back suddenly, her eyes blinking. "The, um, that's the oven timer," she said in a faint voice, before jerking around to fumble with a towel that she used to pull a pan out of the oven.

He watched her movements without really seeing them.

Common sense came back way too slowly, but when it did, he wanted to kick himself.

What was he doing?

She was *Jordan,* for God's sake. Don't-delve-into-those-waters Jordan.

She was working at the counter, scooping up whatever delectable heaven she'd pulled out of the oven, not looking at him.

One of her narrow straps had started to slide off her shoulder, but if she noticed or cared, she didn't reach up to nudge it back in place.

He stared at it. Willing it to fall—to bare her beautiful shoulder even more—or willing it to remain safely where it was, he wasn't certain.

Hell. He should say something. Anything to break the awkward silence that he'd let go on too long. "I shouldn't have done that."

Still she didn't look at him. She opened a cupboard above her head and her shoulder blades worked beneath the thin pink fabric clinging to them as she lifted down a stack of plates. "Then why did you?"

God in heaven, his mouth was watering and it had nothing to do with the aroma of her cooking. "I couldn't stop myself." The admission came without volition. Which left him feeling even more off-kilter.

He could almost hear Jess's soft laughter haunting him from some corner of his mind.

"Not that that's an excuse," he added rapidly. "I usually have more self-control."

Her chin tilted slightly, almost but not quite leading the way over her shoulder to look back at him. She set the plates on the table. "I see."

Did she? Because he sure didn't.

And despite the way he'd pretty much horned his way into her house with the newspaper excuse, his feet were suddenly anxious in the worst way to start inching toward the door. "Maybe I should go."

At that, she did turn to look at him. One eyebrow lifted slightly, and her tousled—just from bed-looking—hair glided over her shoulder where the strap had finally slid off her shoulder, only to get caught on a smooth, golden biceps. "Why?"

He felt himself floundering, and again that was not a familiar place for him. "Because you're upset."

Her other eyebrow lifted, as well. She cupped her hands over the edge of the countertop at her sides and leaned back slightly. Her full, rounded breasts pushed forward, every delectable curve and point clearly delineated beneath the pink knit.

He was a dog.

If Luke were around, he'd give Nate a good shot upside the head.

"Funny." Her tone was frustratingly unreadable. "But I don't *feel* upset."

His hands ached to *feel* her, all over. "Well, why the hell not?"

"I've wondered what it would be like to kiss you for years," she said as blithely as if they were talking about the price of eggs. Then she turned back to the counter and plucked a wooden spoon out of a drawer and started stirring something in a small bowl. "Now I know."

She stopped stirring long enough to slip the strap back up onto her shoulder, then went right back to what she was doing.

Now she knew.

He grimaced. "And what's that supposed to mean? Curiosity abated, no need to repeat the experience?"

Her shoulders rose and fell and she dropped the spoon into the sink. "What do you want me to say, Nate?" She finally turned around to look at him again and her cheeks were flushed. "I've just admitted that I've…wondered about it for a long time. Does your ego need even more stroking than that?"

He stifled an oath. "This isn't my ego—"

"Curiosity *not* abated," she cut in, her voice resigned. "For all the good it does me." She lifted one hand. "You're not going to stick around Amarillo any longer than you feel is necessary. You'll go back to Los Angeles to the fancy, modern condo that Jess described to me and the ninety-mile-a-minute lifestyle you live."

He opened his mouth to counter her, only to close it again.

What could he say to that?

His stay in Amarillo was temporary. Once he'd done what he could to help her father, help the refinery, help his weighted conscience, he'd leave again.

Nothing had changed. She was white-picket-fence Jordan. The kind of woman a man thought about marrying.

Not the kind of woman Nate Aldrich bedded and didn't wed.

"I'd better go." Ironically since, though he'd been anxious to escape, when it was within his reach, he wasn't sure he wanted it.

Her lips pressed softly together for a moment. Her dove-gray eyes looked more like a stormy sky. "If that's what you feel."

He didn't know what he felt. That was the damn problem.

He'd looked at her and felt such an undeniable wealth of…*something* inside him that he'd practically pounced on her. And maybe she could say she'd been curious about kissing him, but that didn't mean she'd done a single thing to invite his advance.

Not now, nor any of the other handful of times they'd seen one another over the years.

"That's what I feel." He said the words as much to convince himself as her, and started for the door. "I need to go out to Chelsey today, anyway. Make sure everything's set for the auditors' arrival tomorrow."

She didn't comment. Didn't try to stop him.

He told himself he was glad. They were both on the same page. Kissing her had been flammable, but neither one of them needed a fire.

Not now.

Certainly not with each other.

But before he made it to the door, a sleepy-eyed Lydia padded into the room. The eyes that were just like her mother's widened at the sight of him. "Are you gonna hang our tire swing now?"

She was looking up at him with such trusting expectation, he didn't have the stomach to tell her he was leaving. He exhaled. "Yeah." His voice was gruff. He let his hand slip over her silky head. "I am."

The smile she bestowed on him was beatific.

And that's when it finally sunk in that no matter what Nate did, he was in way over his head where Jordan Chelsey and her twins were concerned.

CHAPTER EIGHT

THE AUDIT of Chelsey Oil Refinery was done.

Two weeks had passed since he'd seen the last of the team he'd called in to unravel the convoluted knots of Drew's business, and *that* delightful process had taken two weeks.

Now, Nate was staring at the report that he'd read through more than once, desperate to find some inkling that would prove that Jordan's faith in him hadn't been irredeemably misplaced. He'd found none.

"Nate?" Gladys, Drew's patience-of-a-saint secretary, poked her neatly coiffed gray head around the doorway of the small office that Nate had appropriated for himself what seemed an eon ago, but in reality was only five weeks. "I just wanted to let you know that, unless you need anything else from me, I'm leaving for the day."

He roused himself enough to close the report. "You should have left a few hours ago." It was well past quitting time.

"I didn't want to leave until Drew did. But I just successfully badgered him out of his office, so I'm good to go. I really think he's seeming better. Particularly this past week."

"I'm glad." He'd noticed a difference in Drew, too. Not a complete turnaround, but definitely an improvement. The doctor that Jordan had gotten her father to see was obviously doing some good. "You drive carefully, Gladys."

"I will," the woman assured. "Have a good evening, now."

He kept his smile in place until she was gone.

There was no good evenings left to be had, considering the news he needed to deliver not only to Jordan but to Drew.

In the man's tender state, Nate wanted to put that particular task off for about a month of Sundays.

It was going to be hard enough just telling Jordan.

Since that morning in her kitchen a month earlier, he'd managed to regain some measure of self-control where she was concerned.

Oh, he was a helpless sucker when it came to her kids. There was no doubt about that point.

He'd hung the tire swing. He'd helped Henry build a model airplane. He'd taken Lydia out to his grandparents' place so she could pick some storybooks out of the sizable collection his gran had amassed since *he'd* been a kid.

While sharing at least a dozen meals with them, he'd listened to the twins' endless chatter about the day camp that Jordan took them to now that school was out for the summer. Twice Jordan had even succeeded in getting Drew to join them for dinner. Other times, she had people from J's there. Lulu. Maria. Even Mutt and Jeff the cooks, whose real names had turned out to be Marvin and Julia.

Jordan was a born nurturer. It was as plain as the nose on his face.

She'd managed to take him in, more or less, when she had no earthly reason to do so. She owed him absolutely nothing. And he owed her a hell of a lot more than the news that he couldn't see a way for the refinery to avoid bankruptcy.

He also couldn't look at her without wanting her so deeply that his back teeth ached with it, which made every minute he spent with her a double-edged exercise in torture.

He raked his fingers through his hair, stuck the report in his briefcase and left the office.

Under normal circumstances, he would never have considered telling Jordan the news about the report before he told Drew. The man *was* the owner, after all. But these weren't normal circumstances. If they were, the only reason Nate would have to be in Amarillo would be for his grandparents' surprise party that weekend.

Coward that he was when it came to the Chelsey family, he didn't even head straight home. Instead he found himself turning off the highway to head for his grandparents' house.

Neither Jack nor Claire could hide their surprise when they saw him. His grandmother offered to fix him something for supper, though it was hours past the dinner they'd already had, but he declined. His grandfather would have been willing to discuss the refinery if Nate had been willing. He wasn't. Not even with Jack, who'd been an oilman himself.

Instead Nate sat on a chair on their deck with them,

wishing for a cigarette again even though he hadn't had one since the night Jack gave him the pocket watch, and tried to pretend that everything was just hunky-dory.

"So, how is Jordan?" Claire finally asked.

Nate found unusual interest in the wood slats of the deck rail. "She's all right." Beautiful. Caring. Impossibly tempting.

"I've always liked her. She's such a nice young woman. And that ex-husband she had—" Claire shook her head. "I know the attorney who handled her divorce. It was a messy business. It would be nice to see her happily settled with a worthy man."

He could feel his neck flushing. "Yeah." Only that would mean she was happily settling with someone *other* than him, and that was a notion he found unacceptable. "She deserves a lot," he finished.

His grandmother looked knowing. "So do you."

The flush wasn't going to stay confined to his neck no matter how much he wished it would. "Gran, don't go getting ideas about Jordan and me."

"Why not?" Her eyebrows lifted innocently. "You seem to be with each other constantly."

"She spends hours at J's and I spend hours at Chelsey. And don't forget. I live in Los Angeles."

"Have you ever noticed that you don't say your *home* is in Los Angeles?"

"What's that supposed to mean?"

His grandmother gave him an innocent look. "Nothing, dear. But I have heard that you and Jordan have spent every evening together for the past month. There are some who would define that as somewhat constant."

"Give it up, son," his grandfather suggested blandly. "You're defending a losing position."

The back of his neck itched. "How do you know what we're doing every evening anyway?" It sounded salacious, when the reality had been completely innocent.

Completely addictive, he realized.

"I eat at J's at least once a week," Jack reminded. "I've heard."

Nate stared. "Not from Jordan," he said surely.

"Not from Jordan," Jack assured, smiling slightly. "She turns pink whenever she looks at me. Reminds me of your mother when she was a teenager and got caught doing something she knew she shouldn't be doing."

Well, Jordan wasn't doing Nate. Not in any way, shape or fashion. And when she heard what he had to tell her about the refinery, she'd likely feel even more strongly about that point.

"She's probably flushed from the heat in the kitchen," he dismissed, rising. "I'd better get going," he excused himself and kissed his grandmother's cheek; shook his grandfather's hand. They didn't say so, but it was plainly obvious that they hadn't believed his lame excuse. Not for second.

This time, he headed straight for home. He didn't need another detour going so awry.

He parked in Joe's driveway, grabbed the miserable report from his briefcase and headed across the street to Jordan's.

She didn't answer his knock. Nor his second. Or his third. She was home, too. He knew it for certain, because she'd neglected to shut her garage door after she'd parked her car inside it.

Alarm tasted acrid in his throat and he knocked yet again before trying the door. It was unlocked and without hesitation, he went inside. "Jord—" Her name cut off in his throat at the sight of her hurrying along the hallway toward him wearing nothing but a towel wrapped around her torso.

"Nate. What's wrong?" She'd clamped her hands over the top of the towel where it was knotted over her breasts. "I was taking a bath."

It was a needless explanation considering the airy white bubbles still clinging to the tendrils of hair that had escaped the knot she'd made on top of her head, and the slick moisture he could see on her knees below the edge of the soft-looking red towel.

"Your garage door is still up. When you didn't answer, I thought maybe something had happened with one of the kids." But as rapidly as alarm had risen in him, it was forgotten in the killing want that replaced it.

"They're not here. Their day camp is having a lock-in tonight."

No six-year-old chaperones? Alarm of a different sort set in. "What the hell is a lock-in?"

A swallow worked down her long throat. "An over-nighter with all of the kids in the day camp."

"Hank and Lydia are only six!" His voice rose a little. He tried but couldn't recall the matter coming up over any dinner. The day camp included kids through sixth *grade*. "And since when do boys get to have sleepovers with girls at that age?"

"When it's an extremely supervised program run by people I completely trust! And why should it bother you so much?"

"Because I—" He clamped off the rest, knowing he had no right to voice them. "I was just surprised," he excused, tallying up another really big lame excuse for the day.

The death-grip she had on the towel was turning her knuckles white. Her lashes veiled her eyes. "I don't make careless decisions where my children are concerned, Nate."

He stifled an oath and took an involuntary step toward her. "I know you don't. You're a good mother. A great mother. I overreacted."

"Why?"

"Because I—because you and the kids were Luke's family."

Her lashes lifted and that soft gray seemed to slam into him with the delicacy of a sledgehammer. "That's the only reason?"

Who needed methods of torture when Jordan's husky voice and inquisitive gray eyes existed?

"What do you think?" His voice wasn't husky. It was raw. "Have you forgotten the way I kissed you?"

"A month ago," she pointed out in a careful voice. "And you made it plain then that you regretted it."

"Honey, if I had a dollar for the regrets I've got, your dad's refinery would be in the black in a New York minute. Make no mistake, *I want you.* But you said you didn't need a guy like me, remember?"

Her pupils flared for a moment. She moistened her

lips and walked toward him. "That doesn't make me stop wanting you, though." Her damp, bare feet didn't stop until they were nearly toe-to-toe with his boots. "Because my head tells me the reasons why not. But what I feel—" She visibly swallowed again, so hard, he could practically feel it. "What I feel is here." She took his hand and pressed it against the towel. Against her breasts. Against her heart. "And it doesn't care about reason at all."

Her hand was shaking. Or maybe it was his own that wasn't at all steady. "Jordan."

Her lashes were lowered, casting shadows on her cheeks. "Nate."

His fingers felt the knot in the towel. "I don't want to give you reasons for regret."

"Then don't." Her mouth lifted to his, her lips pressing softly. "Don't give me a reason," she whispered again.

He was burning from the inside out as surely as if she'd set a match to him. And the only way to put out the flame was through her.

His mouth covered hers more surely, his hands pulling her up against him. Racing need swept through him as her mouth opened and her hands grasped his shoulders. His neck. His heart pounded, the blood flying through his veins only to pool low and urgent inside him.

She tore her lips away, hauling in a breath. "If you don't put your hands on me, I'll go mad."

But he'd be damned if he'd be rushed. Not now. Not when, at last, she was in his arms.

So he caught her head in his hand, tilting her chin up so he could better explore the fine line of her jaw. The pulse that beat frantically at the base of her neck.

She fisted her fingers in his hair, pulling his mouth back to hers. "Hurry," she groaned, pressing her lips against his while her hands dragged at his shirttails, pulling them free only to slip beneath. "I can't bear waiting any longer."

Waiting? He could give her lessons in the torture of waiting.

Then her knuckles grazed his belly and he nearly came out of his skin. He gave her towel a deliberate, unhurried tug and it slid free, the red terry cloth falling with surreal slowness to drape over his boots. Her toes.

He worked his shirt over his head and tossed it aside, then hauled her back up against him and he could have whimpered like a baby as her full, soft breasts pressed into his chest.

He dipped his head and pressed his mouth against the warmth of her shoulder. She smelled like lavender and tasted like heaven. Sweet, sinful heaven. He'd waited for this for years.

Ever since that party of Luke's.

The thought intruded as effectively as a bucket of ice water dumping over his head.

Damn it to hell.

"Wait." The word emerged low and harsh.

"I can't." Her hands fumbled with his belt and he grabbed her hands, holding them away from him.

"No," he muttered. "*I* can't."

CHAPTER NINE

JORDAN STARED mutely at Nate, because it was quite
evident to her that he most certainly *could.* The dark
blue jeans he wore didn't disguise his arousal in the
least. And every aching cell she possessed urged her
to reach out, to close her hands around him, to draw
him back to her until there was not even enough space
between them to draw breath. "Nate, please—"

He released her and lifted his hand. Beneath the rolled
up sleeve of his white shirt, the corded sinews in his
forearm flexed as his fingers spread in a silent command
for silence. Only the tormented expression on his face
made it more of a plea than a demand. "I shouldn't be
here," he said roughly. "Not like this. Not with you."

Everything that had been on fire inside her went chill-
ingly cold with such abruptness, she felt dizzy with it.

Suddenly, humiliatingly aware of her nudity, she
snatched up the towel and yanked it around herself again.
"Fine." Her voice sounded as brittle as she felt. She'd
basically offered herself up on a platter, and he was
turning her down. Again. "Contrary to appearances—"
like her *begging* "—you could have just said no."

If she didn't get him out of there, she was going to

embarrass herself even more. She could already feel the burning behind her eyes. The words to tell him to leave were in her head, but the confusion inside her didn't let them escape. "At least tell me why. You owe me that."

His sharp jaw canted to one side. "I owe you more than you know."

Her confusion magnified tenfold and even then she didn't tell him to go. "Just tell me, Nate." Her palms lifted, imploring. "Whatever it is, we can work it out."

His lips twisted. "Even the fact that it's my fault your brother and his wife are dead?"

She stared. Of all the things he could have said, this was the last thing she expected. "What are you talking about?"

"They were on their way to meet *me*." His voice was flat. Dogged. "Me and a client. Even though Luke had made it clear he was close to leaving ACFC, I talked him into one more business dinner. Even talked him into bringing Jess along, because she could charm anyone, especially stubborn clients like the one I'd arranged to meet that night. I wanted one more chance to score another deal. Another dollar. *That's* why they were on the road that night. *That's* why they're gone. Because of me."

Jordan slowly let go of her death grip on her towel. The seesaw of emotions rocking through her was leaving her weak. But that was nothing in comparison to the agony she could see so clearly now in his face. "They're gone because a jackknifed semitruck crashed into them," she corrected. "It was an accident, Nate. A terrible, terrible *accident*."

"One that shouldn't have happened."

"That's why they're called accidents."

"How can you be so...accepting?" He sounded almost angry.

Her throat tightened. "Do you want me to yell and scream at you, Nate? Tell you that it *is* your fault? Would that make you feel better?"

"It would at least tell me that you understand the truth." His voice sounded like ground glass.

"I understand the truth just fine," she assured. "I also understand grieving. I've done it, remember? And I can tell you that blaming yourself for an *accident* instead of dealing with the rest of your feelings is not going to make the loss of someone who was important to you any less painful in the end. You're almost as bad as Dad is, except he has the added complication of his depression to give him a better reason to avoid dealing with reality!"

His head snapped back. "You think I'm not dealing with *reality?* Jordan, I'm surrounded by it every second of every day. You don't know—"

"Don't I?" Temper was beginning to gurgle in her veins, which was a good thing, because it was either let that take over, or succumb to sobs and that was something she refused to do.

At least not until she could fall apart in private.

"Don't presume that you have a lock on guilty feelings, Nathaniel Aldrich. My brother and sister-in-law were going to meet you the night of the accident. Okay, so now you've told me this major secret you've been harboring. Only I already knew about your business dinner, because Luke told me so himself on the cell phone, while he and Jess were in the car heading for the freeway!"

He looked stunned. "You talked to Luke that night?"

She crossed her arms over her chest, making doubly certain that her towel wasn't budging. "Yes. He still hadn't given Dad an answer about coming back for certain to Amarillo, and I called him to see if he even *wanted* to. He and Jess loved California. He loved working with you. We all knew that. Even Dad, whether he wanted to face it or not."

She unfolded her arms again and jabbed her finger into his chest, her anger mounting. "How dare you assume that you were the only one in my brother's life that affected him! You want to list the things on his mind that day? Start with his argument with Dad. End with his phone call with me. But don't you dare take on responsibility for a *trucking* accident that even the trucking company is admitting respon-sibility for."

His hazel eyes looked more green than brown. "I—" he broke off, his voice cracking. "I miss them," he finally finished in a hoarse whisper.

Her anger whooshed out and her heart simply broke in two for him.

It didn't matter that he'd turned her down; that he'd pushed her away.

He was hurting desperately, and because of that, she hurt for him, too. "I know, Nate," she whispered. She went to him, slipping her fingers through his hair, bringing his unresisting head down to her shoulder as if he were no older than Henry and Lydia. "We all miss them both."

His arms came around her, tightening like iron bands, but she didn't—couldn't—protest. "I'm sorry." His voice was still rough. Still choked.

A hot tear slid down her cheek, all too quickly followed by another but she let them fall. "Don't be sorry. Just let it go, Nate." She held on to him even more tightly, willing with everything inside her that he could find some ease. Some peace. *"Let it go."*

And then, miraculously, he did.

Holding her as if he never wanted to let her go while his wide shoulders jerked with hard tears. And even though she could hardly bear to witness his pain, she did. Because she realized with a shaft of blinding clarity that she was in love with him.

She always would be.

And when her own tears eased, she pressed her lips to his hard cheek. Threaded her fingers through his chestnut hair, drawing it back over and over from his strong forehead. She murmured soothing sounds of nothing. Again and again. Until finally, eventually, he calmed.

She wasn't sure when his mouth turned to hers. Not even sure when the shudders racking his shoulders ceased, only to be replaced by tension of another sort.

All she knew was the drugging sweetness of his lips on hers. The slow slide of seduction filling her veins when his big, warm palms cupped her hips through the towel and her bare knees brushed the denim of his jeans.

Gone was the mad rush of earlier. In its place was a low, steady flame that burned even more brightly. Even more deeply.

When he swept her off her feet and carried her into her bedroom, there wasn't a whisper of protest inside her. And when he settled her in the center of her bed, she held out her hands to him. "Stay with me," she whispered. "Even if it's just for tonight, Nate. Stay with me."

She didn't realize she was holding her breath, waiting for him to change his mind. But his gaze stayed steady on hers when he reached for his belt buckle and she exhaled as, with a lack of fuss that was impossibly graceful, impossibly arousing, he pulled off his clothes.

Then he bent his knee on the mattress and came down beside her, gathered her close and made love to her with such gentle thoroughness, she felt tears slip down her cheeks all over again.

She could feel his heart charging in his chest as clearly as she could feel him still filling her as he froze over her when he spotted the tears. "Did I hurt you?"

She inhaled a shaking breath. "No. Never."

His thumbs slowly brushed her cheeks. "Then why are you crying?

Her emotions were so ripe inside her, there was no place for them to go, if not through tears. *I love you* pushed at her lips, begging to escape, but she held the words back.

She might have lost her heart, but nothing else had changed. Nate still had a life to return to in California. And her life was here. So she slid her fingers down his hard jaw. Rubbed her thumb over his full lower lip. "I'm not crying. It's just been a long time since I've felt this way. I can't help it." Tears were just a release of another sort after the incredible releases he'd wrought from her so tenderly.

Relieved, Nate let out a long breath and turned to his side, scooping her back against him. He pressed his lips against the silky warmth of her shoulder and his arm circled her waist, his hand pressing against her flat abdomen until he could feel the entire length of her spine pressed against his chest.

He hadn't felt like this ever.

And though it was so tempting to hover there in that land of perfection forever, he knew he couldn't. "I need to tell you about Chelsey," he said quietly. "The report from the auditors came in today."

She didn't try to move away, but he felt the way she went very still. "It's bad," she predicted. "How bad?"

He went to the bottom line. "I think bankruptcy might be the best option."

She didn't flinch. Just remained still. Waiting for more.

He wished he weren't able to provide it. But he wasn't going to spare her the facts now. Not after the way she'd shared herself so trustingly, so totally, with him.

Aside from Drew, Jordan and her children were the last of the Chelseys. And it was the *Chelsey* Oil Refinery.

She deserved all of the truth. "The refinery's been in trouble for years. More years than even Luke knew about, I suspect." His partner would have told Nate if he'd known.

She exhaled slowly. "I'll talk to Dad tomorrow."

"I'm sorry. I wish—"

"Stop." She threaded her fingers through his and drew their joined hands up to her lips. "You're not responsible for this, Nate, any more than you were responsible for Luke and Jess's accident. If you continue to insist on thinking that you are, then work on forgiving yourself."

He closed his eyes for a moment. *Forgiveness.* The word swirled through his thoughts.

"You don't have to tell him on your own," he told Jordan when he thought he could speak without his voice cracking yet again. "I never intended that. I'll be with you."

Her fingers squeezed his. "Thank you." He started to reach for the sheet that had been twisted nearly off the bed and she clutched at his arm. "Wait. You're not leaving?"

The disappointment in her voice would have changed his mind, if that had been his intention. "I'm just getting the sheet," he assured truthfully, and pulled it up over them. "I'm not leaving."

She subsided, her muscles once again soft and loose against his. She pressed her lips to their entwined fingers once again. "Good," she murmured. And after that, she said no more.

But Nate lay there staring into nothing long after her breathing had smoothed into the steady cadence of a deep, peaceful sleep. He would stay with her for what remained of that night.

But what about the rest of their lives?

CHAPTER TEN

"NATE. I've been trying to reach you all day." Rebecca's voice sounded frantic when Nate answered his cell phone the next morning.

Jordan was still sleeping and he'd gotten up to fix *her* breakfast for once. He tucked the phone between his shoulder and ear and poured coffee into a yellow smiley-face mug he'd found in the cabinet. "What's wrong?"

"The caterer for Gran and Granddad's party has pulled out. She has a family emergency somewhere back east."

He hadn't given the party a moment's thought since he'd made love to Jordan. Now, he set the coffeepot down with a thud. "The party's tomorrow night. Doesn't she have staff who can step in to take care of things?"

"She has servers, yes, but no chef. I've called every caterer in Amarillo and nobody's available at such short notice. I've never had anything like this happen before. Your mom knows someone in Corpus we can get, but it would cost a fortune for them to go all the way to Amarillo."

Nate's gaze went toward Jordan's bedroom. "Maybe I can come up with a different solution."

He could practically hear the astonishment in his cousin's silence. "What?" she finally asked. "Who?"

"A friend. Let me do some checking. I'll call you in an hour."

"Sure. Okay." Rebecca sounded still astonished, but at least that was better than hearing panic in her voice.

They hung up and he headed back down the hall. He set the coffee mug he'd filled for Jordan on the nightstand and sat beside her on the bed.

She slept with the same abandon with which she made love. Flat on her stomach, her arms flung wide, her legs tangled in the sheet. He smoothed her thick, long hair away from her shoulders and kissed her between her shoulder blades.

She shifted, mumbling nonsensically.

He smiled a little, though there was a pleasure deep down inside him, and kissed her again. "Wake up, Sleeping Beauty."

She sat up with such a start that he barely had time to straighten before the back of her head could connect with his chin.

She pushed her hand through her tumbled hair, holding it out of her eyes and tucked the sheet against her bare breasts. But the sleepiness in those dove-gray orbs cleared when they focused on him and a soft smile flirted around her mobile lips. "Hi."

He realized he was smiling pretty stupidly back at her. "Hi." He grabbed the coffee mug. "I made you coffee."

She gave him such a look of surprise and gratitude, you'd have thought he'd told her he'd cured cancer. "You didn't have to do that."

"I wanted to take care of you for once." He waited until her fingers brushed against his as she took the mug before releasing it. "Give you the morning off. What time do you have to pick up Hank and Lydia?"

She sipped the hot coffee, still managing to hold the sheet circumspectly against her breasts though he could have told her he was just as hot and bothered by the long, shapely leg that was bared up to her thigh. "Not until ten," she provided. "Why?"

"That means we have hours yet."

Her eyes turned slumberous all over again. A small smile toyed with her soft, inviting lips. "Oh?"

He would have happily tugged aside the sheet and joined her in bed. "Not for that. Not now, anyway. I've got something else in mind."

She narrowed her eyes suspiciously. "And that would be?"

"The caterer my cousin hired for my grandparents' party tomorrow night just canceled on us."

Surprise slackened her jaw. "You're kidding."

"Judging from the panic in Rebecca's phone call a few minutes ago, no kidding allowed. If I find you enough help, do you think you can take it on?"

She sat up more, the sheet falling away from one beautifully rounded breast. "Nate, you told me you were expecting more than a hundred guests! I've catered brunches. Garden parties. Nothing like what you need."

He kept his hand diligently away from her, though it was damn tough. "But do you want to? You said you wouldn't mind having more time to take on some different kinds of jobs. This could be a start, right?"

She slid the coffee mug onto the nightstand. "What kind of menu is it?"

He lifted his shoulder. "I don't know."

"But I thought you were in on the planning with Rebecca."

"I was in on the *paying* with Rebecca," he corrected. "Look. You can talk directly to her. Work out the details together. Just tell me what you need and I'll get it for you."

"I need about twenty-four more hours than you're giving me. Not even *you* can pull that out of a hat." She started to push him aside to slide out of bed, but he hooked his arm around her waist, pulling her back down. Her eyes went wide, her hair spread around her on the mattress like a golden halo. "Nate?

"I've changed my mind," he said huskily. "There is time for *that*. Right now."

She lifted an imperious eyebrow. "You think I'm going to fall in with *that* so easily now?"

He pressed his mouth against hers, one hand sliding up to cup her bared breast, his other hand sliding down that delectable thigh.

She breathed in on a hitch. "Evidently I am," she mumbled against his lips and slid her hands behind his neck and tugged him down beside her.

With a soft laugh, he went.

"OKAY, *what* the hell am I supposed to do with these things?" Nate eyed Jordan across the stainless steel table they'd pulled around in the center of her kitchen at J's, and held up a fistful of asparagus spears.

Ever since she'd gotten off the phone with his cousin that morning, he'd been following her bidding. First to pick up Hank and Lydia from their lock-in, then to pick up Lulu and bring her back to Jordan's house since she'd agreed to watch the children while Jordan dragged Nate through one shop after another in her search for the foodstuffs she needed.

Now, it was nearly midnight and they'd been in the kitchen for hours. Even Mutt and Jeff, who'd been called in for reinforcements around noon, had left.

"Trim the bottom of the spears to the same length," she told him. Her flashing butcher knife didn't so much as hesitate over the leafy weedlike stuff she was chopping. "I'm going to wrap them with sun-dried tomatoes and prosciutto."

He glanced over the trays that covered nearly every section of the kitchen. There were pastries. There were little things she called savories. There were stuffed Cornish hens waiting to be roasted the next day and medallions of beef that were marinating in some fancy sauce. There was a feast for over a hundred people in the waiting and she'd done it in only a day.

"You're amazing," he said above the ends of the asparagus he was carefully measuring and cutting.

Give him a hostile takeover any day.

"You're just saying that 'cause you want to stop for the night."

"I do want to stop. But you are still amazing."

Her lips curved. "Well, as it happens, once we finish the asparagus wraps, we can call it a night."

"Oh happy day," he muttered, and cut green ends off a little more quickly.

"What's this lack of enthusiasm? Does that mean you're not going to want to sign on at J's for the next—" her voice slowed suddenly "—year?"

He stopped his ponderous slicing and looked up at her.

The smile on her face was gone. "I was just kidding," she said quickly. "I know you're not staying in Amarillo." She swept her chopped weeds into a bowl and attacked the mixture inside with a deadly whisk.

He couldn't stay in Amarillo indefinitely. He had a business in L.A. He had employees. Payroll. Contracts. But all he could say in response to her was a paltry, "Right."

She nodded swiftly and turned away from him, placing items in her industrial-size dishwasher. She cleaned the rest of the kitchen, putting everything to rights that could be put, and finally took the knife out of his hands, finishing up the asparagus in mere minutes.

"Show-off," he said, hoping to lighten the somberness that had descended on them both.

"That culinary school I went to wasn't for nothing," she returned, with just as much forced cheer.

Finally, though, the asparagus was tied up in fancy little bundles, she deemed the work done, and they left the restaurant locked tight.

They'd driven to J's in her car earlier and it took only a few minutes to get back to her house. But when they arrived, there was an enormous blue pickup filling the driveway. "That's my father's truck," she said and pulled around instead to park in the street at the curb. "What's he doing here?"

He had no more idea than she did. They had decided that morning to wait until Monday to break the news about the audit to Drew. It wasn't as if the situation would be any worse two days from now. And Jordan had insisted she didn't want the weekend that was supposed to be about celebrating marred.

Nate was hard on her heels as she quickly headed inside. Drew was sitting in a chair reading and Lulu was nowhere in sight.

"Daddy?" Jordan's voice was cautious. "Is everything all right? Where's Lulu?"

He set aside his book and pushed out of his seat. "She's asleep. She shouldn't be keeping late hours like this in her condition. I told her she could go home, but she's stubborn. Wouldn't go any further than the guest room."

Jordan's eyes narrowed a little. "But what are you doing here?"

"I came over tonight to tell you something. The girl didn't know when you might be getting back, so I decided to wait." He made a point of looking at his watch. "Didn't expect to wait quite this long."

"I'm sorry," Jordan said. "If I'd have known, I'd have—"

"What? Put aside your work for me?" Drew shook his head. "No reason for you to do that, girl. I've never put aside my work for you." His gaze turned to Nate. "I'm a mite surprised to see you here, though."

"Nate's my friend," Jordan said smoothly, but quickly. "You know that."

"Men and women aren't friends when it's the middle of the night," Drew countered bluntly. He sounded like the man that Nate had known before. "They're lovers."

Rosy color bloomed on her cheeks. "Whether or not that happens to be true is my and Nate's business."

Drew just harrumphed. Only Nate knew the man could see his daughter's blush as well as he could and he gave the man an impassive look in return to the one Drew aimed at him.

"So what did you come here to talk about, anyway?" Nate gave her points for trying to steer the topic into safer waters.

"Chelsey." Drew's gray gaze moved back to Nate again. "What else?"

"What about it?" Jordan's voice went faint. She slanted her gaze at Nate and he could see the worry there.

So much for safer waters.

"I've decided to sell the refinery," Drew said.

CHAPTER ELEVEN

"*SELL?* Since when?" Jordan stared at her father, looking for signs that he'd had a complete breakdown, but not seeing a single one. If anything, her father looked feistier than he had in a long, long while.

He also looked a little defensive. "Since a long time. I'm an old man, Jordan. Do you think I want to run the refinery forever?"

"Oh, Dad. You're not old."

"I'm sixty-five years old. I've buried a wife and a son. I have a right to feel old if I want to. Besides. There are things I want to do before I die."

Jordan's knees felt weird. She sank down on the arm of the couch. "Like what?"

"Like travel. You know I've never been to Africa? I always swore when your mother was alive that one day, we'd make it to Africa. We never did. She also wanted to own one of them fancy motor homes. Drive around the United States. See every corner of it."

"I think you *should* travel if it's something you want to do," Jordan agreed, feeling utterly bewildered. "But you're not planning to do this alone, are you?"

His lips tightened. "Just because I'm having some

trouble getting used to…to Luke's passing and I've been talking to that doctor you wanted doesn't mean I'm feeble."

She winced. "I never suggested that you were."

"I think Jordan is just wondering if you wouldn't *enjoy* yourself more if you had some company," Nate inserted tactfully.

"Well of course I'm gonna have company."

Even more surprised, Jordan raised her eyebrows, waiting when her father didn't elaborate. "Who?"

"Gladys," Nate guessed before Drew could answer.

"Gladys," she echoed. But she could see the confirmation in her father's face that he was, indeed, talking about his longtime secretary. "That's…that's great, Dad."

"Anyway, I wanted to tell you what I decided. You'll have to agree to the sale once I find a buyer."

She'd agree to anything if it made her father happy. "Are you *sure* you want to sell?" She cast Nate a glance. Given the financial condition of the refinery, she wasn't sure if selling was even an option anymore.

"Unless there's someone around here who wants to take it over, what else is there to do?"

"Hire a good management team," Nate said. "If you want, I can put you in touch with some people. Make some calls."

Jordan's mouth dried. He was talking about the refinery *after* he was gone.

Drew made a face. "Gonna take a mighty fine team to drag the refinery up out of the mess it's in. And don't give me that look, Jordan-girl. Just because I'm tired of the work doesn't mean I don't know what I've let happen to my own business."

"Then you won't be surprised at the results that came back from the audit," Nate said. His hand closed over the back of her neck. It felt warm. Comforting. But it didn't erase the fact that he was discussing something that entailed his exit from her life. "We might be able to file for reorganization."

"Or I can put the settlement the trucking company offered into Chelsey," Drew said with a good measure of composure. "That's the other thing I wanted to talk to you about, Jordan. I want to do what you think Luke would've wanted."

Her vision blurred with sudden tears. Her father was actually asking her what she thought? "I think he would have wanted to save Chelsey," she said when her throat loosened up enough to get out the words. "That's what he told me the last time we spoke. That he wished he could save the company. Not just for us, but for our children. And...and their children."

Nate's finger stroked down the back of her neck. "The settlement isn't going to be enough, Drew."

"Not even if I got them to double it?"

Nate started with surprise. "What?"

Jordan stared at her father. "You negotiated a higher settlement?" The last she'd known, her father had been too grief-stricken to do more than read the letter when the lawyer from the trucking company had delivered it.

"Yes, I demanded more. I'd put the company out of business if I could," Drew said flatly. "No amount is worth the life of my son and his wife."

"Well, given that bit of news," Nate said slowly, "If I add the value of Luke's half of ACFC, you'd be nearly out of the woods."

Jordan jerked. She stared at Nate. "I thought you said that would be like throwing good money after bad."

"Because on its own it wouldn't have been enough to do any significant good."

Drew pushed to his feet. "Okay then. We'll work out the kinks next week." He chucked Jordan gently under the chin. "You're a good daughter, Jordan-girl."

She was still sitting there in a daze when Nate returned after seeing her father out. "That was a surprise," he said into the lengthening silence.

"What?" She pushed back her hair. "My father's state of mind? Gladys? Selling the refinery?" The evening had brought a cornucopia of surprises. Not least of which had been Drew seeking out *her* opinion.

"Gladys isn't such a surprise. The woman's devoted to him."

"She's been Dad's secretary longer than he was married to my mother before she died." She could deal with the stunning announcements from her father. But she knew what she *couldn't* deal with was the impending day of Nate's departure. No matter what she told herself.

He took her hands and drew her to her feet. "Come on. It's late and you've had an exhausting day."

On every level, she thought.

"And tomorrow will be almost equally busy." She carefully drew her hands out of his. "Best thing we both can use is a good night's sleep."

His gaze narrowed slightly. "Alone?"

She pressed her tongue against the back of her teeth for a moment, gathering strength. "The children are here, Nate." As was Lulu. "I have to consider them."

His brows drew together. "I know that. I wouldn't ask you to do otherwise."

She swallowed hard. "Then you can understand why it's better if you're not here when they wake up. They wouldn't understand."

"Even though I'm usually here when they go to bed."

He had to know that wasn't what she meant. "They're already attached to you. They're going to be hurt—" she had to force the rest of the words out "—when you leave."

It was as if a shutter closed over his expressive face. So much so that she was surprised when he lowered his head and brushed his lips, slowly, hauntingly, over her lips. "It's okay, Jordan." His voice was soft. Husky. "I understand."

Then he walked out the front door, closing it softly behind him.

It was one of the saddest sounds she'd ever heard. Because she knew in her heart that he *did* understand.

They'd reached the end.

"To Jack and Claire!" The toast echoed around the country club's beautifully decorated reception hall as a hundred-plus guests lifted their champagne in a toast to the happy couple. The rather stunned couple.

Jack and Claire truly had been surprised. First when Nate's mom had managed to get Claire to the church she and Jack usually attended without arousing her suspicion. At least until she'd found Rebecca's mom already there, holding out the lace mantilla she'd unearthed.

According to Nate's mom, Claire had gone through half a box of tissues before she'd mopped herself up enough to let the women get in the act, fixing her hair and helping her into the long gown they'd rescued from another ancient box of clothing in the attic. Nate's mom had been certain the pale peach gown that Gran had once worn on a date with Jack would still fit. She was the same size as Claire and had snuck the gown away to conduct some discreet but minor alterations. Along with the ivory and peach roses in the bouquet Rebecca had ordered, the antique mantilla and the gown had turned out to be a stunning match on his still-lovely grandmother.

Then there was Nate's granddad.

Despite her legal eagle ways, Jack had been a little cagier than Claire. He'd figured something was up the second Nate asked to meet him for lunch, but until Nate had driven him to the church rather than one of Jack's usual haunts, he hadn't thought Nate's behavior had to do with *him*. But he'd gotten well into the spirit of things and had donned the black suit that had been awaiting him at the church.

"Smartest thing I ever did was marry your grandmother," he'd said as he tied his black bow tie with practiced ease. "Didn't matter a whit that we'd known each other a short time." He'd straightened to look at himself in the mirror. "Man looks at a woman and sees forever, he'd best do something about it no matter what else is going on." Then he'd grinned and clapped Nate on the shoulder. "And even after sixty years, I'm pretty pleased to be able to marry her all over again. Everyone should be so lucky."

Now, Nate raised his glass along with all the rest of the guests who were packed into the country club where they'd reconvened after the touching vow renewal ceremony. "To Jack and Claire," he said along with all the rest, then nearly gulped the contents of his champagne flute.

Every time the door to the kitchen swung open, he spotted Jordan working there.

Her blond hair was tied back at her nape in some sleek, fancy knot. She was wearing black pants that made her legs go on forever and a long-sleeved white shirt that faithfully followed every line of her beautiful torso. She also had a men's black tie knotted at her neck with the ends of the long tails tucked into the narrow waist of her slacks along with the blouse, and it only accentuated the fact that she was not in any way at all mannish.

She was perfectly feminine. Perfectly…perfect and that perfection went way beyond the exterior.

"Hey there, cousin." Rebecca bounced up next to him, her shining brown hair swinging. She looked particularly pretty in her pale blue gown. Or maybe it was the Army Captain who couldn't take his eyes off her that added an even brighter glow. "Guess we managed to pull it off after all." She tipped the rim of her champagne flute against his. "Your Jordan is a positive miracle."

"She's not my Jordan." But God, he wished she could be.

Rebecca's eyebrows rose. "Really? I had the impression that you two were involved."

"I don't do relationships."

She snorted softly. "Oh, please. Maybe you didn't *do* them in the past, but the look on your face tells me that you're *doing* one now. Nothing makes a person look like you do except the big old L word."

He abruptly set his glass on a passing waiter's tray and shoved his hand into his pocket, only to encounter his grandfather's watch. His fingers closed around it like a lifeline. "I have a business in California, Bec."

Her expression softened. "Those are just details, Nate. And you can deal with details better than most of the people I know." The small, live band struck up the first notes of an old song. "I'd better get Gran and Granddad onto the dance floor now." His cousin buzzed off, but not quite in a direct route to their grandparents. She first stopped off to brush her fingers against Ryan's, where he was sitting at a table with her parents.

Nate worked his way through the guests who were crowding around the dance floor to get a delighted glimpse of Jack sweeping his wife into his arms with a stylish flourish.

He pushed through the kitchen door and spotted Jordan immediately. She was directing her crew of servers. Some were from the original caterer and some from her own restaurant. All were dressed like she was, though, and there was no question who was in charge.

He stayed out of the way until the servers were once

more dispersed, carrying their various trays of delectable offerings out to the guests. Then he stepped forward when she was pulling a tray of asparagus bundles out of the refrigerator. "You're amazing." He'd said it before and he still meant it. More than ever.

Her tray hit the counter with a loud clatter. "You shouldn't be in here."

"I'm part of the production crew, remember?"

"The money man," she murmured. She still hadn't looked at him. "Is everyone satisfied with the food at least?"

"Everyone is raving. Why do you think your servers keep coming back in here every few minutes with their trays emptied? Half of the guests are probably already planning to call on you for some gig they've got coming up. If you wanted more catering business, you're sure to get it now."

"I didn't agree to do this today to gain future clients." She pulled out another tray and pointedly nudged him aside so she could set it on the counter beside the first. "Shouldn't you be out there giving a toast or something?"

"The toasts are done." He'd given one. A short, brief one after his parents and Rebecca's had given theirs. "Why *did* you agree?"

She muttered a soft oath when she dropped the tongs she was using to transfer asparagus spears from the storage tray to the serving tray. "Hand me another set of tongs, would you? In that container next to you."

"No." Instead he reached over and grabbed her hands. "I've just watched two really important people in my life reaffirm the fact that they've loved and supported each other for sixty years. I think that's amazing, too."

She tugged her hands free and retrieved the fresh, clean tongs herself. "It is amazing."

"If I started right now, I'd have to live until I'm ninety-five to reach that."

She began filling a serving tray again. "I imagine most people reflect on such things at an event like this."

"Do you?"

She suddenly set down her tongs and gave him a long look. Her eyes glistened like silver. "Nate, *please*."

"Not too long ago, my grandfather told me what he thinks are the three things that get a man through life." He pulled the watch out of his pocket and took her hand, settling the round case in her palm.

Her brows drew together as she looked at the watch. "Fortitude and forgiveness," she read.

Nate lifted her chin. "The third is love. I've realized all three of these things because of you, Jordan."

A tear formed at the corner of her eye and slowly crept down her cheek, only to be caught by his thumb. "I love you," he said softly. "You're the only woman I've ever said that to. And I love Hank and Lydia, too."

She pressed her lips together. Another tear fell.

"The sixty years I want to start on are with *you*."

She inhaled audibly. "In California?"

He shook his head. "I have a house there. But you have a home here. Not just the house you live in. But the life you lead, the people you care about and keep close. That's the home you've created. And I'm hoping it can be my home, too."

Her lips parted. Her gray eyes went soft as clouds. "What about your company?"

"I'm thinking it's time I followed some of my own advice and put a good management team in place. Maybe I'll expand. Open an office here, too. Or maybe I'll see if I can do some good for your father at Chelsey in a more permanent capacity. With the right capital and management in place maybe the twins will have a future there when they're adults if they want, after all."

She was looking at him again with that expression that seemed to believe he could accomplish anything. And maybe he could with Jordan by his side. "So? Will you marry me?"

"You want to marry me?" She looked up at him with amazement.

"What did you think I was talking about?" He ran his thumb along her beautiful lips. "I want to be your husband. I want to be a dad to Hank and Lydia. And maybe even to more children, if you want."

Her eyes flooded and he swallowed hard. "So...will you?"

Jordan stared up at the tall man who'd so easily captured her heart. Who was offering her everything she'd yearned for while his heart was shining in his hazel eyes.

For her.

She swiped her cheeks with her fingers. "If there's anything we've learned lately, it's not to wait when it comes to the things that make us happy. And you do make me very, very happy, Nathaniel Aldrich." She threw her arms around his shoulders, still clutching the pocket watch. "So, *yes*. Yes, I'll marry you."

He laughed exultantly and swept her up in his arms, covering her smiling mouth with his and kissing her as if he would never stop.

Neither one of them noticed when Nate's grandfather poked his head into the kitchen, hoping to find another one of those tasty asparagus things.

What Jack found, though, was a whole lot better and with a smile, he left the kitchen and strolled back out to join his bride of sixty years.

REQUEST YOUR
FREE BOOKS!

2 FREE NOVELS
FROM THE ROMANCE/SUSPENSE
COLLECTION PLUS 2 FREE GIFTS!

YES! Please send me 2 FREE novels from the Romance/Suspense Collection and my 2 FREE gifts (gifts are worth about $10). After receiving them, if I don't wish to receive any more books, I can return the shipping statement marked "cancel." If I don't cancel, I will receive 4 brand-new novels every month and be billed just $5.74 per book in the U.S. or $6.24 per book in Canada. That's a savings of at least 28% off the cover price. It's quite a bargain! Shipping and handling is just 50¢ per book.* I understand that accepting the 2 free books and gifts places me under no obligation to buy anything. I can always return a shipment and cancel at any time. Even if I never buy another book from the Reader Service, the two free books and gifts are mine to keep forever.

185 MDN EYNQ 385 MDN EYN2

Name	(PLEASE PRINT)	
Address		Apt. #
City	State/Prov.	Zip/Postal Code

Signature (if under 18, a parent or guardian must sign)

Mail to **The Reader Service:**
IN U.S.A.: P.O. Box 1867, Buffalo, NY 14240-1867
IN CANADA: P.O. Box 609, Fort Erie, Ontario L2A 5X3

Not valid to current subscribers of the Romance Collection,
the Suspense Collection or the Romance/Suspense Collection.

Want to try two free books from another line?
Call 1-800-873-8635 or visit www.morefreebooks.com.

* Terms and prices subject to change without notice. Prices do not include applicable taxes. Sales tax applicable in N.Y. Canadian residents will be charged applicable provincial taxes and GST. Offer not valid in Quebec. This offer is limited to one order per household. All orders subject to approval. Credit or debit balances in a customer's account(s) may be offset by any other outstanding balance owed by or to the customer. Please allow 4 to 6 weeks for delivery. Offer available while quantities last.

Your Privacy: Harlequin is committed to protecting your privacy. Our Privacy Policy is available online at www.eHarlequin.com or upon request from the Reader Service. From time to time we make our lists of customers available to reputable third parties who may have a product or service of interest to you. If you would prefer we not share your name and address, please check here. ☐

BOB09

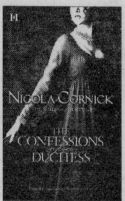